# A Guarded Heart

*(Book IV in the Moon Island Series)*

## Jennifer Fulton

*Yellow Rose Books*

Nederland, Texas

ISBN 1-932300-37-6

First Printing 2005

9 8 7 6 5 4 3 2 1

Cover design by Donna Pawlowski

Published by:

Yellow Rose Books
PMB 210, 8691 9th Avenue
Port Arthur, Texas 77642-8025

Find us on the World Wide Web at
http://www.regalcrest.biz

Printed in the United States of America

Acknowledgments:

My family and friends, as always, have given me love and encouragement. Fel, Jan and JD provided intelligent reading and comments, and Lori L. Lake lent her affable editing support.

**Author's Note:**

Part of the author's earnings from this novel will be donated to the Addis Ababa Fistula Hospital. For more information about this worthy cause please visit their website: www.fistulahospital.org

In memory of Ruth Charters.

# MOON ISLAND

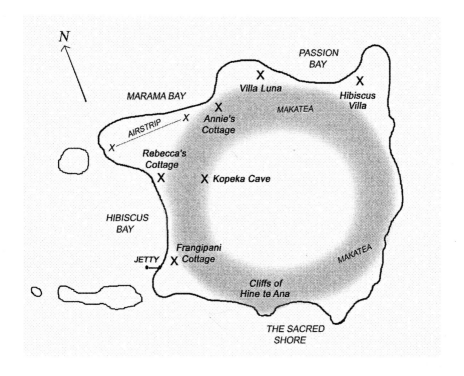

# Chapter
# One


LAUREN RIPPED OFF her mask and gloves and tossed them on the operating room floor. "Am I removing a kidney or a leg?" Her eyes swept her gowned colleagues. "Anyone? The chart says we have renal failure, but the leg is prepped. The chart says Mr. Taylor is an African American gentleman, aged seventy. This patient is twenty-something and whiter than me."

A nurse scuttled to Lauren's side. "I'm sorry, Dr. Chatterley. It's...it's the shooting..." She broke off, tears spilling.

Lauren seized the nurse by the shoulders. "We can't allow a maniac to destroy everything this hospital stands for. Dr. Addams is fighting for his life. Don't we owe him...uh...oh, fuck."

"Cut!" Earl Sternberger clasped his head in his hands and uttered something no one could hear. "Take a break. And while our star is learning her lines, get that dolly set up for the bleeder scene. Ten minutes, people."

Lauren groaned as Earl pointed a finger at her. He didn't have to utter another word. A production assistant handed her a glass of Pellegrino. Thanking the young woman, Lauren sank into a folding chair and contemplated the script. *Don't we owe him more than this? Don't we owe him a St. Hope's that holds true to his vision? With God's help we can do this!* Incredibly, she had delivered crappier lines. You don't work in daytime television for the verisimilitude.

"This came for you, Ms. Douglas." The assistant returned with a lavish Harry & David fruit basket.

Normally, gifts from Lauren's adoring public went straight to her dressing room. A personal delivery on-set could mean only one thing: Her contract negotiations had stalled. Harvey Garfield, the exec VP in charge of Programming, sent fruit baskets to female cast and Scotch to the guys. Lauren knew exactly what he wanted—her ass for eighty percent less than her agent was asking. Dutifully, she read the card.

"Miss Hillman needs your RSVP today," the young assistant said, looking like a shark was snapping at her heels.

Harvey's secretary had that effect on people. Dorothea Hillman was probably eighty, but maintained a reptilian agelessness thanks to Botox and the scalpel. Appropriately, she wore alligator pumps and a matching purse as her signature accessories. Today, being Thursday, they would be slut red to match her acrylic nails, and she would be wearing her pink Bond-girl jumpsuit. Teamed with a ruthlessly teased platinum wig, this look had worked for Dorothea in the Sixties. Evidently she saw no reason to change it now.

Over cigars and cognac, Harvey liked to recount his promotion to vice-president as if he had succeeded to the throne of a minor principality, the legendary Miss Hillman there to crown him and defend him against all comers. His wife was one of the few network spouses who could send her husband to work knowing her marriage was not at the mercy of a league of thong-wearing personal assistants. Miss Hillman could sniff out a home-wrecker at a thousand paces. Everyone knew if a woman wanted access to Harvey, it helped to be over fifty or a frump, preferably both.

Lauren contemplated the invitation. She was summoned to "an intimate gathering" tomorrow evening at Harvey's Connecticut mansion. In other words, it would be Harvey and his henchmen, allies whose job it was to make Lauren feel pathetically grateful to the network for her big break. Such was the fate of previously unknown actors who tried to get a pay raise when their show became a hit.

*Dr. Kate* was about to complete its third season and had clawed its way to the dizzying summit of the daytime television ratings. Lauren's agent, Carter Mack, said Harvey had to show her the money. For the first time in her acting career, she had leverage, which meant people who could not remember her name a year ago were suddenly describing themselves in *Soap Opera Digest* as her best friends.

"Tell Miss Hillman I'm thrilled, but it won't make any difference," Lauren said. "It's a lousy offer and I'm not signing."

The assistant blanched. "You want me to use those exact words?"

"I do."

The girl looked like she was about to throw up. Lauren tried to remember her name. She had only started on the set a week ago, and her shy eagerness was a pleasant change from the fawning ingratiation Lauren was getting used to. Wanting to soften the blow, she lowered her voice and added, "Tell Miss

Hillman you heard Todd Hudson's wife has thrown him out. No one knows yet."

A startled gasp. "She has?"

"Shhh." Lauren made a *keep it down* gesture. "I'm sorry, what was your name?"

"Molly."

"You're new here aren't you, Molly?"

"Yes, Ms. Douglas."

"Well, let me give you a piece of advice. In this business, when someone does you a favor, don't forget it."

"I won't." Molly's face shone with gratitude. "Thank you, Ms. Douglas. You can count on me."

"Excellent. Now go give Miss Hillman the good news."

Lauren could picture Dorothea smacking her collagen-plumped lips over this tasty morsel. There was only one thing Harvey's guard dog reviled more than the signs of aging, and that was Todd Hudson, known to his adoring public as Dr. Lucian Addams, Chief of Surgery and hunky heartthrob of St Hope's General Hospital.

Todd was a scene-stealing camera hog who threw actor's etiquette out the window as soon as the red light signaled "Action." He had spent the entire second season lobbying for equal billing with Lauren, and now that there was on-screen "heat" between them, he was demanding the same rate as hers for the new season. As if that were not enough, Lauren had almost passed out from hyperventilation during their long-anticipated screen kiss last week. Fortunately, while she was fending off his tongue, a disgruntled proctologist ran amok and shot him five times. A bullet had lacerated his proximal aorta, and Dr. Kate Chatterley was now standing vigil at his bedside.

The season was set to end with Dr. Addams on the operating table, clinging to dear life by a thread. A flat line was too much to hope for. On the other hand — Lauren allowed herself a small grin — if anyone could deliver Todd Hudson's demise it was Dorothea Hillman.

A CHILL NOVEMBER wind beat like impatient fingers against the crime scene tape that encircled a stand of pines on the banks of the Delaware River. Winter-bare and limbed up to filter light into the dense forest, the trees stood dark and pencil-straight like mourners around the freshly dug grave at their feet. Overhead, a leaden sky brooded, rain imminent.

Special Agent Pat Roussel stared up through the shadowy latticework of branches, inhaling air musty with the scent of decaying leaves. Her skin felt damp and chilled.

"Looks like he was interrupted." Lieutenant Chuck Cicchetti approached. He sounded almost buoyant. "Got her into the grave and that's it."

"Not like our boy to cut and run before the party's over." Pat shook out a pair of latex gloves. She wanted to be anywhere but standing over another shallow grave, gazing down at the latest victim of the sicko the media had dubbed the Kiddy Pageant Killer.

Destiny O'Connor's body had been found just thirty hours after her disappearance, a fact that leavened the horror of discovery with the hope of a break in the case. It seemed something had flustered the killer. If so, he might have been careless. This time there could be new evidence. No wonder Cicchetti sounded like he'd just won the jackpot.

Bracing herself, Pat lowered her eyes to the body. Winner of the Georgia LaPetite Miss Princess title, Destiny was tiny and fair-haired. She had been restrained with the same lace-covered handcuffs used on all but one of the victims. Her shoes were missing, and her costly peach pageant dress was draped neatly over her naked body. Across the dress lay a white satin sash with hand-stenciled gold lettering: *Little Miss Perfect Petal.*

There was no such pageant, they had learned early in the investigation. With one exception, the killer had bestowed this title on each of his victims, a detail not released to the media.

"It's him. No doubt about it," Pat said. The killer's work was so distinctive, a rookie could have linked the cases.

Members of the Crime Scene Unit milled around Pat and Cicchetti like ants sizing up a pair of beetles with designs on their nest. The Forensic Examiner, Dr. Stephanie Carmichael, acknowledged Pat with her usual mouth twitch. She was one of those women who act like you catch lesbianism off toilet seats. Her hands were invariably knotted together when Pat was around and she took pains to avoid eye contact.

Chuck Cicchetti joked that Pat came across like a natural-born prison guard. If Carmichael's attitude was any litmus, he was probably right. FBI agents were mostly cut from the same conservative cloth as Carmichael herself, straight arrows affronted by sloppy work habits and anyone who rocked the boat. Clearly Pat was made of the wrong stuff, and skipping a few extra weeks between haircuts, as she had lately, would cut no ice with the homophobic pathologist.

Today Carmichael took in Pat's black chinos, turtleneck, ostrich boots and leather coat with disapproving forbearance. "He made her up post mortem," she observed stiffly. "Same lipstick as the others, no doubt."

Carmichael had a bug up her ass about that lipstick. Traces had been found on four of the previous victims. The lab had identified the brand and color. It was one of those exclusive direct-from-Paris types sold in a handful of top-end beauty spas, the kind of clue that could crack open a case. But not this time.

Pat had traced the lipstick to make-up artists Jake & Gilbert, pageant trainers who lived on a fancy spread in rural Pennsylvania. The couple had coached the first victim, Shelby-Rose Dubois. Between sobs, Gilbert had confirmed that the lipstick was in the Tinkerbell backpack that had disappeared with Shelby-Rose the day she won the West Virginia Little Miss Supreme title. He and his partner were quickly ruled out as suspects. These days, they served as a mine of information on kiddy pageant politics and personalities.

"How long before we can move the body?" Pat asked, determined this poor baby shouldn't lie in the cold earth a minute longer than was necessary. Besides, the sooner Carmichael could process her, the sooner Pat would have the autopsy results on her desk.

"She'll be in the morgue tonight." Carmichael finally looked Pat in the eye. "I wasn't expecting another one so soon."

"We're doing our best." Pat knew she sounded defensive. Everyone had sweated blood to get a break in the case before the killer struck again. This was his sixth victim.

"It wasn't a criticism, Agent Roussel. It was an observation. The gaps are getting shorter. He's more confident."

"Yeah. We know." Cicchetti's bland tone disguised a well of frustration.

Three years and six victims later, they had a profile, a partial print, and no DNA. Working with the FBI's cyber crimes unit, they had penetrated child pornography rings, hunting a predator with a jones for six-year-old beauty queens. Their database was crammed with the names of men who routinely purchased one-day photo passes to Little Miss Whatever pageants. These events were a pedophile's nirvana. Where else would mothers cheerfully wheel out their small daughters to pout and strut like truck-stop hookers? Didn't any of these women ever wonder about all the self-described "amateur photographers" in the audience?

Widening the net, Pat routinely trolled an ever-growing collection of pedophile-bait websites set up by parents charging monthly fees for members to see pictures of their daughters in skimpy clothing. *Watch eleven-year-old model Katy groom her horse wearing her favorite thong bikini.* There wasn't a damned thing law enforcement could do to close down those sites unless there was nudity or sexual activity. And they were just the tip of the iceberg. She and Cicchetti had collected so much data on Internet kiddy porn, they could read the files for five years and still not be finished.

Meantime, their killer was planning his next move. And neither Pat nor Cicchetti had a life.

Cicchetti's high-maintenance wife had up and left him soon after he made lieutenant, and Pat had not had a steady girlfriend since she became a Crimes Against Children Coordinator at the FBI's field office in Philly. As for a long-term relationship — that was a joke. If there was a sane lesbian who would put up with being a Bureau-widow, Pat hadn't met her. She knew she was a cliché — the agent who lived and breathed her job. Work made it pretty much impossible to get involved with anyone. Sometimes she wondered if she had intentionally set things up that way.

Pat shook herself. It wasn't like her to navel-gaze at a crime scene. The first drops of rain were falling. She needed to finish her notes and get out of Carmichael's way. Staring at the gold lettering on that white satin sash, she suppressed a welling sense of defeat.

Early in the investigation, hot rage had fueled her efforts. Then the exercise had become intellectual, a contest between her and the killer. Now, for the first time, she was plagued by self-doubt. This case had bankrupted her personal resources to no avail. Yet the clues had to be there. Was she too burnt-out to piece them together? She had promised herself she would never allow ego to compromise an investigation. Was it time to get off the case? Would fresh new eyes see something she was blind to and maybe save a child's life?

She caught a level stare from Cicchetti and knew he was thinking exactly the same thing.

# Chapter
# Two

LAUREN FISHED AN olive from her cleavage and dropped it discreetly into a potted palm. Hors d'oevres were a menace in a dress like hers. Shoving her hand down her front to retrieve cocktail-party jetsam was not exactly in step with her image as the wholesome star of *Dr. Kate*, darling of the daytime audience, recipient of more fan mail than any other cast member. Well, screw her image, she thought, taking another glass of champagne from a passing waiter. And screw Harvey Garfield for trying to manipulate her into taking a lousy twenty percent per-episode raise.

The network big-shot had recently purchased a Greenwich estate once owned by a lieutenant in the Escobar drug cartel. The place was awash with security cameras and bulletproof glass. Harvey had made a point of showing everyone some windowless concrete rooms in the basement he said had been used for *God only knows what*. These days he kept his wine collection down there and jokingly referred to the cellars as Abu Ghraib.

Struggling to maintain her soap-star smile, Lauren surveyed the party crowd and wondered how she could decently escape. Holding court in the center of a throng of men in dinner jackets and black ties was her father, US Congressman Wendall Douglas III, better known as the owner of a pickles empire that printed his grandma's beaming face on every jar. Lauren had gotten her start in television at the age of four years singing jingles for Ma Kelly's Extra Sweet Choice 'N' Chunky Gherkins. Why pay one of those brat actors with a pushy stage mother when he had the cutest kid in the world, her father had said.

It was Lauren's grandfather who had converted Ma Kelly's prized canning recipes into a pickle fortune. When Lauren's dad took over the business in the 1980's, he promptly embarked on a rash of takeovers that had turned the family company into a huge conglomerate. These days they made everything from pickles to frozen baby food.

Wendall Douglas had turned his attention to politics during the Clinton era. Lauren could never figure out whether he'd entered public service because he wanted to improve the world, or because power was a more alluring mistress than wealth. Whatever his motives, these days her father was a fixture at the parties of media moguls. Politics was just another reality TV show, he told Lauren and her brothers. He needed the right people in his corner if he was going to make it to the Senate, and Lauren's boss was one of them.

Spotting one of the so-called right people making a beeline for her, Lauren beat a hasty retreat and promptly collided with a geeky-looking waiter holding a tray of *blinis* topped with caviar and sour cream. Several slid off and plopped wetly to the floor at her feet.

"Oops! I'm so sorry," she said.

"Not at all. It was my fault, ma'am." Red-faced with embarrassment, the waiter knelt to scoop up the mess with a napkin.

"Let me help." Lauren looked around for more napkins.

"No. Please." The waiter cast a browbeaten glance toward the bar, where a supercilious-looking man was adjusting a butter statue of David.

Lauren guessed this must be the catering supervisor. She had probably caused trouble for a guy who really needed his job. Feeling guilty, she hung around until he was back on his feet, then took one of the remaining *blinis* from his platter. "I can't resist these," she said, faking a big smile.

The waiter rearranged a strand of lank mousy hair that had flopped forward while he was on his knees. Obviously grappling with timidity, he said, "If I may take the liberty of saying so, it's a privilege to meet you, Ms. Douglas. I have the entire series of *Dr. Kate* on video. I'm your number one fan."

Trying not to picture Kathy Bates in *Misery*, Lauren said, "Well, thank you. I'm glad you like the show."

His face seemed familiar, she thought. Maybe he was one of those regulars who lurked around the studio doors hoping for an autograph or a few words from their favorite star. Some showed up week after week.

"You should have won an Emmy this time," he announced. "I wrote to them."

"You did?" Lauren didn't know whether to be amused or shocked. It astonished her how some fans reacted when their favorite show was snubbed.

The waiter licked lips already too wet. "I hope you don't mind if I mention something," he assumed a confiding tone.

"Your new hair style...it's obvious where they're going with that."

Lauren had no idea how to respond. She ate her *blini* and listened.

"They're making you look older...you know, compared with that new brain surgeon who, by the way, is not credible. They must think we're stupid. She's right out of high school. Ask yourself this question — would you let a doctor with plastic fingernails prise open your skull?"

"Probably not," Lauren conceded. Diplomatically, she asked, "Why do you think they want me to look older?" In her experience, it was sometimes wise to let a fan say his piece and leave happy.

"Isn't it obvious?" he hissed. "Dr. Addams is going to recover from his wounds and fall for the nymphet. You'll get tangled up in a crazy malpractice suit that could threaten the hospital. The nymphet suddenly gets your lines and voilà. They've got themselves a new lead actress for ten percent of what they pay you." He gripped her arm with a damp paw, his nondescript blue eyes fierce. "Don't let them do it."

His intensity was unsettling, but this kind of fan fervor was nothing unusual   At least he hadn't called her a conniving home-wrecker like that woman in the supermarket last week. Lauren gave her arm a slight tug and the waiter released her.

"Forgive me, Ms. Douglas. That was inappropriate." He looked like a dog caught messing in the house. "I became over-excited on account of my strong feelings about this issue. They have no respect for your talent."

This guy was a trip. "I'll definitely think about what you've said," Lauren promised, edging away.

"I'll be watching. And when they dump the new hairstyle, I'll know we've got them where we want them. Remember," he added as he thrust the platter at a passing guest. "Fans like me are the only people you can trust."

Lauren knew she should dismiss the waiter's paranoia, but she found herself pondering the hair theory as the evening progressed. She decided he was right about one thing. The style aged her. She had discussed this with Earl. He said it gave her *gravitas*. The series was moving away from the usual stereotypes. They no longer had to play so much on her girl-next-door sex appeal. The new look would enable her to create some distance from Dr. Addams, increasing the tension between them. Her hair was a metaphor, symbolizing the struggle between her two selves: the self-sacrificing surgeon and the passionate woman. It sounded like a crock of shit. *And* the up-do had coincided with the arrival of Dr. Farina Fairchild, the breathless coed who had presumably won her board certification in a raffle.

Lauren could not imagine how Dr. Fairchild's character could be developed beyond its current role, that of competing for Dr. Addams' lecherous attentions. So far her inept pronunciation of medical terminology had stymied the writers; despite coaching, she still said Bahrain instead of brain. Surely she would be written out of the series once her novelty value wore off. Maybe it was time to confirm that.

As if he had read her mind, Harvey Garfield presented himself in front of her, all teeth and Italian tailoring. His arm encircled his wife Marcia. That he had married a thinking woman instead of a trophy wife spoke well of him in Lauren's book. They had met in high school and had been married for sixteen years. According to Dorothea Hillman, they were genuinely in love.

"You look wonderful tonight, Lauren," Marcia said, tucking a sleek mahogany wave behind one ear. "We were just speaking with your dad. He's so proud of you."

Lauren smiled. "Only daughter in a family of five. I can do no wrong."

"Blind adoration is a father's prerogative." Marcia cast a fond, wifely look at her husband. "Harvey is walking proof. Simone has him around her little finger and she's only three."

"Hey, now." Harvey objected. "I treat her exactly the same as Lance and Guy."

Marcia raised an eyebrow. "I'm pleading the fifth." She paused, distracted by something, then groaned. "Oh, that's perfect. Cedric Mortimer just turned our butter sculpture into porn. Why do artists think everyone's party is an exhibition? Excuse me a moment..."

For a few seconds they followed Marcia's progress through the guests, then Harvey cleared his throat and refocused on Lauren. "Sounds like your dad actually watches the show. Did he give you a hard time over that kiss?"

"He wasn't impressed. He doesn't like my hair either."

Harvey chewed on that a moment. "Let me share something, Lauren. You're a key part of our new vision. We're looking to attract a new daytime demographic—the stay-at-home professional Mom. You know...lawyers, accountants. They're having their first kids when they're thirty-something, and they're not going to buy a surgeon with big hair and French tips. They want a woman they can relate to—strong values, professional, but also feminine."

"I'm listening."

Harvey had saved the best till last. "We're going to make you the Kate Hepburn of daytime television."

"Then why am I losing lines to a cheerleader with a stethoscope bouncing off her implants?"

"C'mon, Lauren. It's about conflict. She's the antithesis of you. She makes you look even more credible." Harvey sounded sincere.

Unconvinced, Lauren said, "She shouldn't be in the OR when I operate. Her boobs get in my way."

"You want her out. You got it. And, hey, if you hate the new hair, no problem. I'll mention it to Earl."

Well, that was easy, Lauren thought, nonplussed. Wondering how much further she could flex her muscles, she said, "Todd Hudson..."

Harvey compressed his lips. "Dorothea told me. What happened?"

"I don't know. Todd can't keep it in his pants, I guess. And Carole got fed up."

"He had to do this while she's pregnant. What's wrong with the guy?"

"It's not going to help the show's image." Lauren stated the obvious. Rumors were flying already, fanned by the publicists of course. "Everyone's going to think this is about me. The hate mail will be rolling in once the story gets out."

Harvey did his best to look concerned, but Lauren knew he wouldn't be losing any sleep. Publicity was publicity. "Dorothea is handling damage control," he said. "Make no mistake, by the time we're through, no one will believe you had a damned thing to do with that break-up."

"I wish I could share your confidence. But I have to tell you, if my character is going to be assassinated in magazines my mother reads, I'm not sure I can sign on for another season." Lauren allowed that to sink in. "And since we seem to be at an impasse over my rate—"

Harvey winced. "Jesus, Lauren. A five hundred percent raise? I can't set a precedent like that."

"Come on, Harvey." Lauren knew better. "You'll just pass it on to the advertisers. You know, it's not just about the money for me. It's the whole package—my career, the development of my character, my input into the direction of the show..."

"You want co-producer," Harvey interpreted.

"Put that on the table and I'll rethink the salary issue." She smiled breezily. Take *that*, Todd Hudson.

"I'll work on it."

Harvey said something else, but Lauren didn't catch it. Her

scalp prickled suddenly. Sensing someone was watching her, she cast a quick look around. Over by the bar, the geeky waiter gave a brief thumbs up as if he knew exactly what she and Harvey had been talking about. Evading his moist direct stare, Lauren shifted position so her boss's tall frame would screen her.

"It's been good talking with you, Harvey," she said. "If you don't mind, I'm going to step outside. I need some fresh air."

Harvey was instantly solicitous. "You okay?"

"It's been a long day." She longed to go home and crawl into bed with Sara. They would make love the next morning, then go out for coffee and croissants. Maybe she could persuade Sara to come with her to St. Michaels for a couple of days. Sara loved staying at the Douglas family's Chesapeake house.

"Listen. Get out of here," Harvey said magnanimously. "Take it easy this weekend. Have a spa. It's on me."

"That's sweet of you, Harvey, but I—"

"Want Tommy to drive you?" He scanned the room for one of his underlings.

Lauren shook her head. "I could use some time to myself."

"I hear you." Harvey took her hand. "Remember what I said. We've got big plans for you."

Past Harvey's shoulder, Lauren caught her father's eye. He looked gratified to see her schmoozing with the boss. Producing a daughterly smile, she signaled she was leaving and he gave her an *I'm busy* wave. Lauren figured he was talking politics. She passed Marcia on her way out and thanked her, accepted some glib compliments from network staff lower down the food chain, and vanished before the geeky waiter could hunt her down for an autograph.

Once outside, she took several deep gulps of air. Damp misted over her cashmere evening coat, weighing the folds. Shivering, Lauren fastened the buttons and pulled on her driving gloves while she waited for the valet to bring her car around. As always, she promised herself that one day she would no longer come to these parties alone. She would bring her partner, and they would be accepted just like any other couple. Times had changed. There was a lesbian soap, even if most of the actors in it were straight. Ellen was out and *her* career wasn't in the toilet. *Her* public coped. All over America, families were coping better with gay members, partly because famous people gave a familiar face to gayness. Lauren looked forward to the day she could do the same.

A pearl gray Audi TT convertible rolled to stop in front of her, and the valet held the door. With a grateful sigh, Lauren tipped the kid and sank into the driver's seat, briefly closing her eyes.

Giving the heater time to warm the car, she took a small leather box from her purse and flipped open the lid. Nestled in a velvet cocoon, a huge silver-blue star sapphire glowed from a platinum and diamond setting. Sara had been hinting about needing a "statement piece" now that she'd joined a big law firm and had to impress people at social events. She would love the pendant. It was elegant, unique, and obviously costly—the ideal gift for their anniversary in two days' time.

Lauren had picked it up from the custom jeweler on her way upstate and was sorely tempted to give it to Sara tonight. She couldn't believe they'd been together for three years. They had fallen in love virtually the moment they'd met. An attorney, Sara had been doing graduate papers in entertainment law and interning at a production company. Lauren was auditioning for walk-on parts. They'd crossed paths in a parking lot after Lauren tried out for a dog food commercial. Sara had asked her to dinner. Three months later they were living together in the Chelsea apartment that was Lauren's graduation gift from her parents.

Lauren pictured Sara's surprise to have her home from the party so much earlier than planned. Maybe they would make love tonight instead of tomorrow. Sara had promised to make some time for their sex life this week. The prospect soothed Lauren. Pain in the ass contract negotiations aside, life really couldn't get any better.

PAT RESTED HER head in her hands. Her stomach churned. On the desk in front of her, the autopsy report blurred as her mind prowled restlessly around the periphery of an ever-expanding vortex of data. She could not shake the feeling that if she descended completely into that swirling chaos, she might never find her way back. Tonight—too often, these days—she felt displaced. It was as if she were slowly being consumed from the inside out by a succubus bent on evicting her calm, optimistic self. Numbed into the refuge of inaction, she was witnessing her own unravelling like an idle bystander.

She jotted six names on a notepad and stared at them until her eyes hurt.

Shelby-Rose Dubois
Kaitlyn Smith
Jaydeene Harper
Fawn Maxwell
Lashelle Adkins
Destiny O'Connor

Pat was visited by a vision so palpable she could not banish its taunting presence: six little girls sat along the wall of her office like so many broken dolls, dressed in their frilly dresses and white satin sashes. Only their eyes moved, haunting her with their pleading. He had seen this look, she thought, but he was heartless in the face of it. Absent in him was the compulsion that would drive most human beings to return a terrified child to her mother. He behaved as a hunter with prey. If his pleasure demanded the death of a living being, so be it—he was entitled.

Pat got to her feet and paced the room. The man who had murdered these children was meticulous in his work. With the exception of Jaydeene Harper and Destiny O'Connor, he had buried his victims with great care, even marking the graves as if to ensure they would be found. She had wondered if this signified some form of remorse or maybe his way of laying claim to the killings. But the profiler had dismissed this; he thought it more likely that the burial activities were simply a fetish. The killer did what he did because he enjoyed it. It was newspaper reporters and moviemakers who perpetuated the myth that serial killers intentionally left a "signature." In real life, most weren't thinking about how to alert authorities that their crimes were linked.

Few offenders were as ritualistic and methodical as the Kiddy Pageant Killer. He was a Mr. Clean, a guy who lived an orderly life, had immense personal discipline, and came across as likeable. The profile said he was probably active in his church and generally regarded as an upstanding citizen. But he found it difficult to accept criticism and had a superiority complex that had possibly alienated some people. Cicchetti said this described half the white males over thirty in the entire country, which sure narrowed it down.

The case still attracted thousands of tips. Some had resulted in arrests for other offenses. None had brought them any closer to naming a suspect.

Pat stared around her office. It was only midnight but she felt like a zombie. The more she tried to sort through the latest deluge of facts, the more tangled they became. Sluggishly, she packed her briefcase. Tomorrow was another day. If she could face it.

LAUREN PULLED INTO the parking garage. She hoped Sara was home and not working another all-nighter. There had been so many since she'd joined Bernstein Ross. Lauren could understand her commitment. As one of the youngest associates in the prestigious law firm, Sara wanted to make an impression.

But sometimes Lauren was tempted to tell her to pack the job in. It wasn't like they needed the money. Lauren had enough for the both of them. Sara could do *pro bono* work and they could travel the world between seasons of *Dr. Kate*. With a resigned sigh, she let herself into their apartment. She knew exactly what Sara would say to that idea. She was far too ambitious to settle for a life in her partner's shadow.

Lauren turned on the living room lights and dropped her coat and purse on a sofa. Spotting Sara's laptop case, she felt a surge of happiness and crossed the hallway to their bedroom, unzipping her dress as she walked. She pushed the door wide and stopped dead, her smile weirdly snagged in place.

A single lamp burned, revealing a room in disarray. Garments littered the floor. The bed was a tangle of sheets. Lauren caught the distinctive sound of the shower running in the adjoining bathroom. There was another sound, too, the murmur of voices. A cold sweat beaded on her face and for a moment she was certain she would faint. Her pulse hammered in her ears. A whimper emerged from her throat.

Of their own volition, her legs carried her toward the bathroom door. She stood there, frozen. The water stopped running and she heard the voices more distinctly. Finally, the sound of seductive laughter gave her the strength to turn the handle.

White-faced, Sara stared at her. "Oh, fuck."

A hunky, dark-haired man drew a towel hastily around his middle. "Who's this?" he asked Sara.

Lauren imagined herself on set, improvising lines for such an occasion. With icy calm, she informed Sara, "You can tell him who I am while you pack your things. I want you out of here in thirty minutes, or I'll call security and have you both removed."

"Lauren. Please," Sara blurted. "Listen to me. This isn't what you think. It doesn't mean anything..." Sara tried to grab her arm, but Lauren wrenched herself away and slammed the door in her cheating lover's face.

On shaking legs, she walked through the apartment to the study, poured herself a shot of vodka, drained the glass, and poured another. She stared at the marble clock on the mantel. It had stopped; she had no idea when. She'd been blind to quite a few things lately, it seemed.

# Chapter
# Three

TWO WEEKS LATER, Wendall Douglas III stalked into Lauren's apartment and dropped a tabloid newspaper in front of her. A headline shrieked DR. KATE'S LESBIAN LOVE AFFAIR and alerted readers to a double page spread inside.

Lauren whipped the paper open and stared helplessly at an obnoxious photo layout. There was a shot of Sara emerging from a nightclub, and a publicity photo of Lauren. Juxtaposed between them, in a clichéd torn-between-two-lovers format, was Sara's boy-toy. A picture of Wendall Douglas shaking hands with the President was prominently positioned on the opposing page.

"Do you have any idea how much this will damage my campaign?" Her father fumed.

Lauren scanned the text. In other circumstances, she would have laughed to see her apartment referred to as a love nest and herself described as a *Pennsylvania pickle princess*. But this was not funny. "I'm sorry," she said weakly.

"Sorry! How could you be so careless?"

"What was I supposed to do?" Lauren retorted. "Shoot them and dismember the bodies?"

The idea seemed to appeal to her father. He sat down in an armchair and lit a cigar. "Too late for that now. You're going to issue a denial and sue anyone who prints this garbage. I want you out of the country. Do something in Europe. Or join your mother on her next bleeding-heart trip to save the world."

Lauren shuddered at the thought. Her mother was a member of Doctors Without Borders. Until recently, she'd been in Afghanistan. But her organization had been forced to withdraw after local Taliban commanders murdered five of their staff and the government refused to arrest the perpetrators. So much for security. Now Helen Douglas was planning to return to a hospital in Addis Ababa where she'd worked on and off for the past ten years. Lauren felt inadequate just thinking about it.

"I can't leave the country," she said. "I have a career."

"Not any more."

"Times have changed, Daddy. Gay is okay on TV now."

Her father was unimpressed. "I've spoken with Harvey Garfield. They're going to shoot an episode with you in a plane crash. Leave it up in the air for you to return from the dead once everything settles down."

Lauren gasped. "I don't believe this! You can't organize my life. I'm twenty-eight, not twelve."

"There's a morals clause in your contract, or have you forgotten that? I just made sure you're not going to be sued."

"What about my new contract?" Lauren's heart sank. The negotiations had finally been settled and she was expecting to sign the documents by the end of the week. The deal was good. Even her agent was happy.

Her father fixed his steely gaze on her. "Garfield says they're going to wait and see what happens."

Lauren sank down on a loathsome minimalist sofa Sara had insisted they buy from some hip furniture designer. She was probably fucking the guy. In disbelief, she said, "This is a nightmare."

Cigar smoke masked her father's face. Through the haze, he explained, "Here's the deal. Your ex-roommate and her boyfriend are shakedown artists who concocted this bullshit story as revenge after you refused to give them money for his drug habit. My people have done some digging. The guy has a history."

"But, that's not what happened."

"Jesus, babydoll. No one gives a fuck what really happened. This is all about damage control. For starters, you're going to hit anybody who runs that story with a lawsuit. *People* pulled it. They had it planned for next week."

Lauren was speechless. You knew you'd made it when your personal problems were plastered all over *People* magazine along with sleazy revelations about the latest crop of reality-show bimbos.

"By the time I'm done, your ex will be looking for work as an ambulance chaser in Bumfuck, Ohio, and that low-life boyfriend of hers will be in a soup line at the Salvation Army." Her father drew on his Cuban with patent satisfaction.

"Daddy, please. I'm sure Sara had nothing to do with this."

"Think again. Did it ever occur to you that you were a pretty good meal ticket for a girl from Jersey City who had to work three jobs to put herself through law school?"

"Sara's not like that. Just because she had to work hard to

get where she is, doesn't mean she's a gold digger." Lauren fell silent, wondering why she was defending a woman who had brought a man into their home—and had sex with him in their bed.

Her father made an impatient noise. "How do you think she landed that job? I made some calls, that's how. You didn't know she'd asked me to talk to Ari Bernstein, did you?"

Lauren was stunned. Sara had made a huge deal out of getting her new position, telling her family how she beat out a horde of Ivy League applicants. She'd always expressed disdain for people who only got ahead because they knew people. Lauren tried to think of something to say, but her father got in first.

"Look, I don't want to pick a fight with you, babydoll. Your girlfriend thought she could live off you and screw any Tom, Dick or Harry she wanted behind your back. Well, no one treats my daughter like that. Good Lord. Your mother and I welcomed that little tramp into our home."

Lauren felt humiliated. Her parents had been unshakably supportive of her from the time she'd come out. Remaining in the closet was her one compromise, and that was as much about her own career as her father's.

"You and Mom have been wonderful. But you're asking me to deny who I am, publicly. What if this ends up in court? You want me to lie under oath?"

Wendell looked her dead in the eye. "Isn't it a bit late to get a conscience? Up 'til now, you've made darned sure everyone thinks you're a card-carrying heterosexual."

Lauren stared down at her hands. "There has to be some other way."

"There isn't. You're a TV star, and I'm campaigning for the Senate next go 'round. You can get all high-minded about this, or you can get real."

Mouth trembling, Lauren said, "I'm sorry, Daddy. I never meant for any of this to happen."

Her father stubbed out his cigar and slung an arm over her shoulder. "Don't you worry about a thing. No one's going to remember squat about this in six months. Have you eaten today?"

"I'm not hungry." Despondently, Lauren gazed at the newspaper once more.

"Lousy picture of Sara," her father commented. "She should have gotten her nose fixed while you were still paying."

PAT STARED GRIMLY into her beer. "This was a big mistake," she informed Cicchetti.

Why hadn't she just requested a transfer? There was a position open at Quantico; the Chief had said he would recommend her. But Pat didn't want to leave Philadelphia. Taking a complete break seemed like the best plan if she wanted to stay in the Crimes Against Children unit. Burnout was a bitch

Pat was owed eight weeks' annual leave, and the Bureau had approved another twelve without pay if she wanted them. It had seemed like a good idea. But after two weeks at home with nothing to do, she was having second thoughts.

Cicchetti downed a fistful of pretzels. "I was talking to a buddy of mine. Left the job a few years back. He's in private security now. Personal protection. Celebrities, rich people, that kind of deal. He's interested in you."

"Me? What are you talking about?"

"There's a demand for females. Lady clients don't always want a male tagging along, if you get my drift."

"I'm not looking for a new job."

"Yeah, I know. This is just a filler, a short-term assignment type of thing."

Pat shifted in her chair. "I can't take other employment during leave—"

"Here's the thing. This is not, officially speaking, employment. If money changes hands, that's between you and the client. Franco takes his cut is all. As far as the Bureau's concerned, you're doing a favor for a friend."

"I don't know..." She was aware that plenty of former agents and cops made a good living providing personal protection to movie stars and the like. But most so-called celebrities weren't in any real danger. Pat had better things to do than stand around all day acting like the Secret Service for some talent-stricken publicity junkie. Life was too short.

"C'mon. You'll go nuts sitting at home in front of the box," Cicchetti said and started working on his hair all of a sudden.

Automatically Pat glanced toward the door. Yep. Blonde. Stacked. Tight skirt. She finished her beer. "I appreciate it. But I'm not cut out for that line of work."

"Okay, I hear you." Cicchetti wasn't giving up that easily. Eyes flicking between his beer and the reflections in the bar mirror, he said, "How about I tell Franco to give you a call if he's got something. Then you can decide in full possession of the facts. Okay?"

Pat made an effort to sound appreciative. "Sure. Why not." She'd rather say no to this Franco guy than knock Cicchetti back when he thought he was doing her a big favor.

"One condition, okay? If it's Angelina Jolie, tell them you're bringing a sidekick."

"I'll bear that in mind." Pat met his lazy brown eyes. "So. How's it coming?"

Something in his face sagged, and from the corner of her eye, Pat saw the blonde settle at a nearby table with a guy whose hand never left her ass.

"I thought we weren't talking shop," Cicchetti said.

"Just wondering how Agent Sullivan is shaping up."

"So far, so good." Her companion contemplated a neon beer ad suspended above the bar. "We picked up Mulrooney."

"What?" Pat felt winded.

They'd both been sure their third victim, Jaydeene Harper, was the work of a copycat and liked a guy for the killing, a convicted pedophile named Desmond Mulrooney. A Jehovah's Witness, Mulrooney had talked his way into the homes of several Maryland families on the pretext of leading bible study. Once he'd secured their trust, he molested their daughters. Mulrooney had been convicted on three counts of child sexual abuse, served five years, and now lived in Pittsburgh. He claimed to have rehabilitated himself through the power of prayer. Evidently, the Parole Board had bought this story.

Mulrooney had quickly resumed his activities for the church, neglecting to inform the leadership that he was a registered sex offender. He had door-knocked in the Harper's neighborhood two weeks before Jaydeene went missing and had a shaky alibi for the afternoon of her disappearance. But they couldn't get enough evidence to make a case stick, so they'd been keeping tabs on the guy. The media had pegged Jaydeene's murder on the Kiddy Pageant Killer. No one argued. They wanted Mulrooney to think he'd outsmarted the law.

"Got a call from his landlord," Cicchetti said. "Seems he had a plumber in Mulrooney's place last week. The guy sees Mulrooney perusing a kiddy pageant site on his computer and he adds two and two. But he acts polite. Asks Mulrooney if he's got grandchildren."

Pat's heart rate increased. Mulrooney would have figured the heat was off and he could relax and lower his guard. Like most pedophiles, he would find some covert way to relive his cherished crimes in company if he could.

"So Joe Plumber gets our guy talking and he spills his guts about quote unquote, a very special little girl who is now asleep, waiting for Jesus."

"You're kidding me."

"Wait. It gets better. Next thing, he's showing Joe this art-piece thing with an impression of a kid's hand. He's all sentimental like it's his own kid or something."

Pat's jaw dropped. "He made a cast of her hand?" This slimeball was serious about his trophies.

"Had it in plain sight when we knocked on his door."

"Damn, I wanted that interview." Pat couldn't believe it. She takes a leave, and next thing, Cicchetti makes a collar. Perfect; just perfect.

Cicchetti ordered another round. "I knew you'd get all bent out of shape. I shouldn't have told you."

"I'm coming back. I'll call the Chief tomorrow."

"Big mistake," Cicchetti said, sliding a draft along the counter to Pat. "We knew Mulrooney did Jaydeene. It doesn't change anything, us bringing him in."

Pat cradled her chin glumly in her hand. Cicchetti was right. Getting an arrest on the Harper case was a morale boost, but it didn't bring them one iota closer to catching the Kiddy Pageant Killer. She owed it to the other victims to infuse some new energy into the investigation.

Looking awkward, Cicchetti gave her shoulder a squeeze. "Hey, if anything else breaks, I'll call you. Deal?"

Pat raised her glass. A bilious feeling almost choked her. "Deal."

ANTIQUES ROW HAD changed since Pat moved into the neighborhood five years earlier. She rarely had the time to wander through Wash West any more, but after she left Cicchetti, she walked along Camac Street and turned onto Pine. The Row used to be an austere stroll past a procession of antique stores. Most of these had now closed their gated doors, and the street was lined with trendy home stores and cafés.

It was too cold to window shop, so Pat cut through Louis Kahn park, not the safest place to wander after dark. Lately there'd been some incidents involving drug dealers from 13th and Walnut trying to extend their turf. But cops from the Sixth District had increased their patrols and for the time being, the clean-up was working. There were only two other people in the park, a gay couple who lived a few doors down from her on Clinton. They always walked their poodle, Princess Di, around this time.

"Hey, guys," Pat called, her breath fogging. She stopped at the fountain to chat with them.

"Want to come on home?" Gareth asked after a few minutes. The taller of the pair, he managed to look sartorial even in a wool overcoat and muffler. "We're mulling cider."

"Another time," Pat said. "I'm kind of tied up."

"We were reading about that little girl. The latest victim." Gareth's partner, David, lifted Princess Di into his arms, whipped off a glove, and adjusted her plaid coat with plump fingers. "Awful, just awful. You must be devastated."

"Yes." Pat found a tight smile. "It's been a frustrating investigation." She hadn't told anyone she had taken herself off the case.

Despite her attempts to keep a low profile, the entire block knew there was an FBI agent living in their midst. Her presence seemed to engender a mixture of paranoia and gratification. Last year, after she was interviewed on CNN, her neighbors had organized a pot-luck as moral support. Since then, whenever the Kiddy Pageant cases were in the news, someone always showed up on Pat's doorstep with frozen dinners and helpful theories. Pat loved this sense of community; it was something she'd never known growing up. In Wash West, she seldom felt lonely, merely alone.

"Well, we're home if you need a cup of *foie gras* or anything," Gareth said.

Pat grinned. "I'll sleep easy knowing that."

They walked along Clinton together, parting company at Pat's place. She unlocked her door and wandered along the narrow hallway, flicking a few light switches as she went. In the kitchen, she poked listlessly through the refrigerator, discarding the inedible—three-day-old Chinese takeout, a decomposing Caesar salad, sour cream with fungus growing on it. She was not by nature a slob, but lately she'd been too exhausted to deal with domestic trivia.

She found some sliced turkey that hadn't passed its use-by date and made herself a sandwich. Tomorrow she would clean house, buy groceries and stock up on reading material. She had to figure out how she was going to spend the rest of her self-imposed leisure time. Maybe she should go somewhere, Pat reflected. A change of scenery was supposed to lower stress. Mexico would be warm.

Mind wandering, she gazed into the corner of the room. She could almost see her cat Bruno sitting there next to his food bowl, his big ginger face puzzled. Before his kidneys failed completely, Bruno had been on a diet. It had been hell for both of them, and, in the end, it wasn't enough to save him. Pat felt her eyes prickle. She missed the warm heaviness of that feline body in her lap. She missed sleeping with him stretched along her thigh. Velcro-cat, she used to call him. Maybe she could take a trip to the Humane

Society while she was off work and adopt a cat. There would never be a better time to get a new pet settled in.

Bruno had come from a crime scene. The sole survivor of a family annihilation, he had been slashed across the spine. A CSI had found him hiding in an upstairs closet, half-dead. Relatives hadn't wanted to pay the vet bills, so Pat drove the injured cat to the animal hospital, telling herself he would have to be euthanized. But from the moment she'd wrapped him in a towel, they both knew that wasn't happening. Bruno was hers. He would have come to work with her if he could. Instead, Pat used to leave the phone on speaker so she could talk to him via the answer machine while she was working.

That was seven years ago, in the days when she was still kidding herself she could hold down a relationship. Her ex, Wendy, had made it clear they would never move in together if it meant sharing a home with Bruno. Wendy thought Bruno should have been euthanized, especially when his hair didn't grow back properly over the scar along his back. She had pestered Pat to have him de-clawed and had finally issued an ultimatum: If Pat wanted her to sleep over, the cat had to go to the vet. Pat took a pass. It was one of the easiest decisions she had ever made.

The relationship had petered out soon after, and Pat had felt only vague regret. She and Wendy were not meant for one another. Nowadays Wendy was living with a chiropodist and her Mexican Hairless Dog. Pat ran into the happy couple at the supermarket every so often. She always detected a certain smugness about Wendy. *I'm with someone who knows the meaning of commitment* was the message.

Pat chewed on her sandwich. She had concluded a long time ago that she wasn't the type to fall head over heels for any woman. From what she could see, that was a plus. Relationships involved too much risk for uncertain returns. No matter what the couple-cultists wanted everyone to believe, Pat didn't think she was missing out on a whole lot. She was perfectly happy by herself. Occasionally she missed having a sexual partner, but you didn't have to get married to find one of those.

Maybe that was something else she could do for her mental health over the weeks ahead, she decided. Get laid.

# Chapter Four

RETAIL THERAPY WAS supposed to be fun, Lauren thought as she jammed her credit card into her wallet.

A sales clerk wrapped several new dresses in tissue. "I record your show every day," she gushed. "Oh, my gosh, when you and Dr. Addams finally kissed, Mom and I were like...screaming."

"Yeah, that was quite a moment," Lauren said, fingers tapping the counter.

"I've got a friend who's at college, and she wrote an essay about how you should be a role model, not what's-her-name—you know, she's rich and she worked in McDonald's for a day so she'd know how it feels to be poor."

Lauren had no idea who the sales clerk was talking about, but she smiled and nodded. The least she could do was behave like a star. Apparently this young woman hadn't read a newspaper recently. "I'm flattered," she said. "It's fans like you who've made it possible for me to have the career I always dreamed of."

"I can't believe you told that hijacker to get out of your face and let you do your job. That was so brave."

Reprising one of Dr. Kate's lines from the last episode, Lauren said, "It will be a cold day in hell when some lunatic with bad breath tells me to let a patient die."

Buoyed, her young admirer asked, "If it's okay, could I have your autograph?"

"Absolutely." Lauren scrawled her name on the back of a store map.

A small squeal. "Oh, my God, what's going to happen? Are the passengers going to attack the hijackers? I won't breathe a word. I promise."

"I wish I knew," Lauren said as sincerely as she could. "But the writers haven't even told us."

"Well, it has to be a happy ending. I mean, they can't kill off

Dr. Kate, can they?" Laughing, the sales clerk handed over Lauren's shopping bags and added, "I just want you to know I don't believe any of that stuff about you and that woman. Anyway, even if you were gay, so what? I'd still watch the show. I love Ellen and so does my Mom."

Lauren found herself unable to respond. Here was an ordinary young woman who was willing to accept her for who she really was, yet Lauren had to maintain her deception. Would *Dr. Kate* really lose most of its audience if she came out? What was worse — to lie to the decent people who might support her, or to tell the truth and offend the bigots who would not?

Ashamed, Lauren said, "It's great to have your support. I really mean that."

A few minutes later, watching the floor numbers light up inside the elevator, she felt demoralized. Was this to be her life? She was caught in a trap of her own making, and it didn't feel good. They had shot the cliff-hanger episode of *Dr. Kate* yesterday, and Lauren would be packing her bags for an extended European vacation as soon as she got home. By the time the show went to air next week, she would be leaning on a *banco* in Milan, sipping a real *macchiato* instead of the Starbucks version.

Numbly, she stepped back to allow a horde of people into the elevator. As the doors swished closed, she was aware of being recognized, but avoided meeting inquiring eyes. Hopefully she would reach the parking garage before a fan plucked up the courage to talk to her. Or not.

"Excuse me. Are you Dr. Kate?" an older woman asked.

Lauren hesitated. She could almost hear the next question, the one she was asked every time she set foot outside her door. *Is it true that you're a lesbian?* She opened her mouth to reply but was saved by the bell. As the elevator doors opened, a woman in a pink chiffon blouse hissed, "It is her."

With a quick apologetic smile at the older woman who'd spoken first, Lauren set off across the grimy concrete parking lot at a brisk pace. With any luck she would make it to her car before she was asked to pose for a picture. She poked around in her purse, located her car keys, and pressed the remote to unlock the doors. As she lifted the trunk to stow her shopping bags, someone called her name.

Groaning, Lauren closed the trunk and turned. At that moment, there was an explosion and her body was thrown back against the car as if she'd been struck by a sledgehammer. Lauren dropped to the concrete floor, clutching her left shoulder.

"You thought you had everyone fooled!" yelled a man standing about twenty feet away. With both arms extended, he aimed a handgun at Lauren's chest. "God hates homosexuals."

Another explosion followed and the car's rear window shattered, spraying glass in all directions. Lauren lowered her hand from her shoulder to swat the shards away. In shock, she stared at her fingers. They were covered with blood. A tide of red inched down her jacket. It dawned on her that she was shot. Oddly, there was no pain. Time ticked by with exquisite slowness as the man walked toward her, his face contorted by hatred. Lauren dragged herself around the side of her car, reaching for the door. Another shot rang out, and there was a stinging pain in her side. She heard screams, shouts, running feet, the sound of a car motor revving, tires squealing.

A throng of people converged on her, voices shrill and panicked. Lauren caught half sentences. "Call 911...over there...escaped...take down his registration. Oh, my Lord."

"I told you it was her," said the woman in pink chiffon.

"Is she dead?" a man asked.

The older woman from the elevator removed her heavy coat and placed it over Lauren. "Just hold on, Ms. Douglas. The ambulance is on its way." She took Lauren's hand in an urgent grip.

"I know him," Lauren gasped between chattering teeth.

"The man who shot you?" The woman bent close. "What's his name, darling?"

Lauren felt pain stampede through her body, stealing her breath away. Panting, her mind growing foggy, she said faintly, "He's my number one fan."

"I'VE NEVER HEARD of her," Pat said into her cell phone.

"Don't you read the newspapers?" Cicchetti's pal, Franco Giordano, sounded incredulous.

"Not very often."

"Got herself shot by a nutcase fan."

Pat frowned. "I saw that on TV. A soap star. Right?"

"Look at your fax machine. Okay?"

A moment later her printer spat a newspaper article onto Pat's desk. The headline drooled DR. KATE DENIES LESBIAN LOVE AFFAIR.

Pat scanned the printed columns. "Congressman Wendall Douglas III."

"Yeah. The gherkin millionaire. That's who's paying us. Full time personal security for two months. You get sixty K plus expenses. Twenty up front."

"You're kidding me." A bodyguard was a mighty expensive vanity trip if you didn't need one.

"Rates for the elite type service went through the roof after 9/11. Terrible thing." Franco poured cold water on his enthusiasm. No one wanted to sound like they were cashing in on *that* tragedy. "You gotta be crazy to work for the Bureau any more. You wanna think about a career move, just say the word. You'd do real good. My guys, they're making six figures for getting out of bed."

Pat keyed "Lauren Douglas" into Google and ran a search. Every link she clicked brought up publicity shots of an actress with strawberry blonde tresses, indigo eyes, and a girl-next-door smile that underplayed her beauty. *Everyone thinks I'm gorgeous, but I'm really just like you*, it announced. "Yeah, right," Pat muttered.

"Hey. You ask them." Franco thought the comment was intended for him. "Beats the crap out of guarding payroll."

"I'll think on it overnight." Pat tried to picture herself pandering to a self-absorbed soap star 24/7. What a nightmare.

"Sixty large," Franco reminded her.

"Where is this island again?"

"Middle of the fucking Pacific Ocean. There's no way that whack job's gonna show up there. You'll be sitting 'round the pool all day working on your tan."

There were worse ways to make a living; she should know. "I'll think on it and get back to you." She dropped the cell phone on the counter.

Stomach gurgling, she prowled into the kitchen and consulted the refrigerator. The frozen dinner situation was grim. Despite her best intentions, it was now weeks since she'd been in a supermarket. She pulled the nearest box from the freezer and shoved the contents in the microwave. A few weeks of sun and surf was sounding better and better, even if it did mean babysitting a ditz whose lesbian publicity stunt had backfired on her. Lauren Douglas wouldn't be the first actress to spread a rumour that she was gay so she could issue denials and get herself chased by the paparazzi. It must have come as quite a shock to find that some people took her much more seriously than she deserved.

But maybe the shooting was nothing to do with the lesbian revelation. Maybe the fan was just your garden-variety kook who'd built a castle in the air and got hurt feelings when his chosen princess didn't notice. Whatever his story, the guy would be back to finish what he'd started; Pat would put money on it.

She ripped the plastic off her Chicken Primavera and poured

herself a glass of Pinot Grigio. Contemplating her options, she watched the steam rise from her food, took a swig of wine, picked up her cell phone, and called Franco back. "Hey, man," she said. "You hired yourself a gun."

"A BODYGUARD?" LAUREN shook her head emphatically. No way was she buying groceries with some steroid-pumped gorilla in dark glasses and a cheap suit pushing the cart. "Absolutely not. Daddy, really, I don't—"

"There's a crazy out there who wants to kill you," her father said. "Do you think I'm going to let that happen? We're playing it safe until that creep is behind bars. Period."

"But they come everywhere with you," Lauren protested. "You can't even use the restroom without big feet outside the door." She swung pleading eyes to her mother.

Helen Morrow Douglas squeezed her hand. "Your father only wants what's best for you, darling."

"Give me some credit," Wendall Douglas said. "I've hired a female. She's FBI. Graduated top of her class. Black belt in every fucking thing the Japs ever thought of, then some. Sniper training. The whole nine yards. Packs a Glock 23 Compact." An edge of disappointment invaded his tone. Clearly this would not have been his choice of firearm. "Nice piece for concealed carry," he went on as if needing to convince himself. "She probably switches to a .45 ACP when she means business."

"I'm terrified already." Lauren clutched her ribs. Breathing too deeply hurt, so getting agitated was not a good idea. On the other hand, the pain was a small price to pay for being alive.

Her father checked his wristwatch. "She'll be here any minute."

"She's coming here?" Lauren groaned out loud. She already had a police guard sitting outside her private hospital room. And every time her father visited, his security detail lurked in the corridors like sharks at a shipwreck, lifting gurney sheets and getting in the faces of the nursing staff. Just wait 'til this karate expert started throwing her weight around. Lauren would really be Miss Popularity then.

"You bet your life she's coming here," her father said, looking pleased with himself. "The good news is you're getting discharged, and she's going to escort you home."

"Really? I'm going home?"

Her mother smiled. "Isn't that wonderful! We thought you'd want to be in your own apartment tonight, but if you'd rather stay with us at the hotel, that's fine. Tomorrow, if you're fit to travel, we can go back to St. Michaels."

Lauren felt tears prickle. It was funny — since the shooting, her emotions had been all over the place. She cried over complete trivia, yet felt weirdly removed when she contemplated really big things like her break-up and being shot. Wiping her face, she hugged her father. "I love you," she said, inhaling the reassuring scent of his cigars and Truefitt & Hill cologne.

If having a bodyguard meant she could get out of this dump, she could live with that. But there would have to be rules. A bodyguard was an employee, like any other. Lauren would respect the woman as a professional and listen to her opinions, but she would set boundaries. If there was one thing being famous overnight had taught her, it was how to keep people at a distance while appearing friendly and gracious. Celebrity was a balancing act. Perception was everything.

The bodyguard would already have perceptions, most likely shaped by Lauren's TV persona, Dr. Kate Chatterley. She would expect to meet an intelligent, wholesome and somewhat glamorous woman, a dedicated professional with noble instincts and poor taste in lovers. It wasn't far off the mark. But Lauren's public image was a carefully crafted snapshot of who she really was, and at its heart was a huge lie. No doubt she would have to date a few men with the bodyguard in tow to ensure the woman had nothing to leak to the press once her contract ended. It was just as well she and Sara *had* broken up, she thought cynically.

An odd sound drew her attention, and she started with fright. A dark figure stood in the doorway, silently observing. The stranger knocked and entered the room. "Sir, Ma'am." A brief nod. "Patrice Roussel."

Wendall Douglas stood and extended his hand. "Good to see you again, Pat. You've met my wife, of course. And this beautiful young lady is our daughter, Lauren."

Pat's hand was firm and square, larger than Lauren's, her grip businesslike. She greeted Lauren with polite indifference.

"Nice to meet you," Lauren mumbled. It was all she could do not to choke. What was her father thinking? This woman was possibly the most butch lesbian she had ever seen.

No doubt part of the look was for the job. Lauren took in black pants and a cream turtleneck, a tailored leather trench coat, and a thick belt that presumably supported the inadequate Glock. Pat Roussel's straight dark hair was cut very short and she wore no make-up. Long dense eyelashes were wasted on a sensible face with a stubborn jaw and a straight, unsmiling mouth. How typical — it was always guys or unfeminine women who got the eyelashes. And the amazing eyes. The bodyguard's were a mossy shade of green, their expression a mix of sorrow, wariness, and cold detachment.

She's seen it all, Lauren thought, unsettled. Her parents and Pat Roussel were looking at her expectantly. A beat behind, Lauren said, "I'm sorry. Did I miss something?"

Her mother's perceptive gaze shifted from Lauren to Pat and back again. "I asked if you'd prefer to get dressed or go home in your robe, darling."

The tone was benign, but Lauren could almost hear her mother's gaydar bleeping. She knew better than to hope for a reprieve. Helen Douglas was the last person on earth who would raise a fuss over an employee's sexual orientation. In her book, bigotry was a hallmark of profound unintelligence.

Filled with gloom, Lauren said, "I'll get dressed," and buzzed for a nurse.

Her father took Pat aside. In a man-to-man tone, he imparted his plan for a safe getaway. "I'll bring the car around front. There's a couple of my security boys out there by the nurses' station. Just let them know what you want."

Lauren couldn't help but smile. Her father liked nothing better than an occasion he could rise to, preferably one that involved guns and fast cars. Evidently, he saw Pat Roussel as a kindred spirit. Stealing a quick glance at her, Lauren decided he might be right. Pat probably got called *Sir* all the time.

"I can come home with you tonight if you'd like," Helen Douglas offered.

"No. I'm fine, Mom. Honestly. You guys should go see a show while you're in town." Her parents got little enough time together these days. Already they had spent too much of it glued to her bedside over the past few weeks. Lauren waved her parents out of the room, then slumped against her pillows. "The nurse will be here any minute," she informed Pat. "If you'd like to go get a drink or something, I'll be ready when you get back."

Ignoring this tactful request for privacy, her unwanted pit bull paced the room. "I'll need the curtains open while you dress, so I can maintain visual contact. Sorry. I know it takes some getting used to."

"No kidding. Look, I understand you have a job to do," Lauren said with phoney good grace. "But my father's not here now, so you can relax. I'm sure we can come to an understanding about this stuff. For a start, you're not in the room while I'm getting dressed. Got that?"

The green eyes regarded her unflinchingly. "I can appreciate your concerns, Ms. Douglas. However, your father pays my wages, and I report to him. I'm not here to please you. I'm here to protect you."

Speechless, Lauren could only stare as a nurse entered the room and was neatly blocked by Pat, who requested identification.

"She's wearing a uniform," Lauren pointed out.

Like a parent dealing with a problem child, Pat cast a warning look her way. *Don't try my patience*, it said.

Flushed with anger, Lauren greeted the nurse sweetly. "I'll wear the Colette Dinnigan outfit over there, so long as it fits over the dressings. Oh, and please draw the curtains."

EYEING THE PASTEL peach drapes that screened her principal from view, Pat contemplated her options. Under normal circumstances, she would have been satisfied to check the nurse's ID and maintain a watch on the room and its immediate environs. But just as a prison inmate would probe a new guard for weaknesses, Lauren Douglas was attempting to test Pat and assert dominance. The behavior pattern was so predictable Pat succumbed to a half-smile. At this early stage of their relationship, it was Pat's task to define limits and boundaries. Ironically, although her principal would resent this, it would also make her feel secure. At least, that's what Franco's primer on personal security etiquette claimed under the header *Children and Other Reluctant Principals*.

Pat could tell that Lauren Douglas had not even begun to deal with the trauma of her shooting. She was still focused on her physical injuries. When the emotional shockwaves hit, as inevitably they would, she would need to feel safe, and Pat knew exactly how to make that happen. Stepping inside the curtain, she occupied a chair near the bed and trained her gaze on the gap between the curtains. If anyone tried to enter the room, she would see them. Out of the corner of her eye, she kept tabs on the nurse's activities. Lauren was probably in no immediate danger here in the hospital; however, Pat had been trained to expect the unexpected.

Having read the police file on the shooting, she was certain Lauren had been stalked for some time before the shooting, whether she knew it or not. And the guy was still out there. In Pat's experience, stalkers were patient and learned from their mistakes. This nut had tried to kill Lauren in broad daylight in front of witnesses. He was audacious, obsessive, and from all accounts, a religious fanatic. It was a lethal combination. He would try again; no question about that.

"Satisfied?" A fully dressed Lauren dangled her legs over the side of the bed and glared at Pat while the nurse slid shiny black shoes onto each foot.

"Lovely," Pat commented, intentionally misreading the petulant remark.

Lauren Douglas wore a black sweater and tights. Over this was an ivory lace jumper with a gathered skirt threaded with black ribbons. The net effect lay somewhere between beautiful woman and jailbait schoolgirl — in other words, a crazy fan's wet dream.

As the nurse helped Lauren into a wheelchair, Pat said, "Wait here," and stepped into the corridor.

A couple of security guys wearing earpieces stood a few yards away, drinking coffee and eating Danish. US Congressmen weren't important enough to warrant taxpayer-funded protection. But Wendall Douglas seemed to think he needed a security detail. He had told Pat it cost less to employ his own team than to hire specialists every time he traveled overseas on business. On the detail were several former cops, a Navy Seal, and an ex-DEA agent.

"Hey, guys. Babydoll's on the move," Pat told them, adopting their code name for the boss's daughter. Pat wondered if Lauren knew this was her handle. Probably not.

One of the guys spoke into his lapel mic. He gave Pat a nod and she returned to the hospital room and wheeled Lauren out. As they waited for the elevator, she bent and murmured to her principal, "Anything happens, you do two things."

"Okay." Grudging but attentive.

"First. Get down. Hit the deck and stay there." Pat inhaled the scent of Lauren's hair. Citrus and something else; a hint of jasmine. "Second, listen and do exactly what I tell you. No arguments."

"Remind me," Lauren said dryly. "How long do I have to put up with this shit?"

"Your father hired me for two months. After that, who knows?"

A doleful sniff. "He'll probably retain you on permanent staff."

"Don't worry. I won't be available." Pat wheeled the chair into the elevator.

"A better offer?" Lauren shot a quick glance up at her.

"Yep."

Lauren's eyes widened at this casual rebuff. She looked very young without the professional make-up she wore in the publicity photos Pat had seen. Her skin was smooth and almond in tone, her mouth a true bow. Traces of adolescence lingered in the heart-shaped contours of her face. She was not a classic beauty, although her reddish-gold hair was striking. Notably absent was the brittle, prom-queen look most soap stars paid their plastic surgeons to clone. Her slightly snub nose looked like her own, and her smile was a shy display of small pearly teeth instead of the customary expanse of dazzling crowns.

There was a girlish sweetness about Lauren Douglas that was resonant of a different era. No doubt she had been protected from life's harsh realities since the day she was born. She would have sailed through high school and college: popular, rich and pretty. The Laurens of this world were untouched by the turmoil that lay beyond their social bubble. For them, life was not a quagmire in which good slugged it out with evil. They did not agonize over the human condition. They were too busy shopping.

Pat could understand the Douglases wanting to spare their daughter fear and worry. Yet they would not be doing Lauren any favors if they insulated her from the challenges that made people grow. She thought about the web pages and newspaper clippings on her desk at home. Did the wholesome, all-American Lauren they depicted lead a secret life as a lesbian? Had there been a "love triangle"? At first glance, it seemed unlikely. But Pat had been investigating crimes too long to take anything at face value.

After helping Lauren into the back seat of a Mercedes limousine, she slid in next to her and asked, "Comfortable?"

"Shitfaced on morphine," Lauren replied.

Wendall Douglas stuck his head in the door. "She's in your capable hands now," he informed Pat. "Bring her home safe."

"Count on it, sir."

"Don't you worry about a thing, babydoll." He kissed his daughter's cheek, slapped Pat on the shoulder, and waved the driver on.

"WHAT DID HE mean about bringing me home safe?" Lauren demanded some time later, when they were stuck in traffic on Broadway.

"From the vacation, I guess," Pat said.

"What vacation? My trip was cancelled."

Pat paused. "Your trip to Europe was cancelled. Instead you're going to spend a couple of months in the tropics recuperating, remember?"

"I don't know anything about that." Lauren sounded indignant. "When was I told? Was I awake?"

"I don't know."

"Well, tell me what you do know," Lauren insisted. "The

tropics. Where in the tropics?"

"We're flying to the Cook Islands at the end of the week," Pat said. "From Rarotonga, we go to a place called Moon Island. It's a resort. Very isolated. Your father says it's the safest location he could find for you."

Lauren looked dumbfounded. "I can't possibly get organized so soon. We're going to St. Michaels with my mother tomorrow. I won't have time."

"You're already packed. Your executive assistant came around yesterday and took care of that. If there's anything else you need, just let me know."

Lauren was silent for a long moment. "How did this happen to me?" she murmured eventually, as if talking to herself.

Pat did not answer. She was asking herself the same question. It felt surreal to be sitting in a limousine, guarding a TV star, about to embark on the kind of luxury holiday she would never have dreamed of. And she was getting paid for it. Paid handsomely. Nice work if you can get it.

"Tell me something." Lauren looked at her squarely. "Are you gay?"

Pat controlled her expression. She'd expected the question would come up, but Lauren's direct approach had caught her napping. She produced the response she had already rehearsed. "My private life has nothing to do with your security."

"On the contrary," Lauren said. "What if I'm not comfortable with a gay bodyguard?"

"Ms. Douglas, your father is paying me to take a bullet for you if necessary. Maybe you want to give him a call and tell him you'd feel safer with someone who has big hair and wears a skirt."

Lauren blinked. "I'm sorry. I was out of line asking you that. And will you please stop with the Ms. Douglas thing? My name is Lauren."

"Okay. Lauren. Let me tell you how this works," Pat said patiently. "I need to know personal stuff about you for one reason only—so that I can keep you safe. It's not *quid pro quo*. We're not making friends here. All you need to know about me is that I'm qualified to protect you. If you have any concerns about that, feel free to express them."

Emotions played across Lauren's face. She averted her head, gazing out the car window. Pat had the odd impression that she was trying to control tears and reviewed their interaction. Had her approach been too blunt? She was not accustomed to tiptoeing around sensitive feelings. Pat reminded herself that this woman was an actress. Creative types were more emotionally volatile than the rest of humanity. On top of that, Lauren had just suffered a trauma. The situation called for tact and diplomacy.

Pat switched to a kid gloves approach. *Invite the subject to empathize by offering a personal disclosure.* "Lauren, listen, I'm new to working with people like you. Please bear with me."

Her companion shifted her attention from the traffic to glance sideways at Pat. "What do you mean, new?" she asked huskily.

"The last few years, if I ever had to guard anyone, they were in witness protection, or they were criminals. Real assholes. We get taught to use a certain manner with those types so they won't take liberties."

"I'm sure." Lauren looked interested. Tucking her hair behind her ears, she faced Pat more squarely. "So you don't do celebrity bodyguard work very often?"

"The truth? You're my first."

Lauren's mouth parted in that shy smile, front teeth just peeping. "Does Daddy know?"

"It never came up. Your father seemed pretty happy with my qualifications."

The smile grew wider. "I've never had a bodyguard, either."

"I'd hate it." Pat built on the rapport. "Someone hovering around me all day, telling me what I can do and where I can go. Jesus."

Lauren seemed to relax by degrees. "I don't mean to give you a hard time," she said softly. "I can understand why Daddy hired you. I just wish they'd catch the guy. It makes me really nervous to think he's still out there. I can't believe he actually meant to kill me. What did I ever do to him?"

"It's not about you. This guy has problems. You have every right to feel scared, but I promise you something. I will not let anyone hurt you."

Lauren took a deep breath and released it. Pat could tell from her body language that she felt more secure already. Eyes darting to Pat's belt, she said, "You're carrying a gun?"

"Actually, I carry two. This one's a semi-automatic." Pat opened her coat to display the Glock holstered at her side. "And this is a back-up revolver." She lifted the leg of her black jeans. A .38 snubbie was strapped to her calf—a new Smith & Wesson 360 Airlite she'd bought for this assignment. She did not offer up any of the other weapons she concealed on her person. Lauren hadn't asked her about knives, pepper spray, or tasers.

"Oh, my God." Lauren giggled with fetching softness. "You look like an assassin. Are you sure you're not CIA?"

"I considered it once. But no." It had been a close thing. Not long after she'd graduated from the Academy, Pat had set her sights on entering the Clandestine Service. Thanks to her father's engineering career, her family had led a peripatetic existence that included lengthy periods living in the Gulf States. Pat spoke fluent standard Arabic, a fact that had drawn little attention from her superiors prior to 9/11. But she'd always suspected it might open doors for her one day.

Looking to broaden her options and enhance her appeal to special ops recruiters, she had taken FBI sniper training and various advanced weapons courses including hand-to-hand combat and knife combat. Since she was twelve years old, Pat had also been involved in martial arts. Once a hobby, these disciplines now formed part of her résumé. After several high-risk witness protection assignments, she was approached by a CIA Operations Officer. At the same time, the chance came to join the Crimes Against Children unit. In the end, Pat had felt she could do more to help people in an everyday sense by remaining with the Bureau.

"So you left the FBI to become a bodyguard?" Lauren asked.

"No. I'm still an Agent. Officially, I'm on vacation."

"Ahh. So this is kind of a moonlighting thing? That's why you won't be available if Daddy wants to hire you?"

Pat smiled. "Uh huh."

"It's a long vacation." Lauren met her eyes and held them.

"I need some time out."

"You don't want to talk about it."

"Very perceptive."

"We learn about body language in my job, too." Lauren's tone was light, but the message was loud and clear. *Don't assume I'm an airhead.* She yawned slightly and changed the subject. "The police think the shooter's going to come after me again."

"People like him tend to."

"I thought so." Lauren ran a cautious hand over her injured shoulder and shifted in her seat.

She looked sleepy, Pat thought. Whatever they'd given her for pain relief before she left the hospital was kicking in. "Don't worry, they'll have the guy in custody before you get back from this vacation." She injected her voice with confidence. "Meantime, there are some things I'll teach you."

"Like what? Self defense?"

"No, just a few tricks of the trade. So you'll notice more about people. About what's happening around you."

"I think he was watching me," Lauren said.

"What makes you say that?"

"The first time I met him was at a cocktail party. But there was something about him. His face seemed familiar." She closed her eyes and tilted her head back into the cushioned upholstery. "I wish I could remember." Her voice trailed off and she yawned again.

"It'll come to you," Pat said. "Don't force it. Just relax and let your mind wander. Think about your normal daily activities. Driving out of your apartment building. Walking to the store. Filming your TV show. Think about the people you saw without really noticing them...the cars that were always there..."

Pat started slightly as Lauren's body connected with hers. Head drooping, lips softly parted, the young woman had surrendered to exhaustion. Carefully, Pat placed an arm around her, providing a shoulder for her to lean on. As she sank deeper into her drugged sleep, Lauren snuggled contentedly closer, one of her hands curling against Pat's chest. Very gently, Pat stroked the hair away from her face so she could sleep unbothered by the heavy red-gold waves. It was a long time since she'd held a woman. Pat had forgotten how good it felt.

# Chapter
# Five

DR. HELEN DOUGLAS strolled into Lauren's cozy sitting room. "Don't tell me she's still sleeping."

Pat rose politely from her armchair. "Like a baby. I checked on her a few minutes ago."

"Oh, please, don't get up." An impatient gesture. "And my name's Helen." She crossed the room to a small table where the household staff kept coffee brewing all day. "Would you like a fresh cup?"

"Not for me, thanks." Pat resumed her seat near an old-fashioned fireplace. Several split oak logs glowed in the hearth, putting out the kind of heat you never got from the gas equivalent. Stacks of wood on either side and antique fire tools added to the rustic charm.

Located on the eastern shores of the Chesapeake Bay, the sprawling Douglas home had been in the family for generations and was now the Congressman's weekend retreat. Lauren's wing was comfortable and unpretentious. Photographs jammed the walls, bearing witness to the traditions that bound the close-knit Douglas clan. The furniture was solid and smelled of beeswax, centuries-old wood surfaces lustrous with the patina of regular polishing. A family residence drenched in history, it was the kind of home Pat could never have imagined as she grew up. Hers had been a life of impersonal apartments in gated expatriate communities patrolled by heavily armed security guards.

Helen Douglas set her coffee down on a table next to the room's only sofa, prodded the fire, and reached for another log.

"Allow me." Pat took over for her. Feeling self-conscious, she rearranged the logs with a poker and watched as orange flames licked the fresh wood.

For some reason, Pat realized, Helen Douglas awed her. She was not a large woman, but she had a powerful presence. In her finely boned face, Pat caught glimpses of Lauren the way she might look in thirty years if she matured with wisdom, grace and courage. There was something else, too. Helen's clear blue eyes shone with extraordinary candor and perception. Pat guessed she was not a woman who saw anything in superficial terms. Wendall Douglas had mentioned that his wife did foreign relief work. It was only during the drive from BWI airport to the Chesapeake that Pat learned she had just returned from Afghanistan.

She replaced the poker and glanced up to find the doctor observing her intently. Reading faint unease in the summer sky of her eyes, Pat guessed at the cause and said, "You must be worried for Lauren."

Helen blinked, as if shifting her thoughts in a new direction. "I'll certainly be relieved when they make an arrest. I understand he was stalking her for a while."

"The police think so. They've identified a suspect. It's only a matter of time before they find him. Of course, Lauren is not just anyone, so their feet are to the fire."

"Yes." Helen's tone was dry. "I'm not sure how I feel about us getting special treatment because of my husband's influence. I know most women end up fending for themselves in these situations."

"Actually, I was talking about Lauren's TV career. When someone is in the public eye, the police want to be seen to do their job."

"Ahh. Yes. That makes sense." Helen seemed lost in thought for a moment, then she remarked, "My daughter is still a child in many ways. I blame myself. After four sons, it was like a miracle to have a girl. And, you know, when there's a houseful of rowdy boys, one tends to be protective of an only daughter."

Pat wasn't sure quite how to respond without sounding patronizing. "I think Lauren's a credit to you."

"You're very diplomatic." Helen smiled. She had the same small, pearly teeth as her daughter. "I had hoped Lauren might want to come with me to Ethiopia this time. But of course, with her injuries it would not be advisable."

"Well, that's one place the stalker wouldn't follow her."

Helen laughed softly. "Yes, he'd have to be *truly* crazy."

"They'll get him," Pat assured her. "Meantime, Lauren will be with me, and I won't let anything happen to her."

"I can believe that. In fact, I think I'd feel safe in a Kabul alleyway with you."

Pat's cheeks warmed at the compliment. "If I may ask, what made you get involved in such dangerous work, Helen?"

"I'm often asked that, usually by my husband's political

colleagues. I tell them baking cookies just didn't cut it for me."

Pat could just imagine Helen Douglas saying that to a bunch of good ol' boys. She was one of a dying breed. A woman with real class.

"Seriously, though," Helen continued, "my children are grown up, and I'm in a position to be able to make a difference. For me, it would be moral cowardice not to."

"And Congressman Douglas? How does he feel about it?" Pat had trouble imagining her employer cheerfully waving his wife goodbye as she departed for a place where, until recently, women were routinely stoned to death.

"For all his campaign slogans, my husband has a wider view of this world than one might imagine. He knew he wasn't marrying a Stepford wife when he married me."

Wendall Douglas immediately leapt several notches in Pat's estimation. She decided Lauren's parents were quite something. It was hard to imagine how they had produced a daughter who was so — Pat tried to avoid the word *shallow*, but nothing else seemed to fit.

As if Helen could her mind, she said, "None of us is born the person we'll become. We're all forged by our experiences. I'll be interested to see how this one shapes my daughter."

FIVE THOUSAND MILES away, on Moon Island, Annabel Worth reviewed her guest schedule. "Someone booked a Celebrity Seclusion Package. They want adjoining rooms for the principal and her bodyguard."

"There's a connecting door between the bedrooms in Hibiscus Villa," her partner Cody said from the other side of the kitchen counter. "Who's the celebrity?" She added non-verbal parentheses to the word *celebrity* with a flick of each index finger.

Annabel smiled. As always, her beloved was unimpressed that they might be hosting someone famous. "A television star traveling incognito. But the phone number for the reservation is a US Congressman's office. Interesting."

Cody slathered peanut butter across a slice of bread and handed a corner to their two-year-old daughter, who took a couple of bites, then declared, "Enough," and consigned the sandwich to the floor, where it joined an array of chopped fruit scattered beneath her booster seat. Briar Stanton Worth preferred watching food fly to eating it.

"You're going to pick that up," Annabel told the toddler.

With a toss of her glossy black ringlets, Briar declared, "I don't want to." Huge dark eyes challenged Annabel.

"After you've picked it up and put it in the trash, we'll go see Kahlo," Annabel said firmly. There was no reasoning with a two-year-old. After weathering a few screaming tantrums, she had concluded distraction worked much better.

Briar beamed, rebellion instantly forgotten. She adored the dark mare and loved her riding lessons.

Cody lifted the toddler from her seat and brought the trash bin over. Holding the lid open, she looked up at Annabel and said, "So, scare me with the nutty demands. Are we talking just slightly pretentious, or is she one of those do-not-be-fat-in-my-presence twats?"

"Nothing too extreme." Annabel scanned the additional information form for the highlights. "No carnations. Needs the fridge stocked with Pellegrino mineral water. Her make-up artist will be flying in a couple of times to do her hair."

Predictably, Cody snorted with laughter. "She's on an island in the South Pacific where no one gives a damn, but the hair has to be perfect. What planet do these wankers come from?" Cocking her head a little to one side, she said, "A bodyguard in the next room, huh. Did you organize a firearms permit? Can't have Customs impounding her gun. It is a *her*, right?"

"Right. Patrice Roussel. Goes by Pat." Annabel skimmed through the profile form security staff were asked to supply. "Female, aged thirty-four. Five foot ten. Speaks some very bizarre languages...Urdu, Arabic, Mandarin. Interests — reading, shooting, running, martial arts."

"A major jock, huh?" Cody finished sweeping up the lunch debris and led Briar to the kitchen sink to wash her hands.

"I guess in her line of work it's essential." Annabel closed her notebook. "It must be stressful guarding someone 'round the clock."

"Like anyone is interested in attacking these Botox-bunnies. Seriously, if they didn't pay publicists to turn them into celebrities, no one would have any idea who they are. It's pathetic."

"Actors can be targets," Annabel pointed out in a reasonable tone. "Everyone knows their faces. It's pretty hard for them to keep a low profile."

"Oh, please. Getting their faces in the media is their purpose in life. Then they bitch about losing their privacy. My heart bleeds."

"I guess you won't be volunteering to meet her at the airport, then."

Cody paused. "I could make an exception. I mean, if we were talking about a *real* actress like, say, Helen Mirren, that would be a different story."

"Sycophant," Annabel teased.

Cody grinned as she cleaned goo off Briar's face with a washcloth. "I prefer to think of myself as a woman who has her priorities straight."

# Chapter
# Six

LAUREN LIFTED HER hair from her neck and twisted it awkwardly into a topknot. Pain shot through her left shoulder as she struggled to fasten the style with several pins. She and Pat had left the air-conditioned interior of the Rarotonga International Terminal several minutes ago and were crossing an expanse of oozing tarmac. Ahead of them, a group of hangars shimmered in the afternoon heat like a watery mirage.

Strolling along next to her, Pat looked disgustingly cool and comfortable in a loose pale linen suit and Hawaiian shirt.

"God, it's hot," Lauren grumbled.

"Would you like some water?"

"Sure," she said ungraciously, and Pat passed her a bottle of Pellegrino.

The Rarotongan man pushing their luggage cart pointed at an old airplane parked a few hundred yards away. "You can get on board now if you want."

Lauren gasped. "We're flying in that?" Painted khaki green with guns in the nose and tail, the plane was obviously a military vehicle. Did this place even *have* an army? If so, they must be severely under-funded if they had to rent out their planes for tourist transportation. Still, anything was possible in a banana republic where some local crooner played the ukulele in the airport terminal to entertain the tourists waiting to get their passports stamped.

"Where's our pilot?" Pat asked.

"That's him with the tinny and the fag." The Islander indicated a man dawdling across the tarmac toward them.

Mystified, Lauren shot a glance at Pat, who translated, "A can of beer and a cigarette."

"Our pilot drinks on the job," Lauren said tartly. "I feel confident."

In light cotton fatigues and moth-eaten Panama hat, the guy didn't look like much of a soldier, Lauren decided as Pat shook

hands with him and waxed lyrical over the plane. When they
were done with their bonding ritual, the bodyguard remembered
her manners and said, "Bevan Mitchell, meet Lauren Douglas."

"A pleasure, Ms. Douglas." The pilot removed his hat and
aviators and surprised Lauren with a smile that made him seem
almost handsome, that's if you were straight and went for the
Robert Redford type. He shook hands and, in a distinctly British
accent, said, "I must apologize. Ms. Worth was expecting to be
here to welcome you, but she's been held up...faith-healer
protest march in the village or some damned thing. Anyway, if
you'd care to get aboard and make yourself comfortable, we'll
push off as soon as she joins us."

*A faith-healer protest march?* Lauren shot a pointed look at
Pat. What kind of a place *was* this?

Completely unfazed, Pat said, "At least it's not a military
coup." She and the pilot laughed like this was hilarious.

With a pronounced sigh, Lauren climbed the steps of a small
platform and entered the warplane's cabin. There was no first
class; in fact, there were only a few seats at all and half of them
were benches that faced one another. Cargo boxes were stacked
throughout the cabin and a sign taped on the wall said *No
bleeding on maps.*

A stupendously proportioned local woman wearing a floral
skirt and a white cotton top greeted them with a broad smile and
showed them to their seats. "I'm Mrs. Marsters, the housekeeper
for Moon Island. Anything you want, let me know. Okay?" She
handed Lauren and Pat tall, chilled glasses of juice. "Drink this
now."

"Do you have any Pelle—" Lauren began, but fell silent
when Pat elbowed her. Glancing sideways, she whispered,
"What?"

"Drink the juice," Pat whispered back. "Don't insult her by
rejecting her hospitality."

Concealing her annoyance, Lauren took a small sip, then a
longer one. The drink was probably the most delicious she had
ever tasted. Refusing to contemplate the carbs, she said, "This is
incredible."

Mrs. Marsters flashed bright white teeth. "It will make you
fertile," she pronounced, as if this were good news.

"Did she say fertile?" Lauren asked as soon as the
housekeeper had left them.

Pat's mouth twitched. "I believe so."

"Christ, that's all I need."

IT TOOK AN hour and a half to reach their destination, a tiny island in an expanse of ocean so vast it was terrifying.

"This is even worse than I imagined," Lauren said, as Pat helped her unpack a little later in their villa.

"Accessible only by air or sea," Pat observed, pleased by their extreme isolation. "That narrows the possibilities."

"Two months in the middle of nowhere. I'm going to go nuts." Lauren dumped an armful of frilly underwear into a drawer. She looked as beat as she sounded. "God, I need a shower."

"Go take one. I can finish up here," Pat offered.

"It's not your job to unpack my stuff. I'll finish it tomorrow."

"Suit yourself." Pat lifted the cases from the bed and stowed them next to the closet. She checked out the bathroom they would be sharing. White-tiled and austere in its simplicity, it was not exactly the five-star luxury she'd anticipated. But it smelled good, thanks to a huge bowl of creamy gardenias sitting on the vanity counter. And the towels were decent—thick and oversized. "It's all yours," she said from the doorway.

Lauren glanced over her shoulder. Tugging irritably at the zipper of her dress, she asked, "Can you help me with this?"

Pat obliged, and the simple linen garment dropped to the floor. She moved to pick it up, but Lauren said, "Don't. I'll get it later."

Pat could tell she was exasperated. With her left shoulder partially shattered, she had to manage her daily activities barely able to move one of her arms. Dressing was a problem.

Mechanically, Pat unhooked the strapless lace bra beneath the dress and helped Lauren into a silk robe. It felt strange treading this fine line between intimacy and detachment. She could understand why some people found it impossible to keep boundaries in place and ended up having bodyguard-employer love affairs that were splashed all over the tabloids.

That was one eventuality she wouldn't have to worry about. Apart from the fact that Lauren was probably straight and resented the hell out of her, Pat had no plans to compromise her professional ethics any time soon. Fortunately, she didn't have a problem with boundaries. She had learned long ago to compartmentalize her life. Emotions got in the way of work. Attraction could lead to lapses in judgment. Pat simply wasn't going there.

"I'll change the dressings when you're done," she told Lauren.

Lauren hesitated. Holding her robe closed, she turned to Pat with a mixture of frustration and embarrassment. "In the hospital, the nurse helped me shower. It's really hard for me to manage. Mom helped me while we were at St. Michaels, but now..."

"No problem," Pat said impassively. "We can work this out."

Lauren was bright pink. "I should have let Daddy hire a nurse. It just felt kind of crowded, you know. I thought I could take care of myself. I'm sorry."

"Don't be. You have two gunshot wounds."

Lauren perched on the edge of the bed. "The doctor says my shoulder won't close fully for a couple of months and even then I might still have this awful burning pain...what do they call it?"

"Causalgia," Pat said and headed for the connecting door between their two rooms. "I'll change and see you in there in a few minutes. Okay?"

Lauren gave her a grateful look. "Okay."

"TELL ME IF it's too hot." Pat slowly moved the hand shower over Lauren's body, avoiding the dressings on her shoulder and side.

"It's fine." Lauren's throat felt tight.

Pat was sponging her as impersonally as the nurses had, yet the occasional brush of her fingers brought with it a rush of memories. Lauren was suddenly painfully conscious of how much she missed touch, the feel of someone else's skin against hers. She had expected Sara would come and see her in the hospital. There had been one phone call, the day after it happened. It was the last time they'd spoken. After a week, Lauren had asked her father if he was preventing Sara from visiting her, but he said she hadn't tried. Somehow, that had hurt almost more than the cheating. If Sara had loved her, she would have been at her bedside no matter what.

Tears mingled with the water on Lauren's face. So much had happened in the weeks since she had caught Sara cheating. She stared down at the dressing below her collarbone. The gunman had aimed for her heart and missed. That's what the police said. The guy wasn't much of a shot, it seemed.

Pat handed the showerhead to her and closed the glass doors, saying, "When you're ready, I'll help you dry off."

"Thank you." Lauren was grateful she didn't have to explain that she needed some time alone to wash her intimate zones.

When she was done, she turned off the water and replaced the showerhead. She had barely opened the doors when Pat held up an open towel, screening her as she stepped from the shower, then wrapping her, eyes slightly averted.

Pulling a padded bathroom seat from beneath the vanity counter, Pat said, "Sit down," and, with another towel, she dried Lauren's arms and legs, careful not to jar her shoulder.

"It's very nice of you to make this comfortable for me," Lauren said, wanting Pat to know her respectful manner was appreciated.

A fleeting emotion altered Pat's expression. "I've had some practice. I nursed my Mom after a serious car accident."

"Oh. Is she doing better now?"

"She died a few months after it happened. A brain hemorrhage. I think it was connected to the accident, but the doctors weren't sure." Pat dropped the extra towel in a laundry basket and turned her attention to Lauren's dressings.

"I'm sorry for your loss." Lauren held part of her towel across her breasts but allowed the rest to fall aside so Pat had access to her ribs, front and back. She winced as an adhesive cover was removed.

"It was some time ago," Pat said. "My Dad remarried recently, and I have two half-brothers now. Just little kids."

Lauren knew Pat was talking to distract her as layers of gauze were removed, and then the sterile dressings that covered the entry and exit wounds beneath her ribs. Steeling herself for the burn of the anti-bacterial solution, Lauren asked, "Do they live near you?"

"No. They're in Dallas, Texas. Hold tight." Pat swabbed the wounds, front and back.

Lauren tried not to whimper during the torturous process, but she couldn't help herself. "It's okay. Keep going," she urged, as Pat wavered slightly.

After replacing the dressings, Pat squatted in front of her, taking both her hands in a warm, strong grip. "Give me some deep breaths."

Eyes watering, Lauren released the breath she was holding. "I'm fine. You're pretty good at this. Better than some of the nurses."

Pat secured the waterproof outer dressing bellow Lauren's ribs. "You won't be saying that after I bandage your shoulder."

"Now you're really scaring me." Lauren stood and exchanged her towel for a bathrobe.

As Pat helped settle the garment over her shoulders, Lauren reflected on her relative good fortune. The flesh wound in her side was not severe. The bullet had passed right through her, missing vital organs. The wound was clean and healing quickly. Her shoulder was in much worse shape, however. The bullet had not exited originally, and doctors said the full extent of nerve and bone damage might not be apparent for some time. With a shaky laugh, she headed for the door, saying, "Come on. Let's do the rest of this on the bed, since I've fainted so many times sitting up."

LAUREN LAY ON her back and pushed the robe well clear of her injured shoulder. "Knock yourself out," she invited.

This was pretty bizarre, she thought, as she felt the dressing coming off. Pat Roussel's demeanor was impersonal to the point of coldness, and getting her wounds dressed was not exactly a turn-on, yet Lauren felt strangely aroused.

Out of the corner of her eye, she watched the bodyguard in the dressing table mirror, standing over her in a pair of loose-fitting khaki shorts and a white t-shirt so damp it was glued to her muscular shoulders and torso. Around her middle she wore a heavy leather belt, her gun holstered on the right. She was solidly built, not much of a waist or butt.

Lauren wondered if she had a girlfriend, then yelped as she felt the burn of fluid in her wound. "How's it looking?" she asked, irritated by her train of thought. What was it to her whether or not her bodyguard had a girlfriend?

"Pretty good," Pat responded. "It's clean. No sign of infection."

Lauren pictured herself reaching for Pat, the robe falling aside, Pat kissing her mouth, her breasts; that hard body against hers. "Wonderful," she said, trying to redirect her thinking away from sexual fantasy. What was the matter with her? Pat Roussel was not even her type. And maybe she wasn't gay, but was one of those tough, butch-looking straight women. *Yeah, right.* Lauren felt her robe slide back over her body as Pat drew the all-concealing garment considerately across her.

"How does that feel?"

Excruciating. Like a huge, burning cavity in my body...relentlessly painful, a constant reminder of the event it evidenced. "Good." Lauren rolled onto her side and found a weak smile. "Thank you."

"Can I get you anything? Tea, coffee...um, Pellegrino?"

Lauren shook her head. "I think I'll get some sleep." Her eyes dropped to the belt buckle at Pat's waist. Seized by an urge to reach out and unfasten it, she laced her fingers together.

"Sounds like a plan." Pat removed the medical kit and the towels. A moment later, she sat down on the edge of the bed and said, "I'm going to take a look around while you rest." She set her .38 on the dresser next to Lauren. "You won't need this, but

I'm leaving it just in case. Don't open the doors."

"I have no idea how to fire one of these," Lauren said. "I'd probably shoot myself in the foot."

"Don't touch it unless you absolutely have to. The safety catch is off. Just point and squeeze the trigger." Pat handed her a small black box with an orange button. "If you need me, press this. It's an alarm siren."

"God." Lauren laughed softly. "This is like a movie." *The Bodyguard*, her mind suggested. She was wet between her thighs. Hoping Pat could not tell the effect she was having, Lauren drew the covers back and got into bed. "Have fun. I'll see you later."

The epitome of cool, Pat studied Lauren's face, her green eyes assessing. "Sure you feel okay about being here alone?"

"Of course." Lauren did not want telltale pink to flood her cheeks. Neither did she want her heart to accelerate. Both happened. "To be quite honest, I'd like some time to myself. Nothing personal."

With a faint smile, Pat stood and started for the door. "Get some sleep. And don't worry. I've got your back."

As soon as she was alone, Lauren fell back onto her pillows with a loud groan. She felt like one of those geese she'd seen on the Discovery channel, who treat the first thing they see after they hatch as their mother. Was this what happened after a painful break-up? Did the first lesbian you encounter become imprinted somehow?

Lauren decided this gaydar anomaly would pass. All she had to do was ride it out without making a fool of herself. Meantime, she could permit herself a few harmless sexual fantasies. Arranging her pillows so she would not accidentally roll onto her wounds in her sleep, she imagined Pat in bed next to her. She imagined herself cradled in those strong arms, warm and safe, Pat's mouth on hers. How did she kiss? Possessively, Lauren decided. Sensuously and deliberately. Sex with Pat would be nothing like sex with Sara. It would not be slow and sweet and sighing. It would be hot and hard. Intense. Sweaty. There would be no negotiations over whose turn it was to do what. Instinctively, Lauren knew that Pat would take control, and she would surrender. That simple.

Releasing a pent-up sigh, she slid her hand down between her legs and let herself fantasize.

PAT CLOSED THE connecting door behind her and took a deep breath. Peeling off her shorts, damp t-shirt and sports bra, she removed a neatly folded pile of garments from her suitcase and donned dry clothing. It was tempting to dwell on the sensuous ritual of soaping Lauren's body, but Pat wasn't going there. Lauren was attractive, vulnerable, and her job to protect. She was Babydoll. The principal. Pat needed to respond accordingly. That did not include wondering how it would feel to cup those beautiful breasts and bite her neck.

Switching to a shoulder holster, Pat slid the Glock into place beneath her left arm and glanced in the mirror. She felt ridiculously conspicuous. So much for buying a compact handgun so she could carry more discreetly. She opened a heavy, reinforced case and checked that her various accessories had survived the trip undamaged. High powered binoculars. Night vision glasses. Stun gun. She could not imagine needing most of this gear, but Franco insisted his staff act the part. At least it was a tax deduction.

Pat pushed the hefty case out of sight behind a large wooden closet that stood in the corner of her room. Sliding the binoculars over her head, she paced quietly through the villa, checking the window fastenings and making a mental note of the vulnerabilities. The building was a sieve. Might as well throw down a welcome mat that said *Intruders — Please Wipe Before Entering.*

Moving out onto the verandah, Pat scrutinized the environs through the high-powered binoculars. The beach lay a few hundred yards away, down a slope through a belt of tropical trees and bushes weighed down with fruit and flowers. The air was heavy with their scent, a ripe, fruity muskiness that assaulted her senses. Wendall Douglas was dead right about Moon Island. It was probably one of the few civilized places in the world where a minor celebrity like Lauren could hole up and drop quietly off the radar.

Yet the place had its drawbacks. The thick foliage would provide the perfect cover for anyone who had a clue how to camouflage himself. Although it seemed highly unlikely Lauren's stalker would track them down to this remote Pacific Island, he had been cunning enough to shoot Lauren in a public place and escape the scene. Until Pat heard he'd been arrested, she would be taking no chances.

Satisfied with what she had seen so far, she returned to the villa and cracked open the door to Babydoll's bedroom. Lauren was sound asleep beneath the ivory bed covers, her pillows arranged to cradle her without pressure. Pat took a few steps closer to the bed. Hijacked by a strange tenderness, she could not drag her eyes from the inert form. In the half-light of dusk, Lauren was bled of color. Serene in repose, her hands folded on her chest, she seemed sculpted. Pat was reminded of those reclining marble statues she had seen in the great European cathedrals during her childhood. Sleep had stripped Lauren's sophisticated veneer away, revealing the childlike sweetness Pat had seen in her face when they first met.

Pat knew herself well enough to recognize that Lauren's vulnerability aroused her most protective instincts. That the younger woman had survived a murder attempt and was still in peril magnified those feelings. It would be a mistake to read anything else into the rush of warmth she felt looking down at the sleeping woman. As for that lustful moment in the bathroom, Pat was only human. She hadn't had sex in more than a year, and Lauren Douglas was nothing if not alluring.

Retreating from the bedside, Pat silently closed Lauren's door and left the villa once more, locking the front door behind her. Shifting her focus from the woman she was hired to protect to the mechanics of protecting her, she circled the building, assessing every weakness. There was no way to make the place secure, she concluded finally. This was a vacation home, built to shelter its occupants from sun and rain, not deranged psychopaths. To guarantee Babydoll's safety, Pat would need to stick to her like white on rice.

A narrow walking path snaked down through the trees to a white beach. She followed it, glancing back toward the villa at regular intervals. Despite its obvious security headaches, the place had a lot going for it as the perfect hideaway. It wasn't even identified on most maps. Short of housing Lauren on Plum Island, it would be hard to find a more inaccessible spot.

By Pat's assessment, the risks to Lauren were low while she was on Moon Island. Assuming Pat could keep her mind on the game, this would be the easiest money she'd ever made.

# Chapter
# Seven

LAUREN OPENED HER eyes, stretched languidly, and reached into a nearby cooler for a bottle of iced tea. Automatically, she scanned the beach, seeking Pat Roussel's familiar shape. An expanse of white sand extended the length of the bay to a clump of distant coconut palms. The turquoise lagoon was so tranquil the water merely lapped at the beach. Out beyond the glassy calm, waves crashed against the reef in a rhythmic pulse.

Pat had said she was going to swim but she was nowhere to be seen. Slightly alarmed, Lauren propped herself up on an elbow and looked left and right once more. Only a week had gone by, and already she took the bodyguard's constant presence for granted.

"I'm right here." The voice came from a few yards behind Lauren's beach blanket.

Pat was sitting in a deck chair in the shade of a mango tree, reading a hefty book.

Lauren craned to see the cover. "Profiling Violent Crimes, An Investigative Tool," she read aloud. "God, Pat. Take a break. I've got a bunch of trash novels if you want some actual entertainment."

Pat looked unenthusiastic. "Probably not my style."

"Do you ever watch television?"

"Not really. I don't get a whole lot of spare time."

"And when you do, it's still about your job, huh?" Lauren grunted with pain as she pushed herself into a sitting position.

"Sometimes I take in a movie."

"Let me guess. *Silence of the Lambs*."

Pat gave a rueful laugh of admission.

"I knew it." Lauren grinned. "You need to get out more."

"Uh huh."

"I'm serious. It's not healthy to do nothing but work. I mean, look at you. You were supposed to be taking time out.

Instead you're guarding me from a crazy man and reading textbooks about crime. There's something wrong with that picture, wouldn't you say?"

Without answering, Pat closed her book and got to her feet, removing the loose tropical shirt she always wore when they were outside the villa. Beneath it, she had on a midriff-length athletic top and a shoulder holster.

God forbid she sit on the beach without being armed to the teeth, Lauren thought.

"Come on," she said, extending a hand to Lauren. "Let's swim."

Slipping her hand into that reassuring grasp, Lauren felt a shock of awareness. It was all she could do not to stare at the naked band of flesh between Pat's close-fitting top and shorts. Solid and muscular, her torso was as highly toned as the rest of her. How many hours a week did this woman spend working out? Lauren's eyes dropped to Pat's thighs. She wore a folding knife in a waterproof sheath strapped to one of them. The first time Lauren had seen it, she'd spoken her mind, pointing out how superfluous it was, given that Pat carried a semi-automatic.

Pat had listened as if humoring an idiot, and said, "Thanks for sharing." She kept right on wearing the weapon as part of her beach attire.

For some reason, the knife unnerved Lauren almost more than the gun. She supposed it was because knives implied proximity and hand-to-hand combat. It seemed more violent somehow, although that was absurd. What could be more violent than a lethal handgun? An assault rifle, her mind suggested. Pat probably had one of those stashed under her bed. Nothing would surprise Lauren.

As they reached the water's edge, Lauren removed her sarong and tossed it onto the dry sand a few feet away. Her strapless bikini felt even skimpier than usual today. It was silly to feel self-conscious. After all, Pat saw her completely naked in the shower every time she helped her wash, and it was not like she had given the bikini a second glance. Lauren might as well be wearing a sack.

Feeling irritated over her own chagrin, Lauren forced herself to think rationally. What did it matter whether Pat noticed her as a woman? It wasn't like Lauren wanted that kind of attention from her bodyguard. In fact, it would be a real problem. She was just having a reaction to her breakup. Who wouldn't lose confidence having their girlfriend cheat on them with a man? On some level, she supposed she was seeking reassurance that she was still attractive. That's why Pat's lack of interest bothered her. It was not that she was attracted to the woman; far from it. Pat was not her type at all. Lauren had only ever dated other lipstick lesbians like herself. She had nothing in common with women like Pat Roussel. In fact, she had always felt a little uncomfortable around butch lesbians; they were so obvious.

Determined to get her mind off this discouraging topic, Lauren waded out into the warm lagoon until the water was just above her waist. When Pat said swimming, what she really meant was walking alongside Lauren as she floated and kicked her way along. The gunshot wounds were protected by waterproof outer dressings Pat applied every morning. Lauren hoped she would be able to swim without these before they left the island, but for now, healing meant keeping bacteria out.

"Your doctor's appointment is for this afternoon," Pat reminded her after they had completed a length of the beach.

Lauren's medical records had been faxed to the Rarotonga Hospital. Once a week they were supposed to make the trip there for a medical examination. Today Lauren's hair-and-make-up artist would be in Avarua, so she could kill two birds with one stone. Toni would be mortified to see her looking like a low-rent tourist.

Squeezing salt water from her hair as they waded ashore, Lauren said, "Great. I'll be able to get my hair done and make some calls." No one had bothered to warn her in advance that the Cook Islands had only just acquired the GSM network that would enable international cell phone calling, and Moon Island was too remote to connect to this. Incredibly, they still depended on short-wave radio. Lauren could only imagine how many messages she must have waiting.

As they strolled along the beach, she glanced sideways at Pat, marveling that the other woman didn't feel ridiculous wandering around an island resort in swimming shorts and top with a gun in a shoulder holster.

"You know," Lauren said. "You could take the gun off and leave it on the beach when we swim. That way you'd actually be able to get in the water. Just a suggestion."

"Thanks for the thought," Pat said. "But I'm not on holiday."

Lauren rolled her eyes. "I hope my father is paying you well."

"He is." Pat's face gave nothing away. Lauren wished she could see her eyes, but as always, they were screened by a pair of those weightless hi-tech sunglasses spies in movies wore.

"Want to sunbathe some more, or shall we go in?" Pat asked as they approached their umbrella.

"I'll stay out here a while." Lauren fastened her sarong, located a comb and pulled it through her tangled hair. "You can go in if you want. Honestly. Look around. We're the only people here."

"Actually, we're not," Pat said. "There's a boat a couple of miles out, and Cody Stanton is coming down to the beach on that horse of hers.

Lauren stared in the direction of Villa Luna. "I don't see her."

Pat handed her the binoculars she always carried. Lauren focused first on the trees that screened the owners' villa, then out to sea. Pat was right on both counts. "It's quite a big boat," Lauren remarked. "Deep sea fishing, I guess."

"It's too big for charter fishing," Pat said, taking back the binoculars and training them on the speck. "Looks like a marine exploration vessel of some kind." She glanced along the beach. "Wait here. I'll have a word with Cody."

Pat Roussel was way too used to tossing orders around, Lauren decided as her watchdog strode off toward the approaching rider. Niggled, she watched the two women talk and vacillated over whether to join them. It was one thing to go along with Pat's specific safety directives, another to mindlessly obey her every instruction. She wasn't a child.

Resolutely, she marched across the hot sand and greeted Cody with a smile. "Hey, there. Good to see you." Patting the tall black mare so she could avoid looking at Pat, she said, "What a beautiful animal."

"Thanks," Cody said. "Her name's Kahlo. You ride?"

"Not as much as I used to." Lauren could sense Pat's cool regard, but kept her gaze on Cody. It was not a hardship. Their cute host would have drawn a second glance from Lauren any time. "I'd love to take her out one day."

"Sure," Cody responded. "Let me know when and I'll ride over." Her frank gray eyes flicked to Pat, clearly seeking her sanction.

Irritated, Lauren said, "How about tomorrow morning? Say nine?"

"Nine it is." With a casual wave, Cody trotted off.

As soon as she was out of earshot, Pat said, "What are you trying to prove?"

"Nothing," Lauren said coolly.

"I can't permit you to take that horse out."

"You take too much for granted." Lauren's voice rose despite her attempts to keep it steady. "If I want to go for a ride, I shall. I'm not a child."

"Then stop behaving like one. You have a gunshot wound in your shoulder, so one of your arms is useless. It would be irresponsible to ride in your condition."

"It's not the Kentucky Derby," Lauren said huffily. "Just a trot on the beach."

"If the doctor says it's okay, fine."

The doctor. Lauren's heart sank. No self-respecting medical professional would clear her to ride a horse. Yet again, Pat had all the answers.

"I'm going back to the villa." Lauren knew she sounded petulant, but could not help herself.

She'd never realized how much she cherished her space until it was invaded every waking minute. It was not Pat's fault. The woman was only doing her job. It was that creepy waiter who was responsible for this whole crazy situation. Fed up, she stuffed her beach gear and reading material into her bag and slouched her way up the slope to the villa, shrugging off Pat's hand when she tried to help her over a root mass. On second thought, that fan would never have shot her if she hadn't been outed all over the media. And who was to blame for that? Sara Jacobs, that's who.

Lauren retreated to her room and lay on the bed, staring up at the whitewashed ceiling. How could she have spent three years with a woman who was using her, and failed to notice what was going on? She had wanted to believe in love, she supposed, and Sara had told her what she wanted to hear. With the benefit of hindsight, she could see that she had missed countless red flags. All those late nights when Sara's cell phone was turned off so she could "concentrate on work." The glamorous new lingerie she had started buying—stuff she never normally wore: garter belts, bustiers, sheer nightgowns.

Sara had ratcheted up the golden highlights in her light brown hair and changed the style to a sexier, more layered look. And she had starved and exercised herself down to a size four, not an easy feat for a woman who had weighed over 150 pounds when they met. Lauren had attributed the makeover to Sara's new job. But even before she'd joined Bernstein's, Sara had been taking phone calls in the bathroom and keeping all her credit card bills at work, where Lauren couldn't see them.

On and off throughout their relationship, she had pressured Lauren to change the apartment title to joint names. Just weeks before their break-up, Sara had stepped up her campaign, preparing the legal work herself and handing Lauren a set of documents she was supposed to sign. The emotional blackmail had been low-key but unmistakable. With their third anniversary approaching, how much longer did Lauren plan to leave Sara in a vulnerable position should anything happen? Because of their very different financial situations, there had always been a power imbalance in their relationship. Wasn't it time Lauren trusted Sara enough to share every part of her life equally?

Some gut instinct had kept Lauren from signing those papers even when the urge to do so was overwhelming. Had she sensed something was not right? Lauren turned onto her stomach and closed her eyes. She'd been a fool, she thought bitterly.

From the doorway, Pat's voice came as an unwelcome intrusion. "Everything okay?"

"Yes," Lauren mumbled. "Please, just leave me alone."

She knew Pat remained standing there for some time, but Lauren ignored the unspoken invitation to get over whatever it was she was feeling and behave like a regular person. So what if Pat thought she was being childish? She hadn't been through what Lauren was going through. She had no idea how Lauren was feeling. And even if she did, why should she care? She was only here because she was paid to be.

Hot tears ran down Lauren's cheeks. She wanted her life back the way it was — at least the way she had thought it was — before the bubble burst.

A STACK OF thick files sat in silent reproach on the coffee table. Pat had not looked inside them since closing her office door at home three weeks ago. Pouring herself a strong coffee, she contemplated returning the files to her suitcase, locking it, and shoving it out of sight and mind. Instead she sat down in an armchair within view of both the front windows and Lauren's bedroom door, which was ajar.

Babydoll was feigning sleep. From her hunched body language, Pat could tell she was seething, and not just about the horse. Lauren's mood swings were symptomatic of a wider issue. Pat recognized the misdirected anger, having encountered it time and again among victims of crime and their families. Once the initial numbing shock of an attack passed, victims almost always experienced a free-floating anger. Pat knew better than to take it personally. Lauren, like most people suffering the emotional aftermath of a trauma, simply channeled her rage at the nearest target.

Pat sipped her coffee and wondered if there was a psychologist on Rarotonga who could see Lauren. She had attempted to discuss the idea of therapy with Wendall Douglas, but he had insisted that a prescription of happy pills would tide his daughter over until she returned home. Lauren had refused to take the medication, but Pat had the pills in her possession and instructions to administer them if it seemed her charge was slipping into depression or suffering panic attacks.

Flipping open the file on top of the heap, Pat reminded herself that Lauren Douglas would be just fine. The average crime victim could only dream of a situation in which they could feel safe, cared for, and free of the stresses of everyday life. Most were ordinary people who had to look after children, pay the mortgage, please the boss, and somehow survive an inner hell at the same time. Lauren was one of a fortunate few who could allow her life to come to a complete standstill without dire consequences. So she might not be the overpaid star of a banal soap opera any more. BFD.

Pat dropped her eyes to a stack of photographs tucked inside the file. Shelby-Rose Dubois gazed up at her from a modeling agency portrait her dirt-poor parents had spent a week's wages on. Only six years old, she wore false eyelashes and full make-up, including a beauty spot painted just above her glistening scarlet mouth. Like a cloud of spun sugar, her bottle-blonde hair clung to her head, anchored by a diamante tiara. According to Gilbert and Jake, she could actually sing in tune, unlike most would-be Shirley Temples on the pageant circuit. She tap-danced, performed a magic trick involving a rabbit, and could not only recite all fifty states in the Union, but also the first twenty Presidents. Gifted as well as beautiful, the tabloids had gushed, reporting on her death.

Shelby-Rose's parents had planned a glittering future for her, pinning their hopes on starring roles in television commercials and a big break that would launch her career in Hollywood or as a supermodel. Failing that, they were convinced she would at least win a college scholarship and marry a doctor. To scrape up the $20,000 necessary to finance her bid for the West Virginia Perfect Miss Supreme title, they had sold their trailer and moved in temporarily with Mr. Dubois' folks. As far as Pat knew, they were still there, packed into the spare bedroom with their three sons.

It didn't help that John Dubois had now lost his job, along with a couple of million poor schmucks just like him, while millionaires like Wendall Douglas III got a tax break. Reminding herself that she was not too proud to accept a fat paycheck from the Congressman, Pat glanced in at his daughter, then returned her attention to the file.

She had examined and re-examined the minutiae of Shelby-Rose's short life, hoping that their killer was linked to his first victim through personal contact or geographic proximity. Every lead had culminated in a dead end, yet she remained convinced that they had missed something. Statistically, almost all serial killers carried out their first crimes close to home. As they gained confidence, they expanded their comfort zone and moved their activities further afield. Likewise, they adjusted their MOs as they became more experienced, learning from the mistakes they made.

Serial killers fell into different types. Trappers lured their victims to them; stalkers followed a chosen victim; poachers traveled far from home; trollers committed opportunistic crimes while they were involved in other activities; hunters traveled just far enough from their homes to find a victim.

The hunter was torn between a desire to kill away from home where he wouldn't be recognized, and an opposing desire to remain in the comfort zone of familiar territory. Trying to balance these urges meant he operated close to home, but not too close. Working on the premise that the Kiddy Pageant Killer followed this hunter pattern, FBI profilers had mapped his growing activity radius, the locations of attack sites, and the body-dump sites. Their conclusion was not exactly a lightning bolt: The killer lived in the tri-states area.

His psychological profile categorized him as an organized offender. A sadistic, preferential child molester. White, male, probably in his forties. Unmarried. Socially competent. He had completed high school, but probably not college. He was neat and tidy and lived alone but had close contact with his parents. People would find him polite and ordinary.

How had he come into contact with Shelby-Rose? Pat didn't buy the theory her superiors favored—that of the day-pass pedophile. As if any respectable magazine was in the market for freelance photos of six-year-old beauty queens. She recalled her interviews with pageant organizers, always eager to declare their God-fearing, right-thinking, good citizen credentials. These pillars of society saw no problem selling tickets to anyone who wanted to watch little girls posing like porn stars on training wheels. She and Chuck Cicchetti had attended a bunch of pageants to scope out the audience, picking up a few known sex offenders as they went.

These creeps all had alibis that panned out and, unsurprisingly, all claimed to know nothing about the victims. Pedophiles protected one another. To a man, the child abusers they had interviewed expressed righteous indignation over the killings, insisting they would be the first to turn in the depraved individual who killed those sweet little girls if they knew who it was. Some had seemed genuinely offended to be questioned, loudly protesting their innocence and citing their own "lesser" crimes as proof that they were not killers. But Pat had learned long ago not to believe a word any pedophile spoke. To these masters of self-deceit, lying to others was routine.

With a sigh, she dug into the file, locating some of the interviews she had tagged for re-evaluation. In the early stages of the investigation, one of Shelby-Rose's uncles had caught their attention. But the guy's alibi checked out, and once it became obvious that they were dealing with a serial killer, the focus of the investigation had shifted away from the Dubois family. Yet Caleb Dubois, known to all as Duke because of some passing resemblance to John Wayne, had remained on Pat's radar.

It was gut instinct. The only one of eleven siblings who had graduated high school, Duke was the success story of the family. He had joined the military and was honorably discharged after sustaining a back injury during a combat exercise. With an ex-army pal, he'd gone into business and now owned a successful string of hamburger franchises. Duke had never married, and the picture his brothers painted was of a freewheeling bachelor with plenty of money and glamorous women hanging off each arm.

Their wives had a different take. Several had said he made them uncomfortable. Everyone noticed how he had spoiled his niece Shelby-Rose with extravagant gifts, yet virtually ignored the other children in the family. To help out his brother with the pageant expenses, Duke had even hired Shelby-Rose for a television commercial advertising his burgers. At her funeral, it was Duke who gave the eulogy, his grief visible. When asked about his favoritism, he had been perfectly frank. Most children were rude and repulsive, he said. But Shelby-Rose was perfect.

His choice of the word "perfect" had preyed on Pat's mind ever since that interview. It was probably nothing, she had reasoned a thousand times over. But the killer used the same epithet for the sash he awarded each of his victims. *Little Miss Perfect Petal.*

Angry with herself all of a sudden, Pat closed the file and picked up her binoculars. What was the point in taking a break if she was only going to spend all her time thinking about the case? She was crazy to have brought her notes with her. How could she hope to gain new perspective if she couldn't let go long enough to clear her mind?

She stalked to the window and scanned the surroundings. A rush of tension invaded her limbs at the sight of a small outboard approaching Passion Bay. Cody was on the beach, watching its progress. Pat zoomed in on the occupants — two men wearing casual clothing. They didn't appear to be armed, but it was hard to tell. Not about to take any chances, she checked the Glock and slid it back into her shoulder holster, pulled on a loose Hawaiian shirt, and stuck her head in Lauren's door.

"I need to go down to the beach. We have company."

Lauren rolled over. Her face was tear-stained. "Who is it?" There was a note of alarm in her voice.

"Looks like a couple of guys from that boat we saw earlier. Stay put and I'll check them out."

Lauren frowned. "What if someone comes to the door?"

"You're not home." Catching a trace of panic in her eyes, Pat added, "Relax. I'll be watching. I'm going to lock you in. Okay?"

"Okay." Lauren sat up and swung her feet to the floor. "Can I sit at the window?"

Pat hesitated. It would be better if Lauren were out of sight. On the other hand, Pat understood that her principal had become dependent on her presence. Being able to maintain visual contact would give Lauren a sense of security.

Pat crossed the living room and angled an armchair to one side of the window frame. "You can sit here and watch." She handed Lauren the basic binoculars that belonged to the cottage. "I'll be back in ten minutes."

A DARKLY TANNED man with sun-bleached hair cut the motor and waved cheerfully from the small outboard. In a broad Australian accent, he said, "G'day. Mind if we step ashore?"

Cody took her time looking their visitors over. Designer stubble, ponytails and costly Maui Jim sunnies. "That depends," she said. "Who are you and what are you doing here?"

The two men promptly jumped into the shallows and pulled their craft ashore as if this were an invitation.

"I'm Doug Farrell." The Aussie stuck out his hand. "My colleague is Pierre Michaeu. We're with the *Aspiration II* research expedition."

Cody introduced herself and shook hands without enthusiasm. "So, what brings you to Moon Island?"

"We were hoping to speak to the owner," Doug replied.

"Maybe I can help you. I'm her partner." She could almost hear them processing this.

It seemed comprehension dawned for the Australian. Looking past Cody, he raised his hand in greeting. "And I guess this would be the woman herself."

Turning, Cody saw Pat Roussel striding across the sand, her unbuttoned shirt flapping in the breeze, a shoulder holster plainly visible beneath it. "That's not my partner," she said, stifling a nervous laugh.

Both men removed their sunnies and wiped them. Cody guessed it wasn't every day they saw a woman with more muscles than them packing a gun and looking like she could blow their heads off and sleep okay afterwards.

Unsmiling, Pat said, "These men bothering you, Ms. Stanton?"

Cody longed to say yes just to see what Pat would do. Instead, she picked up on her cue and tried to sound as if she employed muscle to mind her beach. "Not so far. Doug, here, was just explaining what they're doing in our waters."

Pat gave a short nod. "Are you gentlemen aware this is a private island?"

"*Merde,*" the Frenchman murmured. "*Elle a l'air d'un assassin.*"

"*Detendez.*" Pat replied with silky self-assurance. "*Je n'ais aucun plan pour vous tirer...à moins que vous me rendiez fâché.*"

Pierre looked startled to be told in his own language that Pat had no plans to shoot him unless he made her very angry. He pushed stray black curls back into his ponytail with a shaky hand.

Doug cleared his throat. "We spoke with a government representative on Rarotonga last week. He explained the situation...you know, your rules and what have you."

"Then you know Moon Island is sacred to women," Cody said pointedly. "There's actually a curse. If a man sets foot on the island uninvited..." She ran a finger across her throat.

"Gotcha," Doug said. "Look, as a courtesy we just wanted to let you know we're going to be in the general area for a while." He hesitated. "And, to be honest, we have a problem. One of our team is not well. We were wondering if there's a doctor on the island?"

"I'm sorry. The nearest doctor is in Avarua," Cody said.

Pat asked, "Exactly how unwell is he?"

"*She* is curled up in a ball, sick as a dog. Vomiting, fever. Severe stomach pain. It's almost like she's gone into shock or something. Could be food poisoning, I guess. Only none of us have got it and we eat the same food."

"Sounds like you better sail back to Raro and get her to the hospital," Cody said, glancing at Pat. The woman was impossible to read.

"How long will that take?" Pat asked.

"Most of the day," Doug sounded uneasy. "I wish we hadn't left it this long. We thought maybe it was...female troubles."

"And you wouldn't want to take those seriously," Cody retorted.

Pat had her binoculars trained on the slopes below Hibiscus Villa. "We have a flight for Raro departing the island soon," she said without lowering them. "We'll take your crew member with us."

Cody nodded. "Good idea. I'll go get Annabel. We can leave early."

Pat returned her attention to the men and issued instructions. "Go get her and wait in the lagoon. We'll meet you in a half hour." To Cody, she said, "Radio ahead and let them know we have an emergency. This doesn't sound like period cramps to me."

MARITIME ARCHAEOLOGIST PENNY Mercer was not just unwell, she was desperately sick. Lauren took one look at her and said, "Oh, my God. I think it's serious. Peritonitis maybe. Damn, I wish I were a real doctor."

"Peritonitis?" Pat sounded skeptical. "What makes you think so?"

"I know this will come a big surprise to you, but I actually research my television role. I read medical textbooks, and I spend time in a real ER observing real emergencies." Pointing at Penny, she said, "This is a real emergency."

"Should we give her something for the pain?" Annabel asked. "There's a phial of morphine on our search-and-rescue craft."

Lauren shook her head. "I don't think we can risk it. We don't know what's caused this. Let's just get her to the hospital as fast as we can." Bending over the balled-up figure on the stretcher, she summoned Dr. Kate's most confidence-inspiring bedside manner. "Penny. Listen to me. We have to move you again. I know it's terribly painful, but just hang on. You're going to be okay. I promise. I'm right here with you." Taking the groaning woman's hand, she said. "Let's go."

The five minutes it took to walk from the jetty to the landing strip felt like an eternity. Penny's grip was crushing, communicating her intense pain and fear. Her companions from the research vessel, Doug and Pierre, gently carried her stretcher along the jungle path. They seemed sheepish, as if her condition were somehow their fault.

"I should have dragged her to a doctor in port last week," Doug said. " She's a stubborn woman."

"And that's probably a damned good thing at this point," Lauren remarked. It was obvious to anyone with a brain in their

head that Penny Mercer's condition was worsening by the
minute. Suddenly shaking violently, she released Lauren's hand,
clutching herself. "Come on. Let's move it!" Lauren urged,
impatient with their progress. "I know she's in pain, but we have
to hurry."

Trying to ignore the cries and moans from the woman on the
stretcher, her colleagues broke into an awkward trot. Lauren met
Pat's eyes and caught a flash of respect in their depths.

As they emerged, panting, from the jungle, and raced
toward the airplane, Annabel said "We can make it in a little
over an hour at full speed. I radioed ahead, and there's an
ambulance on stand-by at the airport."

Without stopping to catch their breaths, they ran across the
strip toward the khaki warplane that was Annabel's pride and
joy. Lauren trailed slightly, trying to stop jarring her shoulder.
She was almost certain it was bleeding.

"I'll be damned." Doug was plainly awed by the sight of
their transport. "A Flying Fortress. I've never seen one."

"She's the real McCoy. You can still see the flak marks."
Annabel unfastened the hatch. "By the way, you didn't mention
what you're doing in these waters."

Doug dragged his attention from the bomber. "Well, I don't
know if you've heard of the *Odyssey*..."

"Sure. The salvagers who found the *SS Republic*, right?"

"Yeah, lucky bastards. We're in the salvage business, too.
Not in the same league as those guys, but you gotta start
somewhere."

"You think there's a shipwreck 'round here?" Annabel asked
as they settled Penny on board.

Lauren felt queasy with pain, but she didn't want to draw
attention to herself. Instead she found the nearest seat and
dropped into it, taking several deep breaths.

Doug and Pat moved the stretcher along the floor of the
plane close to Lauren, then answered Annabel's question. "The
frigate *HMS Jaunt* to be precise. We've been hunting it for nearly
two years."

"And you've found it?" A strained note altered Annabel's
voice.

"I sure hope so. The Pacific is full of shipwrecks.
Worldwide, there are hundreds of thousands. It's not easy to
track down a particular vessel. But we've done our homework.
All we need now is a little bit of luck."

"What happens if you find a sunken treasure ship?" Lauren
asked, belting herself into the hard seat. "I mean, is it like
finders-keepers, or can anyone dive down and help themselves?"

Doug shook his head. "Salvage is an expensive business. It's like mining. You don't want to sink all that money into striking gold if every Tom, Dick and Harry can show up the next day and help himself. So, you arrest the wreck site legally. That means filing an arrest complaint in the local courthouse."

Lauren laughed. "You're kidding."

"And that grants you sole access?" Pat sounded intrigued. "What about the artifacts? What if there are people who have an ownership claim — descendents of the original owners or whatever?"

"The court hears all the claims and decides a final salvage award," Doug replied, helping Annabel strap the stretcher securely to the plane's floor. "Usually the salvage company gets pretty much everything."

Cody, who had been listening quietly, said, "This ship, the *Jaunt*. You think she was in the Cook Islands somewhere?"

"It's a possibility. Ten years ago some unusual gold coins came onto the collector's market. They were auctioned in London but provenance traces to a New Zealand coin dealer. He bought the coins from a Cook islander who had moved to Auckland. This guy said they were passed down through his family for generations. If he's telling the truth, it means the coins must have been brought to the islands by a sailor who probably exchanged them for goods."

From the cockpit, Annabel waved them into silence. "Belt up, people," she instructed. "And someone hang on to the patient during the ascent."

Pat hastily took the seat across the aisle from Lauren, and kept hold of Penny until they were airborne. After the Flying Fortress had leveled out, it seemed everyone released a collective breath, in Lauren's case a gasp.

"Okay?" Pat asked.

Lauren wiped her palms covertly on her pants. "I'm fine. I just hope we get her to the hospital in time."

Pat lowered worried eyes to the semi-conscious woman. "We'll make it."

"Don't worry," Cody added with plastic confidence. "She probably looks worse than she is." When no one replied, she looked slightly embarrassed and changed the topic, returning to her conversation with Doug. "You know, I'm not sure those coins you're talking about add up to anything. A lot of sailors spent money on Rarotonga. We even had the *Bounty* here."

"Well, these aren't just any coins. They're King George III military guineas." Doug extended a hand and gave Penny's shoulder a squeeze. "They were originally struck to pay the

Duke of Wellington's army when they were fighting Napoleon. Most of them ended up in the Pyrenees, but it seems the *HMS Jaunt* had ten thousand of them on board, plus a fortune in gold bars and silver to fund bounty payments for new navy recruits."

"Those coins must be worth a lot of money to collectors," Pat remarked.

"About two thousand bucks apiece."

Lauren couldn't believe they were just calmly talking about gold coins. No one sounded relaxed. Perhaps they were all somehow conspiring to avoid hysteria by acting like everything was normal when there was a half-dead woman lying at their feet.

"What was the *Jaunt* doing in the Pacific?" Cody asked, keeping up her end. "I mean, if it was fighting Napoleon, how did it end up down here?"

"The *Jaunt* was given a last-minute change of orders to escort a merchant convoy after an increase in the French harassment of trade vessels in the Indian Ocean," Doug said. "The last record we have says she picked up survivors from a ship the French sank off Mauritius. Then she took off after some French pirate called Captain Henri Boyer. This Boyer was notorious for attacking ships in the waters between the East Indies and Tahiti. Sounds like he hung out in the Cook islands between times. We did the math and figured these guys probably fought a sea battle somewhere round here."

Lauren was surprised to see Cody looking so uneasy. But she supposed the Moon Island women liked to keep a low profile. If there was a famous shipwreck in their waters, their resort would be mobbed with rubber-neckers. All the same, it was exciting to think of sunken treasure and a piece of naval history. Maybe Cody and Annabel could cash in on it by offering joy-rides out to watch the salvage operation.

She lowered her gaze to the sick woman once more and breathed a silent prayer that they would make it to Rarotonga in time. Penny Mercer was barely conscious, from what she could see. Bending close, she said, "Just hang on Penny. We're nearly there."

# Chapter
# Eight

CHRIS THOMPSON LOWERED her copy of the *Cook Island
News* and gazed out at the ocean. Sitting here, drinking bad
coffee in an open-air café thousands of miles from home, she felt
strangely untethered from reality. Honolulu must have been like
this once, she thought, before Waikiki became a shopping mall
with a beach. It struck her that she had not just journeyed to a
new country, she had journeyed to a different state of mind.

Here in Avarua, capital of the Cook Islands, it was
impossible to be the person she had been back home in
Minnesota — an impatient attorney preoccupied with cramming
as much work into each day as she could, taking for granted the
perquisites of middle-class prosperity in a fast-food, sound-bite
world of instant gratification: widescreen TV with satellite, big
house, endless consumer goods. She had only lived on Rarotonga
for two weeks, and already she understood that hers had been a
life of extraordinary privilege, a life most of the world could not
even imagine.

Relocating to a poor country was an exercise in humility.
Chris could see why most westerners who attempted the fabled
transition to life in the slow lane lasted less than a year before
island madness set in and they scuttled back to civilization.
Rarotonga was littered with the detritus of big dreams turned to
ashes. People vacationed here and were smitten, imbued with a
heady sense of possibility that lent itself to flights of fancy and
lunatic schemes. They rushed back home to abandon the lives
they knew for a tomorrow of tropical sunsets and smiling faces.
Chris had read as many discouraging accounts as she could find
before she'd made the decision to move here. It was one thing to
abscond from your life in your twenties, quite another to do it at
forty-two.

Absently, she glanced around. A handful of diners lingered
in the shade of the verandah. The lunch hour rush, if you could
call it that, was over, and a rooster patrolled the café floor taking

care of the debris. At one time, this place had been the Banana Court Bar, an infamous South Seas watering hole. Now, in addition to housing the Blue Note Café, the bright yellow building boasted a medical practice and a few small stores. These days, the displaced ex-pat Banana Court patrons drank at Trader Jacks, which, Chris had quickly discovered, also doubled as the town's financial center.

On her way back to the main street, she paused in front of a store window, admiring a huge single pearl on display. It was the kind of thing Elaine would have loved. The thought was painful, and in an odd way Chris welcomed that. Recently, acceptance had dulled her raw grief over the death of her lover, and she'd found she could think of her without that familiar crushing sense of loss. It was almost three years since the accident, and sometimes Chris even passed a day without her mind drifting constantly to Elaine. Did that mean she was moving on at last?

With a sigh, she strolled away from the store window, past the traffic circle to a freshly whitewashed storefront with a prominent sign that read:

PACIFIC MINNESOTA TRUST
Principal: Chris Thompson.

"Very impressive," said a voice behind her, and Chris turned to find Annabel Worth standing beneath the tatty awning of the souvenir shop next door. In close-fitting beige pants and a cream linen shirt, her normally ribbon-straight platinum hair in waves to her shoulders, she looked like a displaced movie star from Rita Hayworth's era. "When do you open for business?" she asked in her soft, polished way.

"Officially, next Monday," Chris replied. "But I could make an exception if you need to launder money today."

Annabel laughed. "Alas, nothing so exciting. Can I buy you a drink?"

"I just crawled out of the Blue Note."

"Are you telling me you have other plans?"

Chris shook her head. "I feel like a bum. All I do is wander from one café to the next, reading the newspaper. I have no idea what's going on in the outside world. There's no CNN and no *West Wing*—I'm suffering from withdrawal."

"Welcome to the islands." Annabel tucked her arm into Chris's. "And since you're on a roll, let's go to Trader Jacks. I said I'd meet Cody there in a half hour."

Chris raised her eyebrows. "Wow. What's the occasion?"

Cody seldom budged from Moon Island, claiming she needed to be home with Briar while Annabel shuttled their guests back and forth from Raro. It was clear to anyone who knew the couple that she hated flying and did not suffer Annabel's passion for airborne pursuits gladly.

"We had a medical emergency," Annabel said. "That's the good news."

Chris raised her eyebrows. Annabel sounded flippant, but there was a tension in her body that spoke volumes. Something was bothering her. Chris asked the obvious. "Is Briar okay?"

"Other than being a two-year-old, yes." Annabel removed her dark glasses as they entered the woody interior of the bar.

As usual, the place was packed to the gills, but being local instead of *Papa'a*, or outsiders, meant they scored a table overlooking the harbor.

They were barely seated when their waitress confided to Annabel, "Aunty Mere says she can fix that sick lady up good if you want."

"Tell her thank you," Annabel said. "If they can't help her at the hospital, I'll bring her right over."

The girl beamed. "Hey, your hair looks good like that." Glancing at Chris, she said, "You back again already? Steinlager and *Kati Kati*?"

Chris nodded. "You got it." As the waitress padded off, she returned her attention to her glamorous companion, noting, "News travels fast."

"The faith healers keep tabs on hospital admissions," Annabel explained. "Those tents and shacks out by the airport— that's where they camp. On Sundays, they show up for church wearing nurse's uniforms."

"This place has an encampment of crazies wearing nurse uniforms and claiming to heal the sick? Why am I not surprised?"

Annabel's perfect mouth pulled into the faintest smile. "They think Jesus was here in 1986."

"In Avarua? What happened? Were there miracles?"

"I understand he revealed a cure for baldness," Annabel said gravely.

Chis lay her head on the table and laughed helplessly. "Wait 'til the folks back home hear about this."

A hand tapped her shoulder. Their waitress set a bottle of beer in front of Chris and poured mineral water over ice for Annabel. From her tray, she took a platter of assorted *Kati Kati*, the spicy bar snacks served all over Rarotonga. "Two weeks ago Tutai Karereoa came to Aunty," she announced as she placed a bowl of sweet-and-sour dipping sauce in the middle of the table. "Now he doesn't need his walking stick."

"Wonderful." Annabel politely listened to the sales pitch and took the business card offered.

The girl left with one of those white, perfect smiles that seemed genetically predetermined for all Cook Islanders, and Annabel slid the card across the table to Chris. It read: *Visit Aunty Mere Tiwai for Healing, Potency, and Fragrant Soaps — baldness and lame cures a specialty.*

"I'm sold." Chris helped herself to some coconut shrimp. "Does your medical emergency need new hair?"

"They were taking her into the operating room when I left. Burst appendix."

"Nasty," Chris said. "And maybe not Aunty Mere's field. So, talk to me. What's on your mind?"

"The woman came off a marine exploration vessel. They're in our waters looking for a sunken ship that carried George III golden guineas." Annabel paused, lifting her unearthly lavender eyes to nail Chris in a steady stare.

"Shit." Chris wiped excess dipping sauce from her mouth.

"My thought exactly."

"What's our strategy?"

Annabel reached for her mineral water. "I guess we'll have to wait and see what happens. Maybe they won't find anything."

"Even if they do, there's no way they could make the connection," Chris said, thinking fast. "And maybe there isn't a connection."

"We find, or should I say *you* find, the skeleton of an eighteenth-century sailor in one of our caves. Among his possessions are some George III gold guineas and a map of Moon Island with a big X on it. And there's no connection?"

"Point taken. But the fact is, you have that map locked in a bank deposit box, and the only people who know it exists are you, me, and Cody." Chris fell silent thinking about the fourth woman who had known about the map. It was plain from the shadow that suddenly fell across Annabel's expression that she, too, was thinking about Melanie Worth, her cousin and Briar's mother.

Chris had struck up a friendship with Melanie during a vacation on Moon Island the previous year. Dying from ALS, Melanie had spent her final months on the island, succumbing to the degenerative disease not long ago. Chris had returned to the island for her funeral and had arranged for the legal adoption of her daughter Briar to Annabel and Cody. It was then that she had made up her mind to leave Minnesota.

Annabel intruded on her thoughts. "I'm starting to think there really is a buried treasure. Otherwise why would that sailor have drawn a map and marked a spot? It has to mean something important."

"What do you want to do?"

"Well, you and Cody always wanted to go dig it up."

"Yes, but you were right about the reasons why we shouldn't. If that cross on the map marks a sacred place— maybe *Hine te Ana's* cave—we can't violate the *tapu*. I don't know about you, but I've had enough bad luck for one lifetime without pissing off the local goddesses."

Annabel sighed. "I don't know what to do. I guess what I fear most is that they'll find the ship and the gold will be missing, and next thing we'll have treasure hunters swarming all over the island looking for it. We're not equipped to deal with that kind of craziness."

"Well, let's not panic yet. They haven't even found the shipwreck."

"You're right. I'm getting ahead of myself."

"Try not to worry. If it seems like there might be a problem, we'll take whatever steps we need to take."

Annabel looked heartened. "Did I mention it's great to have you here? There's no one else I can talk to about this except Cody. No one in this town can keep their mouths shut."

"Clearly," Chris said, thinking about the sick woman from the shipwreck expedition. By now, the entire island had probably heard about her. With a population of only 10,000 people, news traveled like lightning.

"How are you finding it here so far?" Annabel asked in a lighter tone. "I mean, it's a huge change."

"I love it. I'm not sure how I'm going to cope in the long term, but right now indolence and inebriation are working out just fine for me."

Annabel folded her napkin, her face pensive. "I was thinking. Why don't you come out to the island for the weekend, before you have to open for business?" There was an odd note in her voice, as if she were making an effort to sound as casual as she could. "You could stay in the villa with us."

Wondering what she was up to, Chris said, "Sounds great. Thanks." Whatever it was, Chris didn't mind. Cody probably needed a hand with one of her many building projects.

Annabel waved as a familiar figure entered the bar. Cody Stanton sauntered across the room, pausing to talk to a couple of people she knew. Chris stood as the athletic Kiwi reached the table, and they hugged briefly.

Dropping a kiss on Annabel's cheek, Cody dragged up a chair, surveyed the few remaining coconut shrimp with dismay, and flagged down their waitress. "Fish and chips and a Steinie, please. Make that extra chips. Oh, yeah, and calamari rings, too. And tell Wiremu I'll come back there and cook it myself if it's more than ten minutes. Okay?"

"Hungry, sweetheart?" Annabel enquired mildly.

"Strangers on our beach, a plane trip, the hospital, *and* John Parker was telling me we lost the match. Three bad calls from that lousy Samoan ref. And Benny Titai was sent off for gouging in the ruck. I need comfort food." Eyeballing Chris after these mysterious rugby pronouncements, she said, "Did she tell you about you-know-what?"

"Yep."

"So we're digging, right?"

"I think we should wait and see if they find that shipwreck first."

"I have a bad feeling about this," Cody muttered, attacking the remaining shrimp. "I was listening to one of those guys talking to someone on the phone while we were waiting for the doctor. He was saying they reckon it's off the southern shelf a couple of miles out from the Sacred Shore."

*The Sacred Shore.* Chris's heart leaped. Just thinking about the night she had spent on that beach was still overwhelming. If she hadn't experienced the extraordinary Hine te Ana rituals for herself, she would never have believed what had happened. What wouldn't anyone give to speak with a person they loved one more time after death? She had spoken to Elaine that night, and Elaine had answered. She had been able to say goodbye, and for Chris, that had been the beginning of her healing.

It was totally plausible that a ship could have gone down off that shore, she thought, picturing the perilous seas and looming cliffs. Cody and Annabel had placed the southern face of Moon island off-limits to their guests for good reason.

"Have they seen something there?" Annabel asked.

"I got that impression," Cody said. "He was asking for money and organizing for someone to fly out here to replace that woman."

Annabel swirled her mineral water around the melting ice cubes. "Well, I guess we'd better make friends with the expedition."

"Keeping your enemies close?" Chris remarked.

Annabel smiled. "Exactly."

"Are you serious?" Cody looked dumbfounded. "I think we should tell them to fuck off."

"And how will that help us spy on them?" Annabel asked with silky sweetness.

Cody groaned. "This gets worse by the minute."

"On the bright side, here comes your food," Chris said.

LAUREN DROPPED THE phone in its cradle and closed her eyes. "Fuck," she said.

"Bad news?" As if Pat needed to ask. Babydoll was fuming.

"My little spy on set tells me they're talking about making an entire season of *Dr. Kate* without me. It's the kiss of death."

"You've been abducted by terrorists, right?"

"Our plane got hijacked. We were flying over Peru. In the final ten minutes, the passengers attacked the hijackers and took back control of the plane. But we're almost out of fuel, so we have to make a crash landing."

"Ah. So, you could be dead or alive?"

Lauren nodded. "The writers are working on a few different ideas for the alive scenario. I could lose my memory and be adopted by the local headhunters who think the gods sent us out of the sky. Or maybe I encounter a rebel army and become their doctor. Then I meet a CIA spy, and he rescues me."

"Those guys get all the glamour assignments," Pat said.

"It's not going to happen," Lauren said gloomily. "If I'm out for a season, I may as well forget it."

"Your fans won't wait?"

"People have short attention spans."

"So titillate them," Pat said. "Use the Internet. Spread rumors. Keep it interesting. What's to stop you running a competition? The person who guesses what really happens to Dr. Kate wins dinner with you and a studio pass."

Lauren's brows drew together. After a moment, she said, almost grudgingly, "That's not a bad idea. I wonder if there's anywhere 'round here we could get online. I could e-mail my publicist and ask her to get the ball rolling. Surely the better hotels have Internet access, or maybe there's an Internet café somewhere."

"I have no idea, but there's one way to find out. Let's take a look around this place."

"What if someone sees me?"

"No one here knows who you are. Your dad's people researched this place pretty thoroughly. They only got television ten years ago, and there's just one channel. They don't even play most US shows."

"Amazing." Lauren wore the startled disbelief Pat had seen a thousand times over in her international travels. It came as a shock for some people to realize that McDonald's or not, the rest of the world didn't live and breathe American culture.

Pat pondered the risks a little more. What were the odds an American soap fan would visit Rarotonga, recognize Lauren, and put in a call to a tabloid? According to her briefing papers, few Americans visited the islands, opting instead for slicker destinations where they could shop in the same stores they had back home. Most Cook Island tourists came from Canada and the South Pacific region, places where *Dr. Kate* was unlikely to have a following. Still, it only took one fan.

"To be on the safe side, how about skipping your appointment with Toni?" she suggested. "If your hair's not styled and you're not in full make-up, you look just like any other cute tourist."

"Except that I have the butch version of Lara Croft tagging along with me," Lauren retorted, ignoring the compliment. "It's not me people look at. It's you."

Pat shrugged. "Better still."

Lauren's mouth compressed. Sounding even crankier than before, she said, "You know, you could draw less attention to yourself. I mean, you must be the only person on this island carrying a gun. Even the police aren't armed. Did you notice that?"

Pat said dryly, "From what I've heard, the biggest crime here is having an overgrown yard."

Lauren sighed and adjusted her topknot. "What time are we supposed to be at the airport?"

"We have three hours to kill. It's your choice. Big hair or we take a drive."

"I do not wear big hair," Lauren shot back indignantly. "That's not my look at all."

"I wouldn't know. I don't watch daytime television."

"Of course you don't. You're too busy being a Secret Agent."

"A Special Agent," Pat corrected, amused by her companion's attempts to needle her. Did Lauren want to pick a fight? Maybe she was missing drama in her life. "It's the Secret Service and the CIA that have covert operatives."

"Whatever. Is it true about the FBI and the CIA? That you don't share well?"

"I think turf wars are a feature of most intelligence organizations," Pat said, choosing her words carefully.

"Too much testosterone and not enough accountability. So whose fault do you think it is that we're in this ridiculous war? Was it the CIA's idea?"

"I'm sure your father would know more about who's benefiting from the war than I do," Pat said, tactful but pointed.

At this Lauren's eyes sparkled. Head tilted slightly to one side, she asked, "Are you always so careful, Pat Roussel? Don't you ever throw caution to the winds and say exactly what you think—or do something crazy?"

"I'm here, aren't I?"

"Oh, come on." Something transparently seductive filtered into Lauren's voice, and the way she was looking at Pat became downright hot. "You were supposed to take time out, so what do you do for recreation? A fill-in gig involving guns and stress. Wow, that's really different from your normal job."

Trying to decide if her principal was simply high from the painkillers she had taken not long ago or there was some other agenda, Pat asked patiently, "What is it you want from me, Lauren? If you're trying to make me leave the gun behind, it's not going to happen."

Lauren paused for a moment, her cornflower blue eyes combing Pat's face. "I don't know what I want," she said, suddenly more serious. "Maybe I want to know you better."

"We're not making friends, remember."

Lauren seemed about to say something, then she lowered her head, as if thinking the better of her impulse. "Let's take that drive," she mumbled after a moment. "I'm sick of hospital smells."

# Chapter
# Nine

IT COST TEN dollars at the local police station to buy a Cook Islands drivers' license—no test necessary if you could show them a valid license from back home. The officer gave Pat two pieces of advice, "Keep left and get extra insurance, Mister."

"I'll do the tip," Lauren offered, opening her purse.

"Put it away," Pat said. "If you try to tip an official here they'll arrest you for bribery."

"You're kidding."

"Maybe. Maybe not." Pat's face was unreadable.

Was this her idea of humor? Lauren wasn't sure why she was trying to get under Pat's skin today. It was as if she wanted to provoke some kind of emotional reaction. So far, there was no sign that she had penetrated her bodyguard's reserve an inch. Pat remained infuriatingly pleasant and just as detached as always.

They rented a Jeep from Budget and set off at a snail's pace on the wrong side of the road. Rarotonga was only thirty-two miles across and the speed limit was thirty-five miles an hour.

"We'll take the *Ara Metua*," Pat said, consulting the map that had come with their vehicle. "It's probably more interesting than the coastal road. Who wants to drive past every motel on the island?" She handed Lauren a tourist brochure that explained the history of the island and said, "Let me know if there's any must-see we need to watch out for."

Lauren read the text with interest. She had never been anywhere quite like this place. It felt like a time capsule. The narrow inland road they were on was built a thousand years ago and was once surfaced in crushed coral. Much of it was still paved in the original volcanic stones. Dappled with the shade of coconut palms, it had connected all the villages of yesteryear, long ago when most of the population lived inland. Back then, the Cook Islanders had raised animals and cultivated vegetables in the cooler temperatures on the mountain slopes. These days, the island's interior was mostly plantation and rainforest, and there was little traffic, other than a few mopeds and the occasional dog or chicken.

"I wish I had my camera with me," Lauren said as they passed through papaya and banana orchards with spectacular mountain views.

Without a word, Pat reached into her pants pocket and produced a tiny digital Canon, slowing down so Lauren could take snapshots.

Below the road, a deep valley spread out like a patchwork quilt in hues so intensely green they seemed painted. Flame trees and hibiscus splotched the verdant canvas bright orange and red. A veil of cloud cloaked the muted mauve mountaintops in the island's center. Hand-carved wooden signs indicated hiking trails that led off the road in all directions.

Just beyond one of these, Pat pulled off at a scenic outlook and halted the Jeep. Opening the passenger door, she cast an indulgent look at Lauren. "A photo op."

"It's like Shangri La," Lauren breathed, absorbing the timeless surroundings. She bailed out of the Jeep and found the perfect angle for her snaps.

They stood in silence for a few minutes. Propped against the Jeep, Pat surveyed the surroundings like a watchful predator. Between photos, Lauren covertly observed her. Today the bodyguard was in loose fitting khakis and a muted floral shirt— her passing-for-a-tourist attire—over a black sleeveless vest. The fluid lines of her clothing could not quite disguise her muscular build. To anyone who paid attention, her coiled demeanor spoke of controlled power and absolute physical self-awareness

Lauren wondered how it must feel to have the kind of confidence Pat radiated. Pat would never have allowed herself to be shot by a crazy fan in a parking garage. She would have noticed something was wrong as soon as she stepped out of the elevator. Somehow she would have turned the tables on the would-be killer, chased him through the parking building, wrestled him down in front of gawping spectators.

Lowering the camera, Lauren asked impulsively, "Pat, have you ever been really afraid?"

Pat's voice registered faint surprise. "Of what?"

"Of anything. I mean real fear. Feeling powerless?"

Pat removed her sunglasses, took a cloth from her breast pocket, and polished the lenses. "My mother's accident terrified me. I had a gut feeling something wasn't right after her surgery. I talked to the doctors, but they insisted she was making a good recovery. All the same, I had this feeling she wasn't going to make it. I was desperate. Completely helpless. I've always wondered if there was anything I could have done differently."

Lauren guessed that this was not a conversation Pat had with many people, perhaps no one. Tentatively, she touched her arm. "You did everything you could. I'm sure your mom felt truly safe and happy in her final days, being with you."

"We were very close. The loss of her changed me." Pat's face grew shuttered, as if she had said too much.

"I'm sorry. I didn't mean to bring it up for you."

"Everyone has something that makes them fearful. It's by confronting our fears and moving through them that we gain more confidence."

"In other words," Lauren translated dryly, "I should hunt this guy down?"

Pat raised an eyebrow. "That's not exactly what I had in mind."

"But that's what you would do, isn't it?"

"I hunt for a living. You, however, attract." Her eyes met Lauren's. "That in itself is powerful. The question is, how can it serve you?"

"You're talking about trapping him?" Lauren felt a rush of nausea. The very idea of seeing that brooding face again made her sick to her stomach.

Pat was running with the idea, her mind obviously engaged. "Only hypothetically."

"So, I'm bait," Lauren concluded. "Perfect. What if it goes wrong?"

"There's always that risk. But the point about taking charge is that you would be writing the rules of the game, instead of him. It's not as crazy as it sounds."

"What are you suggesting?"

Pat stroked her shoulder holster absently. "I'm not suggesting anything—I'm just thinking out loud. There's always more than one way to look at situation like this."

"You don't think it was the right thing to do, to come here?"

"I didn't say that. You're recovering from two bullet wounds and this is a safe location. I'm looking ahead, that's all." Her expression softened. "I'm sorry, Lauren. This is just speculation. If I have any ideas about catching that creep, I should be discussing them with your father, not upsetting you."

"It's not my father he came after," Lauren objected. "I'm not a child, so don't patronize me."

"That wasn't my intention." Pat's tone changed to one of polite deference. Once more she was the distant, unflappable professional. Glancing at her wristwatch, she said, "We should get going if we want to see any more of the island."

Feeling dismissed, Lauren climbed into the Jeep, trying to think what to say. "I like it much better when you talk to me like I'm a responsible adult," she managed.

Pat lifted her eyes. In the brilliant light, her pupils were small, intensifying her gaze to dark emerald. Lauren was certain she detected a flash of heat before Pat's expression was closed to her once more. She slid her sunglasses back on and, in a tone of infuriating benevolence, said, "Now that you've got that off your chest, shall we go find the Internet?"

Lauren had to suppress a juvenile urge to reach across and give Pat a shove. "Sure," she muttered. "Why not?"

They drove in silence for a time, Lauren staring out her window pondering ways she could tell her father that it just wasn't working out with the bodyguard he had chosen. She would e-mail him and explain that although Pat was very good at her job, there was a personality clash, and Lauren needed a bodyguard she could relate to as a woman. Fat chance, she thought cynically. There was no way her father was going to recall his handpicked watchdog and replace her with someone who scored an A in girl-talk.

Resentfully, Lauren cast a sideways look at the woman driving the Jeep. What was it about Pat that got under her skin? On some level Lauren was aware that her reactions were irrational. Pat had done nothing but behave with absolute professionalism. She had also, with good grace, carried out duties not included in her job description, like doubling as a nurse whenever Lauren needed a shower or a change of dressing. It was hardly fair to have her sacked because they hadn't become pals.

Chagrined, Lauren stared down at her hands. It dawned on her in a flash of self-awareness that it wasn't a gal pal she wanted. She felt slighted because Pat had showed no interest in her as a woman. Lauren was not accustomed to being ignored. It was obvious to anyone with half a brain that Pat Roussel was a lesbian. How could she not react at all to Lauren when they lived in such close quarters? Wasn't propinquity supposed to trigger sexual attraction? Or did she find Lauren unappealing?

A different theory presented itself. Pat's lack of interest was so emphatic, maybe it was intentional. Perhaps underneath it all, she did notice Lauren but concealed her attraction because it was the right thing to do professionally. A small smile tugged at Lauren's mouth and she bit her top lip softly to keep her expression bland. Why not find out? If she had to be stuck on an island for the next eight weeks, the least she could do was have some fun.

Stretching indolently, she turned toward Pat and said, with a hint of playfulness, "I don't know how you can do this. Drive on the wrong side of the road, I mean."

"Cheap thrills," Pat said, swerving a little to avoid two Mormon missionaries.

Here was a sight Lauren had not expected to see—a couple of white-shirted cyclists from Utah, pedaling their way around paradise, trying to persuade those who lived there that a better place awaited them in the hereafter.

"I wonder if they get much business," Pat remarked, also struck by the anomaly, it appeared.

"I think the English missionaries beat them to it by a couple of hundred years." In the sweetest voice she could muster, Lauren said, "You know, it's really nice of you to drive me around. You didn't have to."

Pat shot her a quick look. "It's my pleasure." Her tone was laced with irony.

Lauren conjured a crestfallen expression. "Fed up with me, huh?"

"On the contrary. You're much easier than my day job."

"Then you won't mind if we stay here overnight," Lauren suggested ingenuously. "I feel like a change of scene and they have some good hotels here. We could have a decent meal and go see one of those island shows. You know, with the traditional costumes and the dancing and everything." Sounding as meek as she could, she added, "Only if you think it's safe, of course."

Pat's eyes remained on the road. Lauren could almost hear her brain working, no doubt manufacturing reasons why they couldn't do any such thing. "We didn't bring a change of clothes or fresh dressings," she said eventually.

Feeble, Lauren thought. "I can buy anything we need. And we could pick up extra dressings at the hospital."

Pat continued with the wet blanket responses. "Everything's probably booked out."

Lauren shrugged. Trying not to sound wedded to her island overnighter idea, she said, "Then we'll just go back to Moon Island."

They slowed to let a convoy of mopeds pass by in the opposite direction. Feeling Pat's attention flick back and forth between the road and her, Lauren maintained an air of ditzy innocence. For good measure, once they were moving again, she remarked, "I'm bored to tears. Three weeks in the hospital followed by house arrest on a desert island. Bring on the nightlife!"

This time Pat could not conceal a faint shudder. "It's not exactly Vegas, here," she warned.

Reading this as a *yes*, Lauren shook out her topknot and let the wind in her hair. "I hope you like dancing," she said.

"ARE YOU SERIOUS?" Cody took the co-pilot seat and fastened her seat belt. "They're spending the night at a hotel?"

"I wouldn't read too much into it," Annabel said. "It seems Ms. Douglas wants to sample the local nightlife. Pat looked like she would rather eat glass."

"Yeah, I'll bet she's spewing." Cody laughed out loud at the thought of the stern and serious Pat Roussel being dragged from one island hotspot to the next. Small spaces crammed with drunk tourists were probably any bodyguard's worst nightmare. She was surprised Pat had agreed to it. But orders were orders, she supposed. No doubt their resident starlet needed more attention than she was getting on Moon Island. "Did you tell her about the Staircase?"

"Of course. She said Ms. Douglas wants to take in an island show."

"Jeez, I'd pay good money to see the locals drag Pat out of the audience and make her wiggle her hips."

"I get the impression you don't like Pat," Annabel remarked.

"Oh, she's okay," Cody said. "I just don't understand how any self-respecting dyke could do that job. They'd have to pay me a *lot*. Oh, by the way, I found out something interesting."

"I'm all ears."

"Lauren Douglas didn't injure herself in a fall from a horse. Those are bullet wounds."

"And you know this how?"

"Atombomb Mariri at the harbor. His daughter works at the hospital."

"Isn't she a cook?"

"Yeah. In the hospital kitchens. Her boyfriend's an orderly, and he read Lauren Douglas's patient file."

"This place." Annabel groaned. "I wonder how she got shot."

"I guess someone didn't think much of her show," Cody suggested, deadpan.

Annabel gave her a look. "I'm sure it was just an accident."

"Seems kind of careless to shoot someone twice by mistake."

"Well, whatever happened, it's none of our business."

Cody nodded like she agreed. Sometimes Annabel took good manners too far. They had a guest who'd been shot twice and was now holed up on their island with hired muscle to protect her. It didn't take Einstein to figure out that their guests thought whoever had shot her might show up to finish the job. It was probably an ex-husband. Maybe she'd dumped the guy when she got famous and he didn't take it too well.

"I'm serious," Annabel said. "She has a right to her privacy."

"I was thinking we could look her up on the Internet—just for our own peace of mind. I mean, what say there's a nutbag ex-husband gunning for her. We have a right to know for our own safety." Cody played her trump card. "We've got a child to protect."

Annabel hesitated. "I'm not going behind her back. I'll speak with Pat."

Picturing Pat and Annabel in cozy conversation, Cody wished she'd never brought up the topic. She muttered, "That'll make her day."

"You are so transparent."

"I've seen the way she looks at you." Pat Roussel was one of those women who made a show of opening doors and pulling out chairs for femmy types like Annabel. Cody thought that kind of thing was just plain ridiculous in the twenty-first century.

Annabel had a faraway expression on her face. "You're imagining things." She slipped her sunglasses on. "And you ought to know by now that even if some handsome stud crawled across broken glass to give me flowers, I would still be yours."

So much for reassurance. Handsome stud. Was that how Annabel saw their gun-toting guest?

# Chapter
# Ten

PAT USHERED LAUREN into their hotel villa ahead of her, nudged the door shut, and dropped several shopping bags onto an oversized cream armchair.

Lauren hit the fridge right away and pulled out a bottle of her usual mineral water. "Want a Coke?"

"Sure." Pat walked through the lower level, scanning the luxurious surroundings. She could almost hear Cicchetti waxing lyrical about the big favor he did her in setting up this cushy number. Returning to the lounge area, she said, "Nice place."

Lauren handed Pat a bottle of Coke, then poked around in a basket of cookies on the coffee table. "It's perfect." The actress looked as smug as a cat as she uncapped a Pellegrino. Crossing to a wall of glass, she said, "Let's go out on the deck. It'll be sunset soon."

Pat unlocked the sliding doors. Their vast wooden deck was directly opposite the kind of white sand beach she had always envisioned when she heard Hawaiian music. In the distance, she could see several people scattered along the shoreline, but no one was nearby. This part of the private beach had gated access and was shared by just a few villas. The receptionist had assured Pat there was seldom anyone around after dark. They didn't call this a honeymoon villa for nothing.

They had been fortunate to get the room. The happy couple who were supposed to be here had been delayed thanks to an airline strike in France. Pat supposed she should be thankful there were two bedrooms so she wouldn't have to spend the night on a couch.

Standing a few feet away, Lauren was as perky as Pat had ever seen her. "This is great," she remarked. "It's so fabulous having the beach right here instead of being stuck in the trees like we are on Moon Island."

"It's very exposed."

"No one knows I'm here and, as you said, no one will

identify me looking like this, anyway." Lauren gave a dismissive shrug. "Let's just relax and have a good time. Maybe we can catch that bus. The one that goes to all the nightclubs."

Pat grimaced at the idea of a bus full of drunken revelers. "I'll drive us."

"I should get changed. I wish you had let me buy you a set of clothes instead of just a fresh t-shirt."

"I'll survive," Pat said. "It's only for one night."

"I wish I'd thought about this before today," Lauren chattered as they moved indoors. "We could have packed some stuff and stayed longer. Maybe we'll come back." She gathered up her shopping bags, and they went upstairs to the huge king bedroom.

Removing Lauren's purchases from their tissue and laying them out on the bed, Pat made a non-committal sound.

"This one, I think." Lauren lifted a sleeveless dress with a pattern of white hibiscus against a midnight background. "And this in my hair." She handed Pat a decorative comb of carved bone inset with abalone.

Pat stifled a groan. Babydoll wanted a hairstyle. And guess who would have to play hairdresser.

It was even worse than she imagined. After helping Lauren shower and dress, Pat found herself trying to convert the usual topknot into a braided thing. The result hung distinctly to one side of dead center and when she tried to drag it into the right position, the hair loosened, making the problem even worse.

"I guess they didn't teach hair at the FBI school," Lauren said, giggling.

"You got that right." Pat unpinned the braids and brushed the golden red hair out again. It looked pretty good loose, she thought. "How about this, instead?" She snapped off a white hibiscus from the bowl of flowers decorating the dressing table and secured it behind Lauren's ear with a pin. Simple. Sexy. She glanced quickly away, her heart abruptly changing gear.

"You're right. And it matches my dress." With a big smile, Lauren slid her feet into a pair of strappy sandals and made a turn.

"Very nice," Pat said. Her breathing was constrained, as if something had caught in her chest.

"Is something wrong?" Lauren's dark blue eyes were innocently questioning.

Pat carefully schooled her features. "Everything's fine. I'll change my t-shirt and we can go."

"Okay." Lauren studied her for a long moment. Her smile, so delicately contained, broadened. "Pat, I really appreciate this," she said softly. "I mean, I know you don't want to take me out clubbing. It's nice of you to do it anyway."

"You're the boss."

Lauren's smile faded and her face registered slight hurt. Turning away, she picked up her purse and headed for the door, saying tightly, "I'll see you downstairs."

Feeling like a cad, Pat removed her gun and swapped her t-shirt, damp from the shower, for the new one Lauren had insisted on buying that afternoon. Was it really necessary for her to be so tactless? Lauren was trying to have some kind of happy adventure in which Pat was cast in the role of accomplice. What harm would it do to indulge her? They both knew Pat was being dragged into it because she was an employee. Did she have to make a big deal of it?

Refastening her shoulder holster, she checked herself out in the mirror. Already she was looking more tan than she had been in several years. She brushed her teeth and pulled a comb through her hair, noticing the few silver strands at her temples more than she usually did. Why couldn't she be more good humored with Lauren? It was hardly fair to resent her as if she were somehow responsible for Pat not being back in Philly working 24/7. Her time with Lauren Douglas was time she could not spend obsessing over the kiddy pageant case. Wasn't that a good thing?

Determined to stop taking her irritation out on her principal, she buttoned her loose rayon shirt back on to hide the gun and went downstairs. Lauren was standing out on the deck, a breeze playing with her hair. Facing the sea, she stood immobile, apparently lost in thought. For a few seconds, Pat lingered in the doorway, watching her. Then an odd thing happened. Her pulse raced, her stomach fell, and her mouth dried. It was so long since she'd felt this way, Pat had trouble interpreting the sensations. Anticipation.

Taken by surprise, she waited a moment for the reaction to pass. Shockingly, her feelings only intensified, and she found herself unable to return to her normal state of mind. Forcing indifference into her voice, she said, "Let's go dancing."

Lauren looked across her shoulder. Her eyes were wet. She did not reply.

Was this because of Pat's offhand remark? Mortified, Pat crossed the wooden boards to stand beside her. "Why are you crying?"

"I'm not sure." Lauren wiped her eyes on the back of her hand. "I was just standing here looking out to the sea, and I started thinking about what happened...the things he said to me.

Why does he hate me so much? I don't understand it."

Second-guessing her own responses, Pat resisted the urge to place a comforting arm around Lauren. Instead she fastened her gaze on the infinite expanse of the sea, violet in the fading light. "You'll make yourself crazy if you look for a rational explanation. There isn't one. It's not about you or anything you've ever done. You got caught up in a stranger's fantasies. He was writing his own story and including you in it. He believed his own fiction."

"Intellectually, I can understand that. But it doesn't make me feel any better."

"How could it? You're powerless to change his script. And that's frightening."

"I was nice to him," Lauren said in a hurt tone.

"At the cocktail party?" Pat called to mind the lengthy police statement she had read.

"Yes. I think he must have dropped those snacks off his tray deliberately so he could talk to me."

"I'd bet money on it."

"He made me uncomfortable. He was really intense and kind of familiar, as if we knew each other. The way he talked and acted...he was..."

"Possessive?"

"Yes." Lauren looked up. "It was creepy. I should have listened to my gut."

"What could you have done? No one can anticipate something like this."

"I guess you must run into crazy people all the time in your job."

"I don't know if I'd call them crazy," Pat replied. "Evil, maybe."

Lauren shivered. "I couldn't do what you do."

"And I couldn't do what you do," Pat said, intentionally changing the topic. "Trying to remember lines in front of a camera while convincing the audience that you're someone else. I have no idea how you manage it."

"Is that a compliment?" Lauren's eyes sparkled.

"I think it could be," Pat said with a grin. Again she felt those butterflies.

Lauren tucked her hand into the crook of Pat's arm. "Come on. Let's party."

THE VILLAGE OF Ngatangaiia was still and silent when they returned to the hotel many hours later. Dawdling along a winding pathway through lush, manicured gardens, both Lauren and Pat were heavily garlanded with fragrant ropes of frangipani pressed on them by the locals. No one here went without flowers, Lauren had noticed. Even the men in business suits she'd seen earlier, along the main street, wore woven flax wreaths around their heads as if this were as essential to male attire as a shirt and tie.

Senses swimming from Mai Tais and the heady scent of the flowers at her throat, she propped herself against the doorjamb as Pat unlocked their villa. Pools of silvery light illuminated the gardens. The waxing moon hung over Rarotonga like a huge pearly button. Beyond the villa, the ocean caressed the shore, its languid cadence tantalizing.

"Let's go for a swim," Lauren said, following Pat from room to room as she checked the villa. "Take off your gun and come with me."

Pat's face was hard to read. Lauren had the impression she was tempted, but, as usual, she was going to play the personal security card.

Unwilling to have this used as an excuse, Lauren persisted. "It's safe here and you know it. Apart from anything else, we're the only people awake." She marched into the bathroom, unzipped her dress and wrapped herself in a towel. Ignoring Pat's disapproving frown, she let herself onto the deck, and marched down the wooden steps to the pale sand.

"Stop," Pat said. "Lauren. Wait right there."

Exuding resigned discomfort, Pat removed her shoulder holster, pants and shirt. Wearing only her black t-shirt and boxer-style black briefs, she joined Lauren on the beach. It was almost perfect, except that she had the damned gun in her hand. "Give me your towel," she said to Lauren.

Puzzled, Lauren handed it over. She wanted to say *Get your own*. But Pat was already wrapping the gun in its folds. She hadn't even noticed that without the towel, Lauren was naked except for her skimpy lace panties.

Setting the towel down on the sand, and arranging the folds so her gun would be easy to grab, Pat said, "Just in case."

"Whatever," Lauren muttered and headed for the tide. With a quick glance over her shoulder, she called, "Please. I'll feel safer if you come in, too."

I've won, Lauren thought. Pat had taken off the stupid gun and was doing exactly what Lauren wanted her to do. They were going swimming together. Pat had danced with her throughout the evening and kept opportunistic males at bay. She had been friendly, even charming. But Lauren felt peeved instead of gratified. She might as well be a child for all the interest Pat showed in her.

Wading into the warm water, she tried to convince herself that sexual interest from Pat was the last thing she truly wanted. It would be completely irresponsible of her to flirt with an employee of her father's. Yet Pat wasn't just any employee. She had an impressive career of her own. The job of protecting Lauren was just a short-term distraction. Once her contract was over, she would return to her own world, and there would be nothing to stop them from being friends. Or more.

Lauren heard a muted splash and realized her companion was already in the water. Irked that Pat hadn't waited for her, she watched that dark familiar form surge through the waves parallel to the shore. A short time later, Pat emerged from the tide a few yards away and stood dripping, head slick, her grin broad and white in the moonlight. She wasn't even breathing hard after swimming the length of the beach and back.

"It's great," she said, strolling through the water.

For a long moment, Lauren could not drag her eyes from that muscular physique, outlined in stunning relief by her wet clothing. If Pat were shorter, she might have looked stocky. As it was, she was tall and broad-boned, her arms and shoulders well-worked, her thighs powerful. Lauren's stomach lurched. She felt weak. Breathless. She was aware that she was staring but couldn't stop herself. She could not think of any time in her life when she had felt so conscious of another woman, in a purely animal sense. The knowledge shook her, and she backed self-consciously toward the waterline until the tide was washing around her ankles.

"Lauren?" Pat followed her, sounding concerned. "Are you okay?"

Lauren extended her hand, connecting with Pat's arm. "I'm feeling a bit light-headed."

Pat drew nearer still and slid a supportive arm around Lauren's waist. "Let's go back indoors."

A hot shock of awareness radiated from the place where their skin connected. "No," Lauren whispered. "I'm okay. Just give me a moment."

"You're shaking," Pat said. "I can carry you if you feel faint."

Lauren stifled a nervous giggle. She did feel faint, as a matter of fact. But not for any of the reasons Pat might imagine. Succumbing to a wayward urge, she lifted her eyes, drawing Pat's steady gaze. Mouth dry, she said, "Just hold me, please."

Something flashed across Pat's face, dispelling the bland indulgence Lauren had seen there all evening. Clearly torn, she took Lauren in her arms and cautiously held her. As if comforting a frightened child, she said, "Everything's okay. You'll get through this. I know it's difficult."

Lauren turned her head to one side, leaning into the solid wall of that body, listening to the steady thud of Pat's heart. This is madness, she thought, but allowed a hand to drift sensually along Pat's spine. She detected a subtle alteration in the timbre of Pat's embrace, a breath unevenly released. Turning so they were face to face, Lauren drew back just enough to link her hands behind Pat's neck. Arching her body, she moved seductively against Pat, inviting a response in kind.

For a split second, Pat froze, then her arms tightened around Lauren, drawing her closer until their wet bodies were glued together. A wet ache blossomed between Lauren's thighs. She touched Pat's cheek, mutely communicating her desire. Pat stared at her for so long Lauren almost stopped breathing.

Just one kiss, Lauren told herself as Pat's mouth descended on hers. What harm could it do? But no one had ever kissed her the way Pat Roussel did. At first her mouth was tender, sweetly teasing, coaxing Lauren's lips apart, drawing a response that was shy and hesitant. As the kiss deepened, it was as if Pat were ruthlessly peeling back layer after layer to reveal Lauren's most naked self, and it was to that self she spoke. Her kisses grew fierce, passionate, and profound, arousing a need so powerful Lauren could barely stay on her feet. She felt drugged, her pulse a languorous tattoo. Blood, thick and heavy, slithered through her veins.

Pat's hands came to rest flat against Lauren's ass, propelling her firmly against a hard thigh. Gasping, she curled her arms tightly behind Pat's back to brace herself. The pressure against her groin was unbearable. Her nipples felt raw and exquisitely sensitive, grating against the thin cotton barrier of Pat's shirt. When Pat's mouth left hers, she released a sharp cry of dismay and pleading.

Pat kissed her throat. Teeth sank slowly into the sinew that joined neck and shoulder, then moved downward. Pat's mouth warmly patrolled the rise of Lauren's breasts, spreading soft kisses across her goose-bumped flesh. Dazed with desire, Lauren watched as Pat took a nipple between her teeth, tugging it into her mouth and toying with it, barely sucking until Lauren made a small begging whisper. As the pressure on her nipple mercifully increased, Lauren reached for Pat's head, cradling it close, at the same time working her hips, parting her legs wider so she could bear down on Pat's thigh.

Somewhere in the back of her mind a small voice reminded

her that she'd had too much to drink and that maybe she would regret this in the morning, but Lauren could not bear to listen. When Pat sank to her knees, her kisses descending Lauren's belly, it was all she could do to remain upright. Swaying, she caught hold of Pat's shoulders, her fingers biting into the tautly knit flesh.

In that moment, Pat looked up, eyes gleaming black in the moonlight. Her question was unspoken.

Hoarsely, Lauren answered, "Please. Don't stop."

She could hardly keep from crying out as Pat hooked a finger in her panties and drew them down, exposing her. Stepping out of the lacy underwear, Lauren was suddenly conscious that they were in the middle of a beach where anyone could see them. As Pat slid an exploring finger along the slippery cleft and gently parted her, Lauren made a small sound of anxiety. Before she could even articulate her concern, Pat stood.

"Let's continue this somewhere more comfortable," she murmured in Lauren's ear and swung her off her feet.

CRADLING LAUREN EFFORTLESSLY, Pat strode up the beach and into the villa. In the downstairs bedroom, she adjusted the lighting to low and, with one hand, pulled back the bed covers. Instead of lowering Lauren onto the sheets, she held her close and sat down on the bed, Lauren in her lap.

"I don't want to hurt you," she said, stroking the red-gold hair away from Lauren's flushed face.

Lauren blinked up at her, transparent in her desire. "I don't care."

Conscious of those injuries all the same, Pat eased Lauren gently from her lap onto the bed. Stripping off her own wet t-shirt and boxers, she lay full length on her back and stretched out her arms, inviting, "Climb on top."

Even in the muted light, she could tell Lauren had blushed. But she slid a leg over Pat and sat on her belly, her wet core slippery against Pat's flesh. Drawing Lauren down, until she could feel the brush of her nipples and smell the familiar musky floral scent of her skin, Pat cupped her face in both hands. "Are you sure about this?"

Lauren nodded. "Are you?"

"No," Pat said. "But, since I spent most of this evening wanting to drag you off the dance floor and make love to you..."

"Funny, that," Lauren said. "I kept hoping you would."

They laughed softly, and Lauren slid a little further up Pat's torso. Rocking back on her heels, she grasped Pat's hands and lowered them to her beautiful breasts. Pat took the hint and softly squeezed, lost in the feel of her. Her skin was smooth and soft, her body supple and deliciously feminine with its defined waist and girlish belly.

Pat had never been attracted to women with a similar built to her own. She loved softness and curves, the contrast of full breasts against her more muscular body — that seductive combination of strength and vulnerability. Moving her hands over Lauren's flesh, she could barely believe they were making love and it felt so right. Perhaps in another time and place, she might have been able to choose a rigid professional ethic over this. Right now, she couldn't, and she had stopped trying.

Changing position, she lowered Lauren onto her back, automatically arranging the pillows to relieve pressure on her wounds. She longed to feel Lauren's legs wrapped around her waist, to cover her body and move deep within her. But, careful not to allow her full weight to descend, she propped herself on her hands, and rocked her body against Lauren's. Their lips brushed. Eyes closed, they kissed deeply, drinking from one another.

Lauren's hips moved against her in a rhythmic plea Pat could not ignore. Shifting her weight, she slid a hand between those slender legs, finding her wet and open. A rush of arousal stifled her breathing. Heart speeding, she parted the yielding flesh and gained sweet entry.

In the same moment Lauren's eyelids fluttered and she met Pat's gaze. Her eyes blazed hot with anticipation. "Fuck me," she whispered.

It was not like any other first time Pat had experienced; their bodies were so in synch. Somehow Pat could sense what Lauren craved. Decoding her small soft sounds, responding to the insistent cues of body and senses, she adjusted angle and rhythm, and finally moved down the bed a little so she could use her mouth as well as her hands.

Lauren's flavor was sweet and salty, like mulled sea-wine. With lips and tongue, Pat rolled back the protective hood of flesh over her clit to expose the tiny rigid organ beneath. This she delicately sucked and licked until she could feel her fingers drawn deeper. As Lauren's arousal heightened, Pat maintained her relentless focus.

Eventually, she felt Lauren flood and compress, heard her soft moans grow guttural. Sensing she needed no more direct stimulation, Pat lifted her head. Breathing hard, she gazed at Lauren, captivated by the fierce concentration on her face, the interplay of pleasure and yearning. In that moment Pat was consumed with a hunger so intense she broke into a sweat. It was all she could do not to seize Lauren in a hard embrace, ram herself between her legs, possess her with bruising certainty.

Shaking, she murmured, "Come for me, baby," and watched with melting awe as Lauren finally capitulated to bliss.

For a long while, Lauren clung to Pat, quivering. Face to face, they communed in passionate silence: Lauren touched Pat's mouth. Pat cupped Lauren's cheek. Each placed a hand to the other's heart. Lulled by the hypnotic press of flesh and bone, and by the whispered harmony of waves breaking beyond their window, they drifted into sleep.

# Chapter
# Eleven

LAUREN LAY IN contented reverie. She had slept late and awakened alone, but could hear the reassuring sounds of Pat moving around in the villa. Smiling, she rolled onto her stomach. Her body clamored with the memory of Pat's touch. Every nerve ending seemed raw. The very thought of making love again made the blood rush in her ears.

Consumed by wild joy, she pictured the two of them returning home, traveling back to St. Michaels where Pat would be introduced to Lauren's brothers, who would drone on about golf and the economy, like anyone was interested. Her mother would approve; Lauren could see she had warmed to Pat. Her father would decide Pat wasn't good enough for his daughter, as if anyone ever could be. Pat would give up her depressing job and take a nominal position in the family business. Maybe she could be head of security or something. Lauren would return to her career in a blaze of glory with Dr. Kate's amazing survival story topping the weekly ratings. The weirdo who shot her would get twenty-five to life. She would be safe and everything would be perfect.

"Lauren?" Pat stood next to the bed with coffee and plate of chopped fruit.

Thrilled to see her, Lauren sat up and pushed sleep-tumbled hair away from her face. "Good morning."

"Good morning." Pat set the tray down on the lamp stand and opened the blinds. Instead of returning to kiss Lauren, she stared out the window, said, "Shit!" and bolted from the room.

Startled, Lauren got out of bed and ran to the window. Two children were standing on the beach a few yards away. One of them, a flaxen-haired boy no older than six, was holding Pat's gun. He had it pointed directly at a little girl who looked even younger.

"Oh, my God," Lauren gasped.

Frantically, she donned a bathrobe and slid her feet into her sandals. By the time she reached the beach, Pat was kneeling between the two children, blocking the little girl's body with her own. The gun was just inches from her chest.

Very calmly, she spoke to the boy. "Listen to me, sweetheart. That gun is dangerous because it has bullets inside." As she spoke, she gestured to Lauren, who immediately grabbed the small girl and carried her away. "Will you be very brave and do something for me? See that flowery bush? Just throw the gun gently over there. Not hard. Just a little throw."

Hardly daring to breathe, Lauren screwed up her eyes as the boy tossed the gun. Thankfully, it did not go off.

"Good boy." Pat put her arm around the child's shoulders. "It's okay. You're not in trouble. Did you think it was a toy?"

He nodded, fighting back tears.

Pat took his hand. "My name's Pat, and this lady is Lauren. What's your name?"

"Brendon." He pointed at the little girl. "Her name's Amber. She's my sister."

"Okay, Brendon. Where are your mommy and daddy?"

The little boy pointed vaguely toward several villas on the other side of the gardens.

"Wonderful." Pat hissed, eyes glittering with fury. Leading Brendon over to join his sister and Lauren, she said to their small visitors, "I have a good idea. What say you sit here on the beach with Lauren, and I'll get some milk and cookies? Then, we'll go see your mommy and daddy."

"They could come back to the villa..." Lauren began.

Pat shook her head swiftly. Frowning at Lauren, she said in a good-humored voice, "No tricking. Brendon, do you know why that was a trick?"

Brendon nodded uncertainly. "Don't go with strangers?"

"That's right. And do you know what to do if a stranger tries to make you go with them?"

"Say no."

Pat nodded. "Yes. And another thing is to yell very loud. Here's what you say. Help!" Pat yelled. "He's not my father!"

Laughing, Brendon echoed the yell and Lauren clapped loudly.

"Okay. I'm going to go get those cookies." Her face drawn, Pat strolled over to the hibiscus, retrieved her gun, and went indoors.

Shaken, Lauren spoke brightly to the children about any banal thing she could think of. Her skin was damp with sweat, and she felt nauseous. The image of the little boy pointing the gun at his sister replayed over and over in her head. For some reason it disturbed her far more than the subsequent moment when Pat had knelt between the children, risking her life. Lauren had felt a brief sickening terror then. But it was instantly followed by a certainty that Pat would control the situation and no one would be hurt.

She stared out at the ocean, trying to calm her racing heart. She could hardly breathe. A tearing sensation in her chest filled her with fear. Was this a heart attack? Gasping, head spinning, she cast an imploring look toward the villa and was flooded with relief when she saw Pat emerge with the promised milk and cookies.

Handing these to the children, Pat maintained eye contact with Lauren, her expression concerned. "You look very pale," she said.

"I don't know what's wrong with me. I thought I was having a heart attack. I almost fainted. Now my head is pounding."

Pat took her hand. "I think you might be having a panic attack. It's quite normal after what you've been through."

"This is a panic attack?"

"Sounds like it."

"I haven't had this feeling before."

"Some people don't have them until years after a traumatic event. Try to relax. Think of a tune you know and hum it to yourself."

"Raindrops on roses?" Lauren said with wry humor. "Don't worry, be happy?"

Pat grinned. "Whatever rocks your boat. Now, I better take Brendon and Amber back to their parents. You know...before Mom and Dad start worrying and all, being such conscientious parents that they sent two tiny kids out here alone where any damned thing could happen to them."

"You sound mad."

"It pushes a few buttons." Pat changed the subject. "How do you feel now?"

Lauren drew a deep, shaky breath. "I think it's passing."

"Go indoors and lie down," Pat suggested. "I'll be back in a few."

Lauren waited until Pat and the children were out of sight, then retreated into the villa and locked the door. *A panic attack?* She had always imagined these were a simple case of mind over matter. That the people who claimed to have them were probably suffering from some imagined illness. The sheer physicality of the sensations astounded her. There was nothing imaginary about palpitations, sweat, and dizziness. The sensations were all too real.

Lauren took some iced tea from the bar fridge and slowly sipped the sweet liquid, her eyes on the door. It had only been a few minutes, but already she felt like she would start sobbing if Pat didn't return soon. It didn't matter how hard she tried, she could not control a new onslaught of fear. Terrified, she closed the blinds, hurried up the stairs to the king bedroom, and locked herself in the bathroom. For a moment she hung over the basin, splashing her face with cold water, then she began to retch.

"LAUREN?" PAT STROLLED through the empty villa, taking in the half-finished glass of iced tea on the counter and the fact that all the blinds were now closed. Finding no trace of her principal, she sprinted up the stairs to the king bedroom, alarmed to hear audible groans coming from behind the bathroom door.

"Lauren. It's me," she called, knocking. "Open the door, baby."

Almost before she had stopped speaking, Lauren stood ashen-faced and speechless in the doorway, a toothbrush in her hand.

Knowing what she was going through and longing to give her the comfort she needed, Pat enfolded her in a warm embrace. "Everything's okay. This will pass. I promise you."

Sobs racked Lauren's body. Against Pat's chest, she cried, "Why did this happen to me. Everything was perfect. Now it's all such a mess. What am I going to do?"

Wordlessly, Pat led her to the bed and lay down with her, cradling her as close as her wounds would permit. Stroking her hair, she said, "I'm so sorry this happened. I know you're feeling awful."

"I felt so good when I woke up. I just don't understand how it can change to...this."

"Poor baby." Pat had learned, after working with several trauma survivors, that it was more important to empathize than to try and "talk sense" into a person suffering anxiety. It had struck her, after the loss of her mother, that in some ways mourning was a similar process. It simply had to take its course. Fighting it only made recovery more drawn out.

As Lauren's sobs subsided to hiccups, Pat took her hand and said, "If you want to talk, I'm listening."

Lauren was silent for a long while. "It's all true," she said, eventually. "The stuff in the newspapers. I'm a lesbian."

"I had a feeling," Pat teased gently, "after last night.".

Lauren responded with a watery smile. "I wanted to tell you before. I'm sorry."

"You have nothing to apologize for. I wanted to tell you that I'm gay, too. Guess I blew my cover now."

Lauren glanced up at her. "Did you guess about me? Before last night, I mean."

"On some level, I must have. I was attracted to you, and that usually doesn't happen with straight women." She was relieved by the shift in Lauren's mood. One day Lauren would want to talk on a deeper level, but it would happen in its own time.

"Attracted, hmm?" Lauren made a small huffy noise. "You managed to hide it well."

"Not for long," Pat said with dry self-mockery.

Lauren made a small contented sound and snuggled into her. "By the way," a flirtatious note entered her voice, "did I mention how good you were?"

"No. But it's not too late."

Lauren gave her a playful prod. "If we didn't have to check out of here, I'd have my way with you again."

"Oh, really?" Pat grinned. "That's not how I remember things."

"But admit it." Lauren propped herself on her elbow and traced a finger across Pat's lips. "You're secretly begging for it."

"Uh huh."

Lauren's face grew serious all of a sudden. "Pat, thank you for...everything. And for taking care of me. I don't know what I would do without you."

For some reason, the comment jarred. Pat repeated the words mentally. She felt a vague disquiet. She had intended to give Lauren a sense of security, not make her completely dependent. But Lauren was working through profound stress, she reminded herself. It was only natural that she would lean heavily on the nearest grown-up. As soon as she started to come to terms with what had happened, her attachment would loosen. Whatever happened between them in the end, Pat was content to take it one day at a time for now.

# Chapter
# Twelve

THE AROHA GIFT and Flower Shoppe was one of a sea of eclectic stores that lined Avarua's main street. Crammed with everything from shell necklaces and postcards to funeral monuments and real estate listings, it was a just a few doors from the hospital. Chris had dragged herself out of the Blue Note Café in time to meet Cody and Annabel there. Now they were choosing gifts for the woman they were about to visit.

"It sounds like she's doing better," Annabel remarked, hanging up the in-store pay phone. "She was lucky. It was a perforated appendix."

"I can't believe those guys from the boat aren't planning to visit her," Chris said.

Annabel made a small, disgusted noise. "That's why I wanted us to make an appearance."

"Did you say there were some guests we have to pick up later?" Chris asked.

"Yeah, an actress and her hired muscle," Cody chipped in. Not her favorite people, Chris surmised from the grimace that accompanied this statement. "They stayed over yesterday for the, er . . . night life."

Annabel selected a cheery bunch of flowers and a box of chocolates and handed these to her companions. Already weighed down with parcels and pushing Briar in a baby buggy, Cody shied away from the additional burden, leaving Chris to juggle the bouquet and candy with her own shopping selections.

"Have you found a card?" Annabel asked.

Hands full, Chris nodded toward the counter. "I put a couple of contenders over there."

While Annabel studied the get-well cards, Cody sidled over to Chris. In her hands was a booklet called *The Blooming Bride: Signature Flowers For Your Big Day*. Acting like she was reading this, Cody said in an undertone, "I was thinking. It'll be kind of crowded with three of us at the hospital. There's this game I want to take in, so here's the story. I'll tell Annabel I need some parts for the outboard. Briar will stay with you guys, and I'll meet you back at the airport later on. Okay?"

"Why don't you just tell her?" Chris protested. She could not imagine Annabel insisting that her beloved miss a sports match just so she could tag along to stand at a stranger's bedside for a few minutes.

"She thinks I sneak off to rugby every time I'm over here with her." Cody's air was that of a woman misjudged.

Chris could hardly keep her face straight. "Hey, this is between you and her. Leave me out of it."

Annabel turned, and with a quizzical glance at Cody's reading material, said, "Is there something you need to tell me, honey?"

Cody's face was the picture of guilt. "Uh, you won't need me at the hospital, will you? Because there's a couple of errands I need to run."

With an expression of bland forbearance, Annabel checked her watch. "If you go now, you can catch the entire second half."

Cody feigned innocence. "Oh, you mean the Samoa game? I forgot about that. Well, if you think it's okay, and you don't mind if Briar stays with you—"

"Hey, Cody," Chris cut her off before she dug herself into a bigger hole. "Quit while you're ahead."

Trying not to display unseemly haste, Cody rearranged the purchases in the buggy's storage rack, kissed Briar and Annabel, and lightly clapped Chris's shoulder.

Watching the coltish figure scarper out the door, Annabel slowly shook her head. "I don't get it," she said as the store assistant rang up the sale and wrapped the flowers in fancy tissue. "It's not like she's fooling anyone."

Chris grinned. She liked Annabel and Cody. They were so normal.

PENNY MERCER WAS surprised to see them. She was a lean woman with a boat-deck tan and clear hazel eyes so expressive they registered her delight several seconds before the rest of her face caught up. It was worth waiting for that smile, Chris thought as Annabel made the introductions.

Penny was the kind of woman who could light up a room. Not that she was beautiful. In fact, most people would probably find her ordinary. Her light brown hair was parted in the center and framed her angular face in short braids on either side. The ends were sun-bleached to dark honey. Wispy bangs disguised a high forehead and just touched straight eyebrows the same honey color that tinted her hair. Pushing a stray wisp back from her eyes, she urged, "Please sit down. This is so nice of you."

"You look *much* better," Annabel said, taking one of the empty vases from above the hand basin and arranging the flowers.

"Other than a bunch of stitches and a bad case of jaundice, I feel almost human." Penny's hazel eyes settled on Chris. "Did she tell you I was at death's door when they brought me here?"

"Actually she didn't have to. You made the front page." Chris produced the *Cook Island Times* for that day.

Penny read the headline aloud. "*Explorer Escapes Jellyfish Death*." She looked astounded. "Jellyfish?"

"Inventive," Annabel commented. "Makes a change from shark."

"This is nonsense." Penny scanned the page with disbelief. "It's like someone just sat down and made up the whole story. *The glamour-girl ocean expert from Hollywood was allegedly diving in a provocative striped bikini. Warning, ladies! Local fishermen think this could have agitated the jellyfish, causing their deadly attack.* What is this?"

"Well they couldn't interview you," Annabel pointed out. "And everyone knew you were admitted to the hospital. I guess they had to come up with something."

Penny laughed with such unabashed mirth that Chris felt light-hearted just watching her.

"Ouch." Penny winced, clutching her middle. "That *really* hurts."

"Are you saying all those shark stories are bullshit?" Chris asked Annabel.

"Let's face it, nothing gets the tourists opening their wallets faster than a shark scare," Annabel replied. "If you were told a couple of great whites were enjoying their annual feeding frenzy at a beach near you, wouldn't you pay money for a scientifically proven shark-repellent patch?"

"Does it actually work?" Chris had lost count of the youths who'd accosted her on the main street, hawking anti-shark kits at twenty-five bucks apiece. Tomorrow it would be the jellyfish version, no doubt.

"As a member of the Cook Islands Chamber of Commerce, I'm not sure I want to answer that." Annabel lifted Briar from the stroller and sat her on the floor with a chunky jigsaw puzzle.

"Look at it this way," Penny suggested, wiping her eyes against the back of one hand. "Even if it only gives people the *illusion* of safety, it's money well spent."

"How long are they going to keep you in here?" Chris asked,

wondering if Penny had any other visitors. Like, say, a jealous husband.

"Another five days," Penny said. She sounded dispirited all of a sudden. "Doug's replacing me. It can't be helped. We've only got so long before the money runs out."

Annabel nodded. "I'm supposed to be picking up your new crew member at the airport today."

"I wonder how they're doing." Penny sounded wistful. "I don't suppose you've heard anything."

Annabel smiled. "You think your boss would tell me?"

"I'll probably be the last to know," Penny said dryly. "After all, I'm only the person who came up with the historical tide-gauge algorithms and bathymetric change data set that led us to the search zone in the first place."

"Ooh, I want *your* job," Chris said, making a face.

Penny groaned. "I spend way too much time with nerds."

"We can fix that," Chris promptly assured her. "I'm going away for a few days, but when I get back, we'll bail you out of here. Come down to Trader Jacks, and I can promise you, you won't meet anyone with an IQ over a hundred, myself included."

Again, that irresistible smile. "I can hardly wait."

"It's a date, then." Chris lowered her head so no one would see the color that suddenly warmed her face. Helping Briar put her final piece in the jigsaw, she said, "I guess we should be going."

"So soon?" Penny sounded genuinely disappointed. "Come on. Stay and help me eat these chocolates."

Ten minutes later, as they walked from the hospital, Annabel said, "Very slick."

"Even if she's not on the boat, those guys will keep her in the loop," Chris responded with confidence. "And when she gets the news, I'll be there to hear all about it. Talk about killing two birds with one stone."

Deep in thought, Annabel did not respond right away. "What's the other bird?" she asked eventually.

Chris cleared her throat.

Annabel shot a sideways glance at her. "I see. You think she's gay?"

Chris chewed the question over. She had no idea. All she knew was that she hadn't felt a flicker of interest in a woman since Elaine. It was nice to feel alive for a change. "I guess I'll find out," she said.

AS SOON AS Pat met Cody Stanton's eyes, she knew their laid-back Kiwi host had drawn the obvious conclusions from

Lauren's body language and vivacious chatter.

"Did you get to see the island show?" Cody inquired, faking disinterest. At the same time, her gray eyes tracked Lauren's limpet-like hand as it roamed from Pat's arm to her nape.

"It was great," Lauren enthused. "The dancers are so erotic. And when they picked people from the audience, that was hysterical. You should have seen Pat out there with those guys gyrating around her."

"I wish I had," Cody said with conviction.

Keeping a tight rein on her expression, Pat changed the topic. "How's the patient today?"

"Um, she's doing better. Annabel and Chris went to see her." Cody looked inexplicably sheepish. "I had some errands to take care of."

"I was thinking," Lauren said. "We should organize a day when all the guests come over here, and we go to one of those feasts where they cook the food in the ground."

Pat caught a flash of horror on Cody's face before it was supplanted by polite interest. "I'll suggest that to Annabel."

Lauren tucked her arm into Pat's, happily oblivious. "You can put us down for it."

This time Cody was unable to contain herself. With the lucid frankness Pat had found to be the bailiwick of folks Down Under, she observed, "Hey, if you two don't need that extra bedroom any more, I've got some guests who want to swap accommodations."

Unhelpfully, Lauren cast a flirtatious look at Pat. "Maybe we could do that."

Pat could almost hear Wendall Douglas. *What the hell have you done to my daughter? I'm calling your boss at the FBI. You'll never be promoted again.* Lauren was behaving like a teenager, she thought, stunned. Could this kittenish creature be the same woman who held down a television career and had asserted herself with chilly self-confidence just a couple of weeks ago in that hospital room? What in God's name was she playing at?

Not wanting to embarrass her in front of Cody, Pat said, "I think it's better if we stay put."

"No worries." Cody shrugged. "I'll tell the others they'll just have to work it out. It's a bit late to sign up for a romantic getaway, *then* decide you want a divorce."

Lauren heaved a sigh. "I feel really sorry for them. When I threw out my ex, I never wanted to see her again."

Why not take out an advertisement in the local papers, Pat thought. *Lauren Douglas, TV star and Congressman's daughter, flaunts lesbian affair.* Wendall Douglas wasn't just going to destroy Pat's career, he was going to kill her.

Feeling like a deer in headlights, Pat informed Cody, joking but very serious, "You didn't hear that."

Cody held Pat's stare and lifted her eyebrows fractionally. It seemed to be dawning on her that Lauren's behavior was odd. "We're particular about our guest's privacy," she said.

"Thank you." Pat glanced around at the sound of voices.

Mercifully, the rest of the passengers were walking across the tarmac led by Annabel.

"Pat," Cody suggested, "maybe you could get Ms. Douglas settled into her seat so she's comfortable before we board everyone else."

"Good idea," Pat said. As she escorted Lauren to the plane, she demanded, "What are you doing? Do you want the whole world to know we're...involved?"

Lauren looked startled and hurt. "I don't know what you mean."

Impatiently, Pat hustled her onto the plane and showed her to a seat near the tail so they could speak without the rest of the passengers eavesdropping. Trying not to sound as angry as she felt, she said, "We need to talk about this, Lauren. This is not just about you and me. It's about keeping you safe and making sure you are not vulnerable. Gossip has a way of spreading."

"But we're miles from home. I mean, this is like being on another planet. Can't we just be ourselves and enjoy what's happening between us?"

Pat took a deep breath. "What do you think is happening between us?"

Lauren gazed at her, starry-eyed. "Love at first sight."

Oh, God. Pat grappled for a foothold on the slippery slopes of storybook romance. "Baby," she said carefully, "this could be something wonderful. But it's early days. We don't even know each other yet."

"Are you saying you don't feel the same way about me?"

"I don't think I believe in love at first sight. I believe love grows over time between two people who are strongly attracted from the start."

"Was it just sex?" Lauren withdrew her hand.

Pat touched her face. "It was much more than just sex."

"Are you angry with me?"

"No," Pat said. "I'm concerned for you. I don't want us to make a mistake that you might have to pay for. Do you understand?"

Lauren's head drooped. "I think so." She ran a hand across her eyes. "Are you going to leave me?"

"Of course not." Pat found herself reacting to the forlorn tone and defeated body language. Wrapping her arms around Lauren, she said, "Just slow down. I'm not going anywhere. We don't have to make everything happen overnight."

Lauren clung to her. "I don't know what's wrong with me," she choked out. "I'm sorry if I've embarrassed you."

Pat kissed the top of her head. She understood that Lauren's extreme insecurity and neediness were symptomatic of her condition. It was almost as if she had regressed to a younger version of herself. Jumping into the sack had obviously been a huge mistake. Making love had changed everything because it changed the boundaries their dynamic was built on. To Lauren, Pat was no longer the bodyguard paid to protect her; she was a lover — someone who could walk away just like that.

Pat should have seen this coming. Furious with herself, she stared unseeingly at the back of the seat before her. How could she have allowed herself to abandon one of the basic tenets of the job? Don't get involved. Not with anyone — witness, colleague, or, now, client. It was completely unlike her to lose her head this way. She was always the first person to condemn such conduct as weak-minded and selfish. What was her excuse? That she was horny? That her attraction to Lauren had temporarily overwhelmed her principles? That she just wanted to feel like a normal person on a romantic vacation for an hour or two?

All of the above, she admitted inwardly. For once, she had not rationalized. She had not weighed consequences. Not only had her lapse in judgment made Lauren feel less secure, it had almost led to a tragedy. Two small children had found her loaded gun on the beach. Pat felt queasy. She had to get a grip on herself; she had to make this right somehow. What was she going to do?

# Chapter
# Thirteen

*PASSION BAY.* LAUREN imagined a couple so much in love they had named this perfect beach in honor of what they'd shared here. Who were they? On a wall at Annabel and Cody's home, she had seen a photograph of two women and an ethereal blonde toddler, obviously Annabel as a child. Was she the daughter of lesbians? One of the women, dark-haired and overtly butch, wore elegant men's clothing. Her riveting stare seemed a challenge across time, daring the world to deny her existence, the fact of her arm around the waist of the girlish woman next to her, and her hand on the head of the toddler standing between them. There was no mistaking her claim: *Posterity also has a lesbian face.*

Something in the woman's demeanor reminded Lauren of Pat. She decided both were the kind of women brave enough to be self-defining, to live their lives without social sanction or disguise, to risk being outsiders. How very different their choices were from Lauren's. Personal honor meant something to such women. Their integrity was not up for grabs. They would never choose to pass as heterosexual out of expedience. Where did they find that courage?

Lulled by the drowsy motion of the incoming tide, half-swimming, half-floating in the warmth of the salt water, Lauren peered across the silver-gilt sands to a multi-hued beach blanket. Pat, resting her elbows on her knees, sat with the ubiquitous binoculars trained on the lagoon. She had finally ceased insistence on wading with Lauren as she swam, instead sitting beneath the palms, intermittently reading the grim volumes she'd dragged along with her to paradise.

Lauren raised her arm in a languid wave, and Pat waved back. Her calm presence was comforting, yet Lauren was troubled. It had been two days since their return from Raro, and they had not made love again. Instead of moving into Lauren's bedroom, Pat had remained in her own. They were together all the time, yet Lauren had an odd feeling that Pat was avoiding her. She'd even stopped the regular "be aware, be prepared" lessons. When Lauren asked what was wrong, Pat always said the same thing. *Let's take it slowly.* Was that a euphemism for *Let's not go there again*?

Despondently, Lauren flipped onto her stomach and mooched along the shoreline in a mutant version of sidestroke. The memory of Pat's touch brought with it churning butterflies and a longing so desperate she was forced to redefine her entire sexual history as little more than a practice run for the real thing. When she thought about Sara, she felt humiliated. How could she have set the bar so low? How could she have read so much into Sara's lukewarm attentions?

Even if she never slept with Pat again, just one night in her arms had provided Lauren with a whole new frame of reference. Having felt so alive, so awakened to herself with a virtual stranger, she could see that her relationship with Sara was at best sterile and at worst, a farce. She had spent three years in a hiatus of unconcern because she knew no better. Recalling Sara's forceful attempts to have her sign over half of her property, Lauren finally understood why she had balked. On some deep level, her spirit had resisted. Part of her knew something was not right and that she deserved better.

Lauren's eyes prickled. She thought about her father's cynical words. The way he saw it, Lauren was little more than an apartment and an ATM card to Sara, a whistle-stop on the road to the American Dream. Sara's single-minded pursuit of the trappings of social success had seemed almost admirable to Lauren. Her lover had not been handed a gilt-edged future on a plate, as Lauren had. What was wrong with her being ambitious? Wasn't Sara's way the American way?

Even now, Lauren found herself justifying her ex's actions. Who was she to judge a woman who had to tread on some toes to carve out the opportunities Lauren and her friends took for granted? Sara was no better or worse than any of that legion of women who chose their partners for cynical, self-serving reasons. All the same, it hurt. Lauren hated to think that she did not exist for Sara but as a means to an end, that Sara hadn't loved her, but had only envied her.

What stung Lauren most was not that she had loved this woman and been betrayed. It was that she'd been made a fool of. She had seen what she wanted to see—just like the maniac who'd shot her. Lauren supposed it was the human condition to deny reality when it flew in the face of fondly held belief. Her father and his politician friends counted on it. Lauren must have heard them discuss the "lemming factor" a thousand times. Finally, she understood the expression.

Well, she was not blindly running over any cliffs again in the near future. When she had her next long-term relationship, it would be with someone who had a very different set of values, someone who loved her for herself. But how would she know? Lauren steered herself into shallow water and lowered her feet to the sea floor. Automatically, her eyes fastened once more on Pat.

Every instinct she possessed told her Pat Roussel would never feign love where it did not exist. But perhaps she was deluding herself yet again, seeing what she wanted to see. Pat was dead right. They should slow down. If nothing else, Lauren needed time to process everything that had happened in the past two months and make some decisions about her life. A new relationship would be a tempting distraction from all that was painful and difficult about the present. But it was time to grow up. It was time she took responsibility for herself.

Out of the corner of her eye, Lauren caught a movement in the water a few yards away. Coming straight for her, a dorsal fin cut the gleaming blue surface. Shocked into a piercing scream, she splashed her way frantically out of the water and collapsed on dry sand, her heart pounding violently. A shark! At the airport, she had seen a front-page headline in the local newspaper about a great white sighting. Maybe the terrifying predator had smelled her wounds and come into shallow water looking for a quick meal.

She was shaking uncontrollably when Pat grabbed her and turned her over, urgently looking her up and down. "Baby, what happened? Are you okay?"

"There's a shark." Lauren pointed at the tranquil lagoon. "Over there. I saw it. Just a few yards away."

Pat released her. "I believe you." She got up and stalked into the water, scouring the bay.

"Please don't go in!" Lauren pleaded. "They can attack people in knee-deep water."

At that moment, the lagoon erupted and a silver form shot high in the air in a rolling somersault. Whistling and screeching, a dolphin crashed back into the sea and surfaced a moment later, staring at Pat and Lauren as if expecting something.

Lauren's fear subsided into astonished delight. Feeling foolish, she scrambled to her feet and hurried to Pat's side. "I'm such an idiot."

"No, you're not. Better safe than sorry." Pat dropped her sunglasses into her front pocket and slipped her arm around

Lauren. "I think it wants to meet us."

Slowly, they advanced toward the graceful visitor. As they drew near, the dolphin flipped onto its back and swam a few feet, waving its flippers and making soft clicks. Keeping pace, Pat and Lauren followed, moving into deeper water. The dolphin circled them and swam so close, Lauren felt the cool, sandy brush of its skin. In disbelief, she extended her hand and the dolphin butted it very gently with the top of its head, then stood upright in the water, gazing at her.

Propelled by a strange conviction that this was what the dolphin sought, Lauren moved toward the animal and embraced it. A strange joy flooded her, and her eyes filled with tears. It was almost as if she could sense what the dolphin was thinking, yet there were no words to express the mystic content of its message. Lauren closed her eyes and made some clicking sounds, trying to imitate its language, wanting to say something back.

She was aware of Pat staring at her, eyes bright with an emotion Lauren could not fathom. She released her hold on the dolphin, and it glided away from them, flicking its tail just enough to propel it slowly through the water. Lauren stared after it, committing to memory the distinctive dorsal fin, pale silver with a dark, featherlike stripe. If she saw that fin again, she would recognize it.

"You two seemed to hit it off," Pat remarked with gentle humor.

Lauren hesitated. "I felt like it was speaking to me."

"What did it say?" Pat sounded genuinely interested.

Lauren struggled to give shape to her thoughts. "This will sound silly. I felt love." Detecting no trace of mockery, she continued. "It was like being wrapped in a blanket when you're really cold — you know, kind of warm and peaceful and content."

Pat smiled. Taking Lauren's hand, she steered them out of the water and back along the beach. "I guess it thought you needed that."

Lauren felt stunned. She had wondered how she was supposed to recognize love, how she could tell if someone truly loved her, and it was as if the dolphin had answered. A strange joy seeped through her. Blinking up the sun, she said, "Have you ever been in love, Pat?"

Pat was quiet for a few seconds, then, in a neutral tone, she answered, "It's hard to say. At the time I thought I was."

"Don't we all?"

"Well, everyone wants it to happen." Pat sounded philosophical.

"You think we just convince ourselves?"

"Sometimes, maybe. Hell, I'm no expert." Pat shook the sand from their beach blanket and repositioned it, along with their cooler and Lauren's bag and towel, in the shade of some coconut palms.

Lauren sat down and pulled a bottle of water from the cooler. She took a long swig then passed the bottle to Pat, who had elected to share the blanket with her instead of returning to her deck chair and weighty reading matter. Relaxed, but watchful as always, the bodyguard leaned back, propped on her elbows, strong legs extended. Her tan was deepening by the day, making her eyes seem greener. Her hair had grown. Thick and dark, it now fell slightly over her forehead.

Lauren was reminded of a young Greek sailor who had once manned a yacht owned by friends of her parents. He and Pat shared the same disturbing androgynous beauty.

When Lauren was twelve, the two families had spent a summer holiday together, cruising the Aegean Sea. The sailor, Leonidas, had befriended her, eventually escorting her and her mother to a *panigirias,* or festival, at his village on the island of Sifnos as a guest of his family, who were hosting the event. Lauren remembered the evening festivities as one of the happiest times of her childhood. Leonidas' four sisters, feminine versions of their striking brother, dressed her in village costume and taught her local dances. They had urged her in broken English to come back one day and bring her own children.

In her mind's eye, Lauren could see the terraced, scrub-dotted reddish slopes with their ancient stone walls and whitewashed houses, the donkeys dozing under anything that passed for a shrub, the profound cobalt of sea and sky. She could hear goat bells and children laughing. Sifnos was timeless, the simple camaraderie of village life as remote and unreal as if it took place on Mars. By contrast, her life seemed cluttered and frantic, bereft of meaning. And it had almost been taken from her.

Lauren confronted that simple, shocking truth squarely. Had she died there in a department store parking garage, what would she have lost? What would she have regretted not doing with her life? What would her death have meant to anyone other than her family?

The answer was disturbing. Her life was essentially worthless. She was a woman playing the role of a doctor, tending imaginary injuries, faking emotions she did not have, making statements she did not believe, for an audience of people she would never know. And in order to live out this farce, she had to lie about who she really was. All for money she did not need, and so-called fame, increasingly the province of the professional attention-seeker.

Did she really want to spend the rest of her life competing for media-play with people whose contribution to humanity was inversely proportionate to their need for ego-pats? Lauren cast a sideways glance at Pat and wondered what this woman, who lived a life that was actually about making a difference, really thought of her.

Impulsively, she asked, "Pat, am I the kind of person you would make friends with? You know...if we weren't in this situation."

Pat was silent for a moment, then said, "If you and I had just met somewhere, I doubt we'd have gotten to know one another enough for a friendship. We don't have much in common."

Well, that was frankly spoken. "Do you like me?"

Pat seemed cagey. "I care about you."

Lauren let that sink in. Pat was paid to take care of her. Was that all Lauren was to her—a job and a one-night stand? Refusing to believe that, she asked, "Why aren't we sleeping together? Is it because you don't like me as a person?"

"No. It's nothing like that. Damn, I wish our situation was different."

"What do you mean?"

Pat took her hand. "Listen to me. I like you. I care for you. But I'd rather things were on a professional footing between us from now on."

"You're breaking up with me?" It was not as if they had a relationship, Lauren thought as soon as she had spoken. She wasn't really sure what they had. Nothing, from the sound of it. She withdrew her hand. Pat did not resist.

"What I'm saying is that, while we're here and while I'm your father's employee, I would prefer that we don't blur the boundaries."

"Then why did you sleep with me?" Lauren demanded, angry at Pat's calm logic, her after-the-fact misgivings.

Pat's face was shuttered. "I made the wrong choice—for both of us. Lauren, wait," she said as Lauren threw her things together and got to her feet. "Sit down. We need to talk."

"I've heard enough. You've made yourself quite clear."

"I don't think I have." Pat scrambled to her feet and seized Lauren's arm. "I'm trying to be sensible. Maybe too sensible. I would love to sleep with you again. But if we do, if we have this...interlude, I think it's all we'll have. And I'm not sure I could settle for that."

Lauren stood still, struck by the conviction in Pat's voice, the stark emotion in her face. "Why couldn't we have more?" she whispered. "I don't understand."

"You have to trust me on this," Pat said, releasing her arm. "It's the wrong time for either of us to get involved. Even if you feel ready, I know I'm not. There's something I'm dealing with, and until it's over, I..." Pat broke off, as if she had said too much.

Lauren could tell she was truly upset. How little she knew this woman. Pat had taken time out of her job because she needed a break. Only now did Lauren understand what that must mean to someone like Pat. She wasn't taking time out because she felt bored, or wanted a tan. Something profound must have happened, and, selfishly, Lauren had never even tried to guess what it might be. "Can you talk about it?" she asked carefully.

"There's no point." Pat was her detached self again. "It's something I have to resolve for myself."

Lauren bit back a frustrated protest. Clearly Pat found it difficult to discuss her feelings. Given her line of work, she had probably trained herself not to show vulnerability. At least she hadn't said she wasn't interested in a relationship at all. Lauren was willing to bide her time, to build some trust and see what happened. She slid her hand into Pat's and tried to rise above her own disappointment. "I understand. Thank you for telling me. Friends then? For now?"

Pat squeezed her hand, relief visible in her face. "I'd like that."

CODY SANK DOWN onto a crush of rotting vegetation and retrieved a water bottle from her backpack. "This is hopeless," she said, studying the photocopy they had taken off the original map Annabel kept in a bank deposit box. "X should be right over there, but there's just that bloody great rock. We're never going to find it."

Chris's eyes roamed the jagged formation Cody was glaring at. They had explored the area around it at length, using their hiking poles to probe the terrain for suspicious openings. "At least the views are good from up here," she said. "I'm going to take some photos."

"Knock yourself out. I'm not moving." Cody slumped against her pack and pulled her hat over her eyes, apparently planning a nap.

Chris picked her way along the *makatea* toward the cliff edge and stared down at the Sacred Shore. One hand strayed to the heavy gold locket she always wore. She drew a sharp breath, then exhaled slowly. Is it okay? She cast her silent question to the winds.

An odd sorrow had settled on her since meeting Penny Mercer. Her attraction to the marine scientist rattled her. The thought of acting on it filled her with guilt. How could she be disloyal to Elaine's memory? Chris had come to believe she would never feel anything for a woman again, and in a way that was a relief. On an intellectual level, she knew her late lover would not have wanted her to spend the rest of her life alone. Last year, on the beach hundreds of feet below, Elaine had come to her in spirit, and she had released Chris. She had told her to be happy, to live her life without regret.

Chris had tried to convince herself that her inexplicable experiences on the Sacred Shore were merely hallucinations. She had certainly felt drugged by the bitter-tasting drink the island women passed around during the rituals dedicated to Hine te Ana, a goddess who protected the island. But, in her heart, she believed the impossible—that Elaine's ghost had been present that night, that they had shared a final goodbye.

Chris opened the locket and gazed down at Elaine's picture. Give me a sign that it's okay. No answering gust of wind shook the palms. No shadow crossed the sun. The birds did not fall silent. With a sigh, Chris dropped the locket back inside her t-shirt and resumed her careful progress.

The *makatea* on the southern face was the most dangerous on the island. Precipitous cliffs faced an ocean torn by rip currents and restlessly pounding the shore. From her vantage point, Chris could not imagine how anyone could swim in to the small beach below, yet according to legend, the goddess Hine te Ana had done just that. And last year, while Chris was holidaying on the island, so had one of the other guests—Olivia Pearce. Chris wondered how she was doing and hoped she and her lover Merris were happy. Last she'd heard, they were somewhere in Italy, and Olivia had been hired to write songs for a movie.

Once more Chris stood at the base of the rock formation and gazed up. If anybody had buried a treasure here, it would have to be in a fissure or cave. So far, she and Cody had uncovered nothing but a beehive and a shred of what looked like someone's lacy underwear.

Annabel's theory was that the map Chris had found when she was caving was not a buried treasure map at all. She was convinced the X on it marked the entrance to the cave of Hine te Ana, the island's most sacred site. According to legend, there was a magic pool in the cave that could grant wishes, but anyone who looked into its waters uninvited would be cursed. After lengthy discussions, they had agreed Chris and Cody would dig up the spot and see whether Annabel was right.

Based on their futile attempts so far, Chris felt sure there was no danger anyone would ever stumble across this sacred cave while they were hunting for treasure. It was time to turn back. Annabel had no need to worry. The island's secrets were safe.

Chris had an idea. She would take some photographs of the inaccessible terrain to prove her point and set Annabel's mind at ease. Lifting her camera, she took a few steps back and framed a wide-angle shot of the rock formation and the dense jungle that skirted it. She snapped a couple of pictures then zoomed in, wanting a closer shot of the jagged, fissured wall. As she prepared to take the photograph, she froze, transfixed by the sight of a huge bird emerging from what looked like solid rock about thirty feet up. The bird stood surveying its domain from a narrow ledge straight above the spot where they'd found the torn lace. They hadn't climbed any higher.

"Cody," Chris yelled. After a few seconds of silence, she stumbled back to the reclining woman and shook her awake. "I've seen something."

Cody's wide gray eyes blinked foggily at her. "Is it treasure?"

"That's what we're going to find out." Chris yanked her to her feet and handed her a pair of protective gloves. "Let's go."

They scaled the sharp rise to the point at which they'd turned back last time and looked up. From where they were standing, it was impossible to see any kind of gap, certainly nothing a sea eagle could have nested in.

"Let's try the north side," Chris said.

Grunting and cursing, they scrambled over a boulder and up to a ledge that snaked behind the western face of the rock wall. The ledge broadened and channeled into a vertical seam that had been invisible from where they'd stood earlier. It was barely wide enough to admit a person. At the entrance to this was a substantial bird's nest with two eggs in it. Just above eye level, several strings of white shells hung like markers from a small protrusion.

"Check this out!" Cody touched the shells and stared into the dark opening. "We've found it."

They stood in awe, staring at one another. Hine te Ana's cave was *tapu* — forbidden.

"Let's just conceal the entrance and go back," Cody said, casting nervous glances toward the sky as if expecting to be struck by lightening at any moment.

"No way," Chris said. "This looks like just the place for someone to hide treasure." Besides, she wanted to see this legendary cave, *tapu* or not.

Cody looked pained. "Okay, but first..." She unclipped a pocket knife from her belt and calmly sliced into her forearm, just enough to draw blood. She painted a small triangle on the rock next to the shell marker and closed her eyes, mumbling something Chris could not make out. Then she passed the knife to Chris, instructing, "Ask permission from the goddess to enter, and promise you won't tell anyone where the cave is."

"Can't I promise without the bloodletting?"

"It's an offering," Cody said, deadly serious. "It symbolizes *mauri*...life force."

"If you think that's going to stop us getting cursed, who am I to argue?" Chris took the knife and followed suit, half in earnest, half astonished at herself for buying into absurd superstition. "Okay. That's my O positive. What are we waiting for?"

Cody dug around in her pack, produced a couple of flashlights and rappelling gear, and after leaving most of their stuff outside, they squeezed warily along the narrow crevice for a few feet. Abruptly this fell away in a steep drop, and they heard the sound of water gurgling.

Training her flashlight down the entry shaft into the darkness below, Chris was astonished to see what looked like mats and quilts around a pool of water. "This is definitely the place. I can see the pool."

"Jesus. How far down is it?"

"About thirty feet."

"Well I'm not jumping. Let's get roped to that boulder and we can rappel down." Cody vanished back the way they came.

A few minutes later, they descended into a cool, dark chamber unlike anything Chris had ever seen. A shaft of bright sunlight spilled from a chimney high above, bouncing off crystalline walls. Flowering creepers and fleshy plants trailed down from the cave entrance, scenting the air. Necklaces of shells hung from rock and crystal formations and water seeped from some source deep in the earth, spilling into a glassy pool in the center. If there had been candles around the walls, the grotto would have passed for a religious shrine.

"This has to be the cave Olivia talked about," Chris marveled. "I thought maybe it was just wishful thinking or something. You know, after everything she went though."

"Don't look in the water," Cody warned, averting her face as they approached the pool. "Man, I am so creeped out."

"We're not going to be cursed." Chris elected herself the voice of reason. "We donated blood, and we haven't done anything wrong. I guess we should search the pool in case that's where the treasure is." She felt distinctly uneasy about that prospect.

"No fucking way. I am not touching that water."

"Okay. We'll leave it 'til last. Let's take a look over there."

They crossed to the other side of the cave, where there seemed to be another way out. Cody pulled herself over a ledge, aiming her flashlight ahead. "There's a path." She sounded excited. "And carvings. This must lead down to the beach."

Gripping the hand Cody extended, Chris hauled herself up and over, wishing she were thirty pounds lighter. Since Elaine's death, she had blimped in front of the television and comforted herself with junk food. Every super-sized burger meal seemed to have landed around her middle. It was time to stop that.

The path was a series of steep steps carved into solid rock, each about two feet tall. On either side, the walls were etched with a recurring motif. Chris's fingers traced triangles and long curved feather-like shapes. She recalled the geometric tattoos she had seen on the priestess and some of the local women present at the rituals. The design was the same.

"This is incredible," she said, shining her flashlight around. "I wonder when they carved this out. It must be hundreds of years ago. Maybe thousands."

Cody paused on one of the huge steps, catching her breath. "Whoever they were, they had really long legs." She sank down onto the step below Chris's. "Want a drink?"

"You bet." Chris sat her flashlight on the step, leaving it turned on to provide them with some light.

Cody passed Chris the water bottle "I don't think there's much point us going all the way down to the Sacred Shore."

"I agree. There's nothing down here." And frankly, she could do without having to climb hundreds of feet if they could avoid it, Chris thought.

"Maybe there's no treasure after all." Cody sounded a little deflated.

"The dead guy with the map probably wasn't a pirate," Chris theorized. "He was probably a navy deserter from this ship they're talking about. He must have rowed ashore, climbed this cliff, and found his way in. Maybe he left some stuff here in the cave and decided to explore. He made a map so he could come back."

"You think he went looking for signs of life on the island

and fell into that cave where you found him?" Cody said. "Broke his ankle, couldn't get out?"

"It makes sense. There's no way he could have climbed up here with thousands of gold coins. Imagine what they'd weigh. I'm guessing the ones I found in his boot were his wages."

Cody stood. "No one ever has to know you found that skeleton."

"That's right. He's not going anywhere." Chris got to her feet and did a couple of stretches. She was so out of condition her legs ached.

Cody sighed. "It would have been cool to find a real buried treasure."

"It's all at the bottom of the sea," Chris said, struggling up the first carved step. "God, I can't believe we have to climb back up fifty of these suckers."

Cody shone her flashlight past Chris, the beam illuminating the carved relief of the walls above. "Take it slowly."

Chris laughed. "I don't have much choice."

"Let's cut the lights and save our batteries so we can have a really good look in that cave. Can you feel your way okay in the dark?"

"Sure." Chris flicked off her torch, closed her eyes for a moment to adjust, then opened them again.

About twenty yards ahead a sliver of sunlight pierced the darkness, filtered from a gap high above. She hadn't seen it so plainly on the way down, with both their flashlights illuminating the steps. Cody was climbing like a mountain goat, taking two steps for every one of Chris's. Embarrassed over her own sluggish progress, Chris picked up her pace.

This also had to change, she decided. With Elaine, she'd kept herself fit. She would never be thin—her build was naturally solid, and besides, she didn't feel right without some meat on her bones. But these days the meat was running to fat and she had almost no physical stamina. They had only hiked for a couple of hours and she was exhausted. A woman like Penny Mercer would not be caught dead with a couch-potato lover, Chris guessed. Not that they were necessarily going to be lovers. For all Chris knew, the woman was straight.

She hoisted herself onto yet another step and halted, panting. She had a stitch, and it felt like one of her hamstrings was about to pop. "Hey, Cody?" she called. "I need to stop a minute."

"You okay?" A disembodied voice floated down. It sounded like Cody was miles away.

"I'm fine. Go on without me."

"No way, mate. Take it easy. I'll wait here."

Chris took a few deep breaths. She had never felt claustrophobic before, but she did right now. All she could think about was reaching the light of day. Trying to calm herself, she fixed her gaze on the shaft of sunlight and headed for it. Soon she would be out in the fresh air. They would go back and tell Annabel the good news. She would have some delicious snacks ready for them. Chris would take a long, warm bath. They would sit out in the shady verandah at Villa Luna and drink a little wine.

Annabel had invited the other guests on the island to a barbecue. One of them, she had breezily informed Chris that morning, was single and seemed really nice. Chris had to smile. She had sensed Annabel had something up her sleeve; apparently she fancied herself a matchmaker.

Chris reached the sunlit step and sat down to take a drink.

"How are you doing?" Cody called, this time sounding closer.

"Let's just say, I won't be entering the local iron-woman this year." Chris capped her bottle and got to her feet.

Something caught her eye—a bright glint to her right. She stared at the spot. The sunlight was playing off something that looked metallic. Curious, Chris moved sideways and almost lost her footing. The step fell away into a void. Lucky they'd been sticking to the opposite wall, where the carvings guided them, she thought, reaching for her flashlight.

Standing near the edge of the step she trained a beam into the darkness. Round bright golden eyes stared up at her. "Cody!" she yelled. "Get down here."

"YOU'RE KIDDING ME," Annabel said as Chris and Cody sat on the verandah steps, removing their hiking boots.

To her horror, both women reached into their pockets and dumped a handful of large golden coins onto the wooden planks at her feet.

"There are thousands of them," Cody said. "We're rich."

"*I'm* rich," Chris corrected her, laughing. "I found them, remember."

"I was about to come down and help you," Cody said. "I would have seen them."

"This is just perfect." Annabel groaned. "Now they'll find that damned wreck, discover the missing coins, and draw the obvious conclusions. They'll be all over this place like a rash."

"What obvious conclusions?" Cody asked. "Couldn't someone have found the wreck first and taken the money? Why would they assume it's here?"

"Because the ship sank off our shores," Annabel said patiently. "Think about it, you're the captain, and you're under attack by pirates. What do you do? You keep the enemy busy, load as much gold as you can onto a lifeboat, and row for the nearest shore."

Chris nodded. "You're right. That's exactly what those salvagers are going to think."

Annabel poured iced tea into two tall glasses and handed these to her sweaty companions.

"At least we didn't have to search the pool," Cody said, sinking into a cane chair.

"And we made a blood offering before we went in the cave." Chris pointed to a cut on her arm.

"We have to get the treasure out of there," Annabel said, thinking out loud.

"Forget it," Cody said. "Jeez. No one's ever going to find that cave. Honestly, babe. We only found it by accident."

"If you could find it, so will someone else." Annabel felt bad about sounding discouraging when Cody and Chris were so thrilled by their discovery. But she couldn't get excited. The gold would have to be moved. She couldn't risk having Hine te Ana's cave exposed.

"I know what we'll do," she said, an idea percolating. "Penny Mercer. She'll be leaving the hospital in a few days, and I think she should come here to recuperate."

Chris gave her an odd look. "You want the enemy staying on the island?"

"Absolutely. And not just staying. I want her exploring." Annabel sat on the chaise lounge and sipped her tea. "Picture this. There's Penny in the Kopeka Cave. Chris, you're her guide to the natural wonders of the island. You both stumble across a few golden guineas—"

"In the vicinity of that slippery slope down to the other little cave." Chris caught on right away.

" — where she finds Mr. Bones, our resident pirate, and a big swag of treasure."

"Imagine that," Chris said dryly.

Cody looked appalled. "You're going to give the treasure to them?"

"No. I'm going to give the treasure to *Chris* and them," Annabel said. "It's only fair. After all, if Chris hadn't found Mr. Bones and the map in the first place, we'd never have found Hine te Ana's cave."

Chris started to say something, then seemed to think the

better of it.

"Why don't we just split the treasure with Chris." Cody was indignant. "It's on *our* land, after all. I can't see why we have to give anything to Doug and his mates."

"Because we don't need the money, and I want the *Aspiration* people to leave happy and let the whole world know there's nothing left on this island to be found. Anyway, it would be nice if Penny could be the hero of her crew." She caught another look from Chris and smiled innocently.

It was the perfect solution, Annabel thought. Chris gets to impress a woman she is interested in, Doug and his pals won't need to send out the search parties when they find a few thousand coins missing from their shipwreck, and any public attention will center on Mr. Bones and his cave. All they had to do was retrieve hundreds of pounds of solid gold from a cursed cave up a dangerous cliff, row it out across incredibly treacherous waters under cover of darkness, then transport it on their backs halfway across the island and conceal it deep within the Kopeka Cave. What could be simpler?

# Chapter
# Fourteen


"ARE YOU SURE you don't want me to carry something?" Lauren asked, guiltily watching her bodyguard approach.

Pat was carrying all their gear in a substantial backpack. Not that the weight seemed to bother her. She had barely broken a sweat in almost two hours of hiking. The expedition had been Lauren's idea—something *friends* would do—a scenic hike into the center of the island where, according to their hosts, there was a beautiful waterfall.

As Pat made it to the crest of the ridge, she handed Lauren one of the spare water containers she had dangling from her hip, as if this would lighten her load. "You can carry this," she said. "It's kind of annoying bouncing around."

Lauren wanted to point out that lugging a gun probably didn't make Pat's belt comfortable, but she held her tongue, having already made her opinion about hiking with a firearm perfectly clear. She tied the canteen to her belt and briefly studied the hiking map Cody had provided. "I think we're coming to the path," she said, peering ahead and spotting a bright pink coconut shell wired to a tree. "The pink markers are for the waterfall trail and the yellow ones lead to the bird cave."

As they descended from the sparsely treed ridge, the jungle air was once more thick and moist, the vegetation so dense that it seemed the creepers and shoots were engaged in a perpetual struggle to reclaim the pathway. Lauren could see that the track to the waterfall had been cut recently. The greenery on either side was littered with severed palm fronds and tangles of dead creeper. These would soon rot down and form part of the cycle of regeneration that was so apparent in this wild, natural place.

Like Rarotonga, Moon Island's interior seemed untouched by humanity. The route they had taken led them inland across the *makatea*, a fossilized coral reef that had once been under the sea. The formation was razor-sharp and slow to traverse, thanks to numerous small holes disguised by the fleshy creepers and ferns that covered the jungle floor. Cody had insisted they take steel climbing poles with them to ensure safe footing, and Lauren quickly saw why. This was such a beautiful place, it would be all too easy to forget it was also dangerous. She wondered how many guests had broken their ankles trying to explore without the right equipment.

Lauren stopped for a moment, enchanted by several pretty little birds that were hopping from branch to branch as they proceeded along the trail. She was amazed at how tame the creatures of the island were. The mynahs and fruit doves that lived around the villa showed no signs of fear when she approached, and some would even sit on her shoulder. They had no reason to think ill of human beings, she supposed. And there were no predators on Moon Island; the place was a veritable Garden of Eden. She extended an arm and to her delight, a small apricot-breasted bird landed on her palm and studied her as if she were a curiosity.

"It's a *kakarori*," Pat said, coming to a halt behind her. "They're an endangered species that's making a comeback here. I read about it in the visitor guide."

The gregarious little bird made a rapid twittering sound and flew off, joining several companions in a papaya tree a few yards away.

"I wonder what other animals live here," Lauren mused, sensing they were being watched, probably by countless tiny creatures invisible to the human eye. She just hoped none of them were giant jumping spiders.

"Birds, lizards, bats, small mammals. We're the only dangerous species on the place."

"It's amazing." Lauren picked her way carefully down a slippery gradient. "It feels so prehistoric. All you can hear is squishy noises and birdcalls. I don't think I've ever been anywhere that there's no cars."

Moon Island must be one of the few places in the world without a single road, she thought. And the only power supply came from generators. It was amazing that Cody and Annabel had been able to do so much with the place. Lauren was surprised she wasn't missing the comforts of home more; who knew how quickly a person could adjust to lukewarm showers and no television? In this faraway place, the days seemed longer, the nights more restful. Except for the last few.

Despite their agreement to be "just friends," Lauren still lay awake yearning for Pat. Sometimes she even contemplated sneaking into bed with her in the small hours, just so that she could smell her and feel her. But that wouldn't be enough. She would want to make love, and knowing that was not going to happen, it was easier to sleep alone.

Lately Lauren had found herself wondering if Pat had only said she still wanted her sexually, just to soften the blow. If it were true, surely she must be just as frustrated as Lauren was. And wouldn't a woman like Pat do something about that? In her darkest moments, Lauren suspected that, for Pat, the encounter on Rarotonga was just a hot one-nighter, no matter what she said about wishing they had met under different circumstances. Talk was cheap. If she really wanted Lauren, keeping her at a distance made no sense.

Slowing down, Lauren mopped her face on her t-shirt. The dull pain of her shoulder was starting to wear her down. She hoped they would reach this waterfall soon.

Pat caught up with her. "Tired?"

Lauren cast a quick look back. "I'm fine."

"As soon as we get there, I'll find the painkillers." Pat checked her watch. "It's been more than four hours since your last dose, and causalgia is no picnic."

"I feel like a junkie," Lauren muttered.

"Trust me. You're not a junkie. Let's slow it down some. This isn't a triathlon."

"I suppose you do those in your spare time."

"I used to."

Lauren rolled her eyes. "Of course you did." The woman was a chronic over-achiever. When did she have a life?

Abruptly, Pat unclasped her pack and lowered it to the ground with a thud. "I'll get those painkillers now."

"No. I'm fine. I can wait."

"You're grumpy as hell, and you're bracing that arm like every movement hurts." Pat withdrew a first aid kit from a zipped compartment on top of the pack. She shook a couple of pills from a bottle and handed them to Lauren.

She *was* being grumpy, Lauren realized as she washed the tablets down with a swig of tepid water. Maybe it was her shoulder that was the main problem and not the celibate footing of their relationship. Pain could make everything harder to bear. She probably had things out of proportion. And after all, she had accepted Pat at her word and agreed to settle for friendship, hadn't she?

Avoiding Pat's penetrating stare, she tightened the cap on her water bottle and said, "Thank you. It has been bugging me."

"No problem." For a moment it seemed Pat was going to say something else, then she shouldered the pack once more and they walked on.

A short while later, Lauren heard the unmistakable sound of water against rocks. It sounded so inviting she could hardly wait to get there and cool off in the pool Cody had described. Increasing her pace, she all but slid down the final incline to a small clearing. Someone had erected a hand-carved sign that said *Te Wai o Aroha*. Probably some kind of goddess reference, Lauren assumed. The island was littered with them. She was only grateful the place was not marked *tapu*, which meant either sacred or forbidden, usually both. She hadn't come all this way to miss out on a swim in cold, fresh spring water.

A narrow pathway skirted the clearing and led through a stand of sweet-smelling frangipani trees to a secluded pool so beautiful it took Lauren's breath away. Water cascaded down a dark rock face, over huge moss-clad boulders into the tranquil waters below. Surrounded by overhanging mango trees and gleaming stone ledges, it was almost like a magical grotto. White hibiscus flowers drifted across the surface of the water, cast off by the many bushes that clung to the steep rock walls. Tiny birds hopped from branch to branch, their calls reverberating like dulcet wind chimes.

Captivated, Lauren sank down on one of the overhanging ledges and set about removing her boots. Hearing Pat's approach, she called, "I'm over here. Isn't it incredible?"

"Unreal." Pat dropped the pack next to her and stood, a thumb hooked over her belt, taking in the surroundings. Looking delighted, she crossed the boulders to stand nearer the falls and got down on her belly, hanging over a lip and running a hand through the water. "It's pretty cold."

"Fantastic." Lauren rid herself of her shorts, t-shirt and underwear. Her skin was sticky, and the areas beneath the dressings itched. "I'm going in."

"Wait a second. I'll help you as soon as I'm done." Pat pulled towels and drinks from the pack and spread them out under the shade of a tree.

"I can manage by myself," Lauren said, knowing she sounded edgy. She clambered down to an overhang and peered into the water below. It looked deep and clear. Cody had said the pool was safe to dive into. Lauren started to lower her legs but did not have the strength in her injured shoulder to hold herself poised on the ledge for a controlled drop. Unwilling to risk injury, she drew back.

"I have a better idea." Pat now shared the overhang. Stripped down to her sleeveless t-shirt and boxer shorts, she stretched out her hand. Her face registered no response to Lauren's nakedness. "Come with me."

Wounded by this indifference, but accepting she needed help into the water, Lauren allowed herself to be led around the pool to a gap between two boulders.

"Look." Pat pointed to the right of the waterfall. "There's a shelf of rock. If we go in here, we can swim over to it." Before Lauren could speak, Pat dropped into the water, sinking out of sight. A few seconds later, she surfaced and kicked her way back to Lauren's feet.

Lauren swung her legs over the ledge and let go. She'd barely broken the surface when Pat caught her beneath the arms and drew her up. Spluttering slightly from the shock of cold water against hot skin, Lauren shook the hair from her face and automatically clasped her hands behind Pat's neck, allowing herself to be half-carried, half-floated along. They had swum this way so often, it seemed instinctive. But Lauren hadn't been in Pat's arms for almost a week, and the feeling brought with it a stampede of sensation.

She closed her eyes and breathed in Pat's scent. If she turned her face slightly, her mouth would graze Pat's skin, ostensibly by accident. Lauren gave in to the urge, imprinting Pat's taste and smell. Memory toyed with her nerve endings. She opened her eyes and met a steady emerald gaze. Neither woman looked away. Languidly, they kicked their way around the perimeter of the pool, an unasked question drifting between them.

Lauren could feel every inch of the skin she occupied, from the prickle of her scalp to the slithering sensation of water between her toes. She tightened her grip around Pat's neck, then her feet were no longer gliding and she was upright, standing on solid rock in the shimmering spray of the waterfall.

Sunlight seeped through the tree canopy above and refracted in the cascading water, casting a myriad of tiny rainbows. Noise receded, supplanted by the drum of Lauren's heart, the ebb and flow of blood in her veins. Between them, the air grew hazy with feeling. Something in Pat's expression altered. She stroked the sensitive hollow at the base of Lauren's spine, and Lauren tilted her head. Pat's tongue traced the seam of her mouth, and Lauren's lips yielded like lock to key.

Still they stared at one another, anchored in the certainty of this beat in time, this kiss, this place; unburdened by what should be, by the dictates of sterile common sense. The kiss deepened. Pat's hand slid between Lauren thighs, parting flesh. Opening to her, taking her in, Lauren felt like a witness to her own undoing. Contentment blended with fire. The soft sounds in Pat's throat echoed her own. She was falling, and trusted implicitly that there was a net waiting for her.

Lauren wrapped her legs around Pat's middle, taking her deeper inside. Sensation magnified, doubt receded, as they worked together in the primal embrace of lovers. Lauren had thought she knew her own body—the tides of her arousal, the familiar climb before release. But with Pat, she found herself in a landscape as foreign yet familiar as a dream. Her body spoke another language, a mother-tongue long known to her soul. It bared her from the inside out; she could pretend nothing, conceal nothing.

*I love you.* Lauren tried to form the words, but all that broke across her lips was a cry from deep down, as her body contracted and flooded, and her eyes closed against the impossible brightness of what she now knew.

"Baby?"

Time had passed; Lauren had no idea how much. She felt Pat's fingers ease from the flesh that enfolded them, leaving their impression within. Her feet found substance and she stood, wobbly but safe in Pat's embrace. Blinking, she focused on Pat's face and took a mental photograph so she would always know the truth. It was there in the shadowed green of those eyes. Shock and recognition. Pat's defenses were breached—an arrow had pierced her guarded heart.

Lauren lifted a hand to her face. Wordlessly, Pat transported her through the water, to the gap between the boulders, and had her wait, gripping the overhang. After hoisting herself from the water and up over the rock, Pat got to her feet and bent to help Lauren up into the warm afternoon air.

They lolled on their soft towels. Pat took Lauren's hand and kissed the palm. She still didn't speak. Lauren guessed she couldn't.

# Chapter
# Fifteen


LAUREN SAT ON the corner of Pat's bed, her expression uncertain. "Can I sleep with you?"

"Of course, baby." Pat drew back the covers, accepting the inevitable with as much grace as she could.

Neither of them could pretend this afternoon hadn't happened, and that it hadn't changed everything. Pat had spent the entire hike back to the villa trying to reason with herself that they were just two red-blooded women stranded together in an impossibly romantic environment. Who could be surprised that they could not keep to their agreement about boundaries? She should have known better than to bathe in a pool whose Maori name meant "the waters of love."

Pat took complete responsibility. She was older and wiser. She had a professional obligation to conduct herself in the appropriate manner. Now she had not only had sex with the boss's daughter, but seemed to be falling for her as well. How had this happened? It was one thing to be horny after months of celibacy and briefly lose the plot, quite another to break every rule in her own book. Emotional involvement was bad news.

The bottom line was, even if she wanted to see Lauren Douglas after this assignment was over, she would be kidding herself if she thought it could work. What she was going back to was an investigation that left no room for anything but eating and sleeping, a case that had stripped her of emotional energy for anything else. If she tried to have a relationship, she would fail, and they would both be hurt. That was a sure thing.

Heavy with sadness, Pat flicked off the bedside lamp. "Come here," she murmured, one arm extended.

Lauren rolled onto her side, her head on Pat's shoulder, a small hand curled over Pat's heart. "Pat, can I ask you something?"

Dreading the question, Pat said, "Yes."

"What are you thinking about? You've been so quiet. Ever

since...this afternoon."

"I'm thinking about you."

Lauren lay very still. "You are?" The tension left her body, and Pat could feel the muscles in her face move to form a smile. "You've been on my mind, too. I was thinking, when we get back, I could maybe come stay in Philadelphia for a while. I could commute for filming."

"You're very sweet." Pat kissed the top of her head. She could not bring herself to say anything that would cause pain. And part of her, against all rational thought, insisted that maybe there was a possibility it could work out and she would be a fool to burn her bridges.

Nestling closer, Lauren continued with her happy conjecturing. "I don't have to stay at your place. I'll look for an apartment near you. Would you like that?"

"My place *is* on the small side," Pat said, avoiding a direct answer.

"This is amazing," Lauren murmured, her hand sliding to Pat's breast, the fingertips rolling back and forth across her nipple. "I had no idea it could be like this." The hand trailed down Pat's body to her belly, then to her thighs, caressing so delicately that Pat's skin erupted in goose-bumps.

"That feels good," Pat said, her voice husky. "But it's late. Let's sleep."

Lauren stiffened. Her exploring hand stilled for a moment, then she slid her leg over Pat's, laughing softly. "You can sleep through it if you want."

Stealing between Pat's thighs and nudging her legs apart, she stroked with teasing precision, just firmly enough to make Pat crave more.

Despite the delicious sensations, Pat's mind and body were at odds, voices in her head growing louder by the second, urging her not to give in to her own physical needs, reminding her that things were moving too fast. Already Lauren was talking about something more permanent. It was a charming daydream, but it couldn't happen. Pat had to nip these illusions in the bud, find some way to let Lauren down gently before they both got in so deep that getting out would be ugly. Allowing their intimacy to become completely mutual was not the right signal to send.

As Lauren continued her persistent caresses, Pat forced herself to detach. As she so often did in the field, she distanced herself emotionally and became clinical in her responses. She had allowed everything to get out of control this afternoon at the waterfall. Even now she was giving Lauren mixed messages. It was time to put the brakes on.

Lauren's hand grew still. "Is something wrong?" she asked, her voice muffled against Pat's breast. "You seem far away."

"I'm sorry. I'm just kind of tired."

"Is there something else that would please you more?"

"No, baby." Pat drew Lauren's hand to her mouth and kissed it tenderly. "Another time. Okay?"

Lauren was quiet for a few beats. "Okay." She sounded confused and hurt. "If that's what you want."

"It doesn't have to be turnabout, you know." Pat injected a little humor into her tone and felt the tension seep from Lauren's body.

"I just don't want you thinking I'm some kind of pillow princess."

"I don't." Pat kissed her cheek. "Relax. Everything's fine."

She held Lauren close until she felt her breathing deepen and her limbs grow heavy. Then she eased her onto her back and slipped quietly out of bed. She had to talk with Lauren honestly, explain that they had no future and it would be best if they ended this fling before someone got hurt. Maybe the right moment would present itself tomorrow.

LAUREN OPENED HER eyes with a start and reached for Pat. But the other side of the bed was empty, and the pillow was cold. She surmised Pat must have gone to the other room to sleep. Maybe Lauren had been hogging the bed, or tossing and turning. Pat had said she was tired. Being the practical person she was, she would have done the sensible, unromantic thing and slept alone.

Lauren turned onto her side and listened to the sounds of the island — wind rustling the palms, the steady pulse of waves against the reef, the unmistakable plop of mangoes falling to the ground. She closed her eyes and tried to return to sleep, but a pressing disquiet hummed like the chorus of a song she wanted to forget. Her mind drifted to Pat's withdrawal during their love-making, and she bit her lower lip.

Lauren knew she had not imagined her sudden sense that Pat was no longer fully present in her own skin. She hadn't seemed tired until Lauren started making love to her. What was really happening? Lauren tried to come up with some possibilities. Perhaps Pat was one of those women who preferred to make love to her partner and did not enjoy reciprocation. Or maybe she had issues — perhaps the kind of work she did made it hard for her to relinquish control.

Lauren wished she had pressed Pat for the truth instead of accepting her excuses about being tired. How would they be able to take their relationship to a deeper level if Pat felt she had to pretend in their intimate life? Lauren was an adult. She could have an adult discussion with her lover. It was time Pat trusted her a little.

Restless, she threw back the sheets and got out of bed. She hesitated at the adjoining door between their rooms, but decided three in the morning was not the time to have the deep and meaningful conversation she wanted. Instead, she padded quietly into the kitchen, poured herself a glass of juice and retreated to a sofa near the verandah doors. This was one of the few times since coming to the island that she really missed television. Right now, an episode of *Seinfeld* would be just the thing to take her mind off Pat.

Lauren flicked on a lamp and tried to remember where she had left the paperback she was reading. Scanning the room, she caught sight of a stack of books and files that belonged to Pat. Curious, she wandered over and opened the file on top, expecting to see official-looking papers. What greeted her was a color photograph of a child's body in a makeshift grave.

With a start of horror, she dropped the file cover over the shocking image and took a deep, steadying breath. Then she opened it again and leafed slowly through photographs too ghastly to take in, and page after page of explicit notes detailing crimes no ordinary person could bear to contemplate. She tried to imagine how anyone could live a normal life seeing this every day of the week.

Lauren carried the files over to a small table by the sofa and spent the next hour or so reading through them. From what she could piece together, Pat was investigating a string of murders by a fiend who chose child beauty queens as his victims. Lauren could remember seeing some of these cases on CNN. This was why Pat had needed time out, she reflected, and this was what she would be going back to after they left the island. No wonder Pat seemed remote so much of the time. This was what preoccupied her. These were the images that haunted her every waking hour, and perhaps her dreams as well.

Lauren could not imagine how stressful it must be. She was filled with shame over her own self-pity and the petulant behavior she had indulged in when Pat first came on the scene. With a sense of shock, Lauren understood that Pat's world was much larger and more complex than she had imagined. It was not as if she had bothered to find out. She had been perfectly content to know almost nothing about the woman she'd allowed inside her body.

Suddenly, Lauren was aware as never before of her own

narrow experience of life. Here she was, happily fantasizing a relationship developing between them, yet what did she bring to the equation? She was attractive and owned an apartment, superficial attributes that were important to a woman like Sara. But Pat was a far cry from the likes of Sara; that much was apparent.

Gnawing on her bottom lip, Lauren returned the files to the stack on the sideboard and quietly opened the sliding doors. What would Pat seek in a partner? She knew Pat found her sexually attractive, but was that the extent of it? At the waterfall that afternoon, Lauren had been certain they were connecting on a deeper level. Now she wondered if the intense emotion she'd glimpsed in Pat's eyes was merely a trick of the light.

She strolled out onto the verandah and gazed into the darkness. A half moon glowed like a cat's eye against the infinity of the night sky. Millions of years away, in a Morse code of light, stars left their footprints in the history of the universe. Somewhere, on one of them, an intelligent creature was probably gazing up just as she was, wondering who was out there.

A corrosive melancholy settled on her. Impulsively, she slipped into a pair of sandals, descended the steps, and took the path to the beach. She wished she could still feel the joyful certainty she'd experienced in Pat's arms just hours ago, or even the confidence she'd felt soon after they arrived on the island. Things had been so much simpler when they were on a strictly professional footing. Now, Lauren realized, she didn't know where she stood with Pat.

Well, that could change, she decided as she reached the water's edge. They had plenty of time left on the island. She would make an effort to draw Pat out. She would find out who she really was. By the time they were ready to leave, she would be much more than a pleasant distraction; she would be part of Pat's life.

PAT WOKE WITH a start. On the fringes of her consciousness, she was aware of having heard something—a sound that was wrong for three in the morning. Automatically she picked up her gun, flipped off the safety catch and silently opened the door to the other bedroom. The bed was empty. She entered the room cautiously and slipped a hand under the covers. It was cold. She opened the bathroom door a crack and said, "Lauren?"

Her next port of call was the refrigerator. Even before she'd made it that far, she saw the open sliding doors and panic surged through her limbs. Hastily, she pulled on sneakers and loped down the ocean pathway toward the beach. She'd barely made it to level ground when she spotted Lauren wandering along the waterline, heedless of the rules Pat had set in place to keep her safe.

Angry, Pat skirted through the trees, then removed her shoes and silently crossed the sand. As she came up behind Lauren, she caught her in a mock stranglehold and hissed in her ear, "It's that easy. Now try and fight me off."

As Lauren struggled, Pat relaxed her hold and released her.

"How could you!" Lauren rounded on her. "You gave me such a fright!"

"How do you think I felt looking in your bedroom and finding the doors open? We have agreements in place so that I can keep you safe."

"I am safe!" Lauren yelled. "This is just stupid. No one is coming here to kill me." She turned her back on Pat and flounced off along the waterline.

"Oh, no, you don't." Pat caught her arm and steered her toward the cottage. "We are going back indoors, and you are going to promise me you will never do anything like this again."

"Or what?" Lauren tossed her head.

Pat felt like throwing the pouting woman over her shoulder and carrying her back home. She also felt like kissing her. Neither was the appropriate response. In the coldest tone she could muster, she said, "Or we leave for home tomorrow and you don't just have me on your tail; you have your father's entire security detail. Round the clock. Because you were— uncooperative."

"You wouldn't do that to me."

"Try me."

Lauren glared at her for a long moment, then her body language changed. Head drooping, she touched Pat's arm. "I'm sorry." Her confrontational tone was supplanted by one of appeasement. "You're right. I shouldn't have gone out by myself." She hesitated. "Please come back to bed with me. I don't want to be by myself."

Pat vacillated. If she wanted to send Lauren a clear signal, here was the perfect opportunity. But the timing didn't feel right. She sensed she had already hurt Lauren's feelings in bed just hours ago, and now they'd had words. It would be better to wait until things were less emotional. She would talk with Lauren tomorrow.

Resigning herself to walking on eggshells until then, she slid her arm around Lauren's waist and said, "Okay. Let's go get some sleep."

# Chapter
# Sixteen

"WOW, I'D LOVE to spend some time on Moon Island."
Penny's face lit up. "That's so sweet of Annabel."

Chris made a noncommittal sound. She felt like a rat,
knowing the real agenda. Today's mission was to get Penny
Mercer to Moon Island no matter what. The *HMS Jaunt* had been
found, and it was only a matter of time before the divers
discovered there were several thousand missing golden guineas.

"I can't wait to get out of here," Penny said, pushing her
wispy bangs off her forehead. "I'm going nuts reading the same
ten issues of the *Womens' Weekly*."

"We could leave today if they're ready to discharge you."

"I'll discharge myself if they're not." Penny's hazel eyes
danced. "I'm serious. Enough is enough."

"Alrighty, then." Chris found her heart racing at the thought
of having Penny all to herself for a few days.

She allowed her gaze to dwell on Penny's body outlined
beneath the thin cotton nightshirt she was wearing. Lean and
neatly muscled, she looked like a woman who had been lanky in
her teens and had never quite lost her awkwardness. Chris could
imagine an eighth grader with the same honey-streaked brown
braids and candid smile, only with braces on her teeth and a
shyness in her manner.

What was Penny's story? Where was she from? What were
her dreams? Chris had a feeling Penny was a lesbian, but
wondered if this was just wishful thinking. It had to be pretty
obvious to Penny that Chris was gay, although these days no
thinking person made assumptions based on short hair and
gender-neutral clothing.

"So when are we leaving?" Penny asked, snapping Chris's
attention back to the matter at hand.

"I told Annabel we'd be at the airport around three this
afternoon. Assuming you can get out of here."

Penny swung strong, sinewy legs over the side of the bed.

"I'm going to go see the head nurse now. What say you meet me back here in a couple of hours?"

"I don't mind waiting," Chris said, then realized she sounded like a moonstruck high-school kid.

This time Penny's smile was as sweetly coy as a note pressed into Chris's hand. "I need to shower and see the doctor and stuff."

"Sure. Of course. And I've got things to do in town." Chris looked at her watch. The battery had run out a few days ago, but Penny wouldn't know that. "See you later, then."

Penny startled her by extending both arms. "Give me a hug."

Chris hesitated, then took Penny in a polite embrace. She had never been one of those touchy-feely people who engaged in air-kissing and needed to hug complete strangers. Elaine always used to tease her about not holding hands in public, but displays of affection made her uncomfortable.

Releasing Penny, she cleared her throat and said, "You're going to love it on the island."

"And we'll get to spend some time together, too." Penny held Chris's stare with frank deliberation. "I'm looking forward to that."

"Me too," Chris said, slightly unnerved. She could feel those hazel eyes boring into her back as she strolled from the room.

Penny had just let her know she was interested. It was not her imagination. Chris took a couple of deep breaths as she exited the hospital. She was gratified but also surprised. Somewhere along the way, she had lost any sense that a woman might find *her* attractive. It was as if she had relegated that part of herself to a shelf a long time ago.

Well, it was time to dust off the old animal magnetism, she thought. She was still grinning when she reached Trader Jacks.

ANNABEL SLAMMED THE restroom door and shoved the bolt across. Leaning back against the peeling wood veneer, she caught her breath. She could hear her pursuers on the other side, testing microphones, yelling instructions at underlings, calling her name, and ignoring the pleas of Trader Jacks' waitresses to leave the premises.

Someone pounded on the door, almost dislodging it from the rickety frame. "Two thousand per night, cash," a male voice bellowed.

"I said no," Annabel yelled back. "We have nothing available."

She sized up the tiny restroom window and pictured herself

stuck halfway, a horde of television reporters and treasure hunters swarming in the alleyway below, demanding accommodation on Moon Island.

Since Doug's announcement yesterday morning about the discovery of the *HMS Jaunt*, foreign media, naval historians, coin dealers, and a gaggle of amateur treasure hunters had descended on Rarotonga. The *Aspiration II* had already filed its legal claim and had hired round-the-clock security to guard the site. Annabel had agreed to provide meals and a limited amount of hospitality. So far, Doug and his team had shown respect for Moon Island's women-only tradition. Crew members came ashore strictly at Annabel's invitation. The *Aspiration* team was not the problem. The problem was publicity.

Annabel knew Doug's hands were tied. To attract the extra investment dollars he needed for the salvage operation, he'd had to make a big announcement to the press and talk about millions of dollars in sunken treasure. The *National Geographic* had promptly dispatched a team to record the discovery and requested rights to film on Moon Island. Uneasily, Annabel had granted these, figuring the staff of such a notable publication could be counted on to conduct themselves with sensitivity around sacred sites.

Besides, if their treasure-in-the-cave ploy was going to work, it would probably be a good idea to have a prestigious media team nearby who could authenticate Penny's "discovery." She hoped Chris had been persuasive and that Penny wouldn't want to rush straight back to the *Aspiration* instead of recuperating on the island.

Noticing that the noise outside the restrooms had abated, Annabel placed an ear to the door and listened carefully. Someone was talking in a low, authoritative voice. Then there was a knock.

"Ms. Worth?"

Recognizing Pat's voice, Annabel released the bolt and gingerly cracked the door open. She'd never been so thankful to see a brawny butch packing a gun.

"This way, please." Somehow Pat managed to clear a path through the crowd, her arm around Annabel, hustling her along like she was someone important.

"You're good at this," Annabel murmured, thankful Lauren's medical treatment had made it necessary for Pat to come to Rarotonga today.

"I watch Clint Eastwood movies," Pat said with a tinge of amusement. She held open the door of a rental Jeep, and Annabel climbed in. The vehicle was immediately surrounded by people thrusting their business cards at her.

Chris and Lauren were in the back, with Lauren in deep cover — big sunhat, oversized dark glasses, and her distinctive copper-gold hair in a single braid at the back. Annabel didn't know why her guest bothered. Without cable television, no one on Rarotonga would recognize an American TV star, let alone pester her for autographs. Cody was probably right; it was an ego thing.

"What in God's name is going on?" Chris asked, fending off arms that kept straying into the Jeep.

"Everybody and their dog wants to camp on the island," Annabel said.

Pat wasted no time. After a couple of warning revs, she stuck her hand on the horn and drove through the human tide, heading for the airport. "I figure you can hole up in the terminal while we go do what we have to do," she told Annabel.

"Sounds good. Thanks for getting me out of there." Annabel shot a glance over her shoulder toward the back seat passengers. "I suppose you're used to this kind of thing," she remarked to Lauren, who was now minus the all-concealing sunhat.

"No, I'm not that big of a deal," Lauren said, exchanging her Miami-widow shades for less obtrusive eyewear. "Although, when I was outed in the papers, it was the pits."

"Hey, wait a second. You're Dr. Kate? I didn't recognize you." Chris stared, almost open-mouthed. "My sister is totally addicted to your show."

Pat's discomfort with this topic was palpable. "Lauren is here incognito."

"I can still get your autograph, can't I?" Chris waved a pen and notebook. She tapped Annabel on the shoulder as Lauren obliged. "By the way, Penny will be coming back with us if she can get discharged."

"That's great." Annabel was flooded with relief. All they had to do now was get the woman inside the Kopeka Cave. Hopefully, she wasn't claustrophobic.

"She looks so much better, doesn't she?" Lauren chipped in. "We stopped by on our way to the doctor."

"She looks great. Really, good." Chris colored slightly.

Pat pulled into the airport drop-off zone and got out of the Jeep. "I'll walk you in," she said, opening Annabel's door.

"There's no need." Annabel swung a quick look around. "I think we lost them."

Pat took a long hard look down the road. "Seems that way."

"I'll see you back here by three. I'll be in the hangar." Annabel exchanged a covert glance with Chris, who gave an enthusiastic thumbs-up.

Heading for the entrance doors, she smiled to herself at the prospect of killing two birds with one stone: set Chris up with a girlfriend and ensure no one ever found Hine te Ana's cave. She was a genius.

"ARE YOU SERIOUS?" Cody surveyed the *National Geographic* team with a show of disbelief. "You want to go down the drop shaft with all that camera gear?"

"It's not so bad," Penny said. "I slid down there on my ass. You just have to put the brakes on once you're close to the bottom."

"No worries." Doug upended his pack. He had enough climbing gear for an attempt on Annapurna.

"Well, if you insist," Cody said. "But remember, you've all signed disclaimers. If you break any bones, we're not paying."

This only seemed to whet their appetites. Cody cast a quick look at Chris, who was wearing her unflappable lawyer's face, then led the group into the Kopeka Cave.

Penny and Chris had made their big discovery the day before, and Cody had promptly escorted Penny by boat to the salvage site to electrify Doug with the news. He and the *National Geographic* team had been chomping at the bit ever since. Now, entering the Kopeka Cave, they were feverish with anticipation. How often did an explorer get to find a shipwreck *and* a buried treasure along with the skeleton of the poor bastard who took the loot, all in the same week! It was going to get them the cover photo.

"Jesus! Look at this!" One of the photographers plucked something from the floor of the cave. Displaying a gold coin triumphantly in his palm, he asked Doug, "Hey, man, do I get to keep this?"

"Legally, no. But since you guys are going to get us all kinds of publicity, and that means more investment dollars, we'll see what we can do."

Chris could not quite conceal a smirk. It had been her idea to salt the cave with a few extra guineas. Cody had grudgingly done the deed with several of the coins she and Annabel had kept as souvenirs after they'd transported the haul across the island using sleds Cody had rigged up.

"The shaft is right here." Penny shone her torch at a narrow opening. "There's not much room down there, so one person at a time." She gestured at Doug, inviting him to go first.

The camera crew lowered him by rope, and after a few minutes there was a shout. They pulled the unhitched rope back up, ready for the next guy. Already they could hear yells echoing up.

"Sounds like he's hit the jackpot," Penny said happily. "I still can't believe it. I mean, it's amazing no one found this chamber before. Most of your guests come here, don't they?" she asked Cody.

"Yeah, but I don't think they go looking down dark holes. You were just in the right place at the right time."

"I can't take all the credit," Penny said. "It was Chris who found the coin. She almost threw it away!"

"I thought it was a bottle cap or something," Chris said with slippery conviction. "Penny was the one who made the ID. Really, it was her discovery. I don't think I did anything to earn twenty percent of the find."

"Of course you did," Penny protested. "Anyway, Doug won't hear of anything less. If it wasn't for you, I'd never have come here, and the *Aspiration II* would be stuck searching the ocean floor for bullion we'd never find."

Once Penny and the *National Geographic* guys had all descended below, Cody poked Chris in the ribs. "Ooohh," she mimicked, "I don't deserve my twenty percent."

Chris grinned. "Yep. I'm a disgrace to the legal profession."

"Penny totally bought it. No one suspects a thing."

"Why would they?" Chris shrugged. "I just hope no one ever gets to hear that I actually found Mr. Bones last year, and there was no treasure then."

"Who's going to tell them? The only people that know are the guests who were here at the time. I guess we could drop them a line with the official version."

"Yeah. I can say I didn't happen to notice several thousand gold coins crammed into a tiny space. Guess who's *not* going to buy that? Guess who's going to *know* the coins must have come from the sacred cave."

Cody grimaced. "Dr. Howick, I presume." She could just imagine what the UCLA anthropologist would have to say. Glenn Howick was fixated on Hine te Ana's cave and firmly believed Annabel and Cody had conspired to prevent her finding it during her research trip the previous year.

Chris laughed. "She wasn't real happy leaving the island without seeing it, *tapu* or not."

"My heart bleeds. If she'd had her way, Moon Island would be some kind of women's spirituality theme park."

"Oh, come on," Chris objected. "She meant well."

"The problem with these ivory tower types is they don't live in the real world," Cody shot back. "If she'd published a paper about the cave and the magic pool, do you really think everyone would have said: *Hey, we better respect that this place is sacred.* Hell, no. We'd be invaded by hordes of people wanting wishes granted. The sick, the lame.... Next thing, someone has a vision of the Virgin Mary, and the Vatican takes us over."

"Our Lady of Moon Island." Chris snickered. "I can see it now. The candles in jars, little statuettes with hibiscus around the base..."

"You think I'm kidding?"

"No. Not at all. Annabel was dead right about moving the treasure."

Cody sighed. "I still think we could have tossed it over the side of the cliff and made like it washed up on the beach, instead of lugging it all the way over here." She had tried to convince Annabel that was a good alternative, but her lover was a stubborn woman. After six years, Cody knew that once Annabel made up her mind about something, arguing with her was more trouble than it was worth. Cody preferred to take the path of least resistance.

"Well, it's done now and everyone's happy," Chris said diplomatically.

"What's your twenty percent worth, anyway?"

Chris frowned and counted on her fingers. "A million plus."

"Jeez, mate." Cody whistled. "Next time you're buying the beer."

"ISN'T IT INCREDIBLE about the buried treasure?" Lauren marveled as she and Pat strolled along Passion Bay.

"Amazing," Pat said.

"How come Annabel and Cody are letting them have it? If it's found on their land, wouldn't it belong to them?"

"I'm not sure what the law is in this part of the world."

"Apparently it's worth millions." Lauren wished they could have gone to the cave that morning to see what was happening. But Cody and Annabel said the salvage team had to make their assessment and secure the site first. Guests who were interested would get the chance to see what was happening tomorrow, when the pirate skeleton and some of the treasure would be brought out of the cave.

Pat stopped walking and squinted out to sea. "I need my binoculars."

Lauren spotted a fleck on the horizon. "It's probably one of those boats from the *Aspiration*." Whenever someone from the crew needed to see Annabel, they came around by outboard and anchored in Passion Bay.

Pat looked doubtful. "Seems a long way out," she said and turned her steps toward their sun umbrella.

Lauren dawdled after her. Pat had finally started leaving her binoculars with their towels most of the time. Lauren had given up hoping she would do the same with her weaponry. She watched Pat focus the powerful lenses on the ocean and was lust-struck. It happened often. Pat would be doing something innocuous, like reading a book or removing a crawling insect from their villa, and Lauren would find herself dry-mouthed with yearning.

She re-tied her sarong, burdened with a creeping unease. Something was not right between them. Technically, they were lovers. Yet even in their most intense lovemaking, she sensed that Pat was somehow at arm's length. She was attentive, passionate and intuitive, the perfect sexual partner. Yet she still did not invite Lauren to make love to her and discouraged her careful overtures. Lauren hesitated to persist, not wanting to pressure her if indeed there was some kind of issue. There were women who did not want to be made love to. Maybe Pat was one of them.

It was time they had a real conversation about this, Lauren decided. Over dinner, she would ask Pat to be honest with her. The weeks were slipping by. They should be talking about their relationship, about their future. Yet it seemed they had both tacitly agreed to forgo discussion in favor of sex, and to pretend there was no tomorrow.

"I think it's a charter boat," Pat said, lowering the binoculars. "Probably tourists hoping to get a look at the shipwreck."

Collecting her thoughts, Lauren said, "Well, I'm going to stay out here and read for a while." The boat was drawing closer. They probably didn't know which bay to look for.

"Fine." Pat was already walking toward the water. "Stay where I can see you."

As if she needed to be told. Lauren rearranged their beach towels and stretched out on one of them. She shook out her topknot, removed her sunglasses, and covered her face with her hat. Maybe she would just sleep. The late morning heat was already building toward an afternoon high. Lauren scratched warily below her ribs where the second bullet wound had closed properly at last. It was so itchy sometimes it almost made her crazy.

The doctor at Rarotonga Hospital had said this meant her skin was growing and she needed to leave it alone. Refraining from more purposeful scratching, she rolled onto her stomach and opened her book. This week's trashy reading was Kitty Kelley's much-hyped exposé of the Bush clan. Lauren couldn't see what all the fuss was about. Why was anyone surprised that a powerful oil-rich family seemed more like the cast of that old TV show, *Dallas*, than a wholesome Rockwell calendar portrait? Being in the business of manipulating her own public image, she knew all about the difference between reality and propaganda. The only thing that ever surprised her was the public's willingness to buy almost anything they were told by a celebrity.

She'd bought this book at the airport after a woman tugged it from her hands and told her indignantly that it was unpatriotic. Apparently she thought it was just crazy-talk that a President might hide stuff about his past. Lauren had been too startled to remind her the guy was only human, and that no one got ahead in politics by being a boy scout. Her father had once told her the most important rule in politics was *Cover Your Ass*, closely followed by *Surround Yourself With People Willing to Lick It*.

Lauren sighed. In the past, she had at times judged her father harshly for peddling the party line even when his personal views differed. Yet, was she any less a hypocrite? It took courage to be truthful when the truth might have negative consequences. For people in the public eye, those consequences could be extreme; Lauren had the bullet holes to prove it.

Hearing the whine of a motor, she closed her book and peered down the beach. Just beyond the reef, an up-market cruiser had dropped anchor, and a small outboard was barreling across the lagoon toward Pat. Lauren sat up and pushed the hair out of her eyes. There were several men in the boat. As they drew close to the shore, two of them started shooting with video cameras and telescopic lenses.

Startled, Lauren lay down once more, her face turned away. Surely they weren't shooting film of her. She didn't think so. They seemed to be panning all around.

Pat's raised voice floated across the sand. Someone wound the throttle, and the motor noise gradually retreated. Whoever the photographers were, Pat had gotten rid of them. A shadow fell across the sand in front of her, and Lauren rolled over.

"Who were they?"

"Freelance photographers."

Lauren shuddered. "Paparazzi?"

"Not the kind you've encountered. Just some guys looking to get wreck footage before the major agencies muscle in. I sent them to the site. Doug can handle them." She moved her deck chair around for more shade and opened the chiller. "Drink?"

"Yes, thank you."

"Are you okay?"

"I'm fine." Lauren took the bottle of Pellegrino she was offered. Pat had removed the cap.

This was part of the problem, too, she thought. When they were not in bed, Pat treated her with polite formality. The connection palpable between lovers was missing. There were no warm looks, no oblique references to passion shared. Pat's body language was that of a stranger. Lauren felt disoriented. It was as if each day made a lie of the night that preceded it.

On an impulse, she extended a hand and stroked Pat's thigh. When her touch was ignored, she drew herself up a little onto her side, and placed her head in Pat's lap. After a long moment, Pat absently stroked her hair.

Lauren looked up at her, trying to read the face beneath those sunglasses. "You seem uncomfortable," she said. "With this...with me being affectionate."

Pat gave a small shrug. "There's a time and place."

"We're all alone, and you're my lover. What's wrong with this time and place?"

Pat was silent for a long moment. She removed her sunglasses and lowered her eyes to Lauren's upturned face. "Having sex is something we do when it feels good. We're two consenting adults."

"And your point is?"

"When we're not making love, I'm your bodyguard, and I have a job to do. We've had this conversation, Lauren."

"Yes, and we've made agreements, then broken them, and now we're lovers. Why can't we just accept what's happening between us, and enjoy it like everyone else does? Why do we have to compartmentalize?"

Pat released a weary sigh. "Lauren. I wasn't lying when I said this is not the right time for me. I know you want more. You have every right."

"Yes. I do want more. I hate feeling like we're strangers except when we're in bed. Even then it's not...mutual."

Pat touched Lauren's face. "I'm sorry I can't give you what you need."

Lauren knocked Pat's hand away and scrambled to her feet. "I don't believe that. I think this is all about control. No one can look into the future and predict what's going to happen in any relationship. And you can't handle that. So you have to control it. This way, you know what's going to happen. We're just going to go back home and never see one another again. And that suits you, doesn't it? You can go back to your cozy little life chasing the bad guys and everything can stay just the same." Turning on her heel, she strode off toward the villa.

"Lauren, stop." Pat came after her. "Please listen to me. If I thought I could offer you more, I would. I don't want to hurt you."

"Too late!" Lauren threw her sunglasses onto the sand and wiped the back of her hand across her eyes. "Don't you get it? I'm falling in love with you. I don't want to go back home and pick up where I left off. I want to be with you."

Pat looked pale beneath her tan, her facial muscles taut. "I'm sorry. Lauren, listen..."

Shaking with anger, Lauren tried to process what she was hearing. She had just told a woman she was falling in love with her and the response was: *I'm sorry.* "Fuck you!" she said. "I would never have taken you for a coward. But that's what you are. I want to go home. And once we're back, I don't want to see you again."

PAT STARED AFTER the limber figure retreating up the pathway and prevented herself from giving chase. There was a dusty taste in her mouth, as if she'd swallowed ash.

Here, right in front of her, was the reason she didn't get involved with women. What in God's name had possessed her to forsake ethics and common sense? That Lauren would end up hurt was inevitable from the moment Pat had chosen to ignore her own unease and reach for the forbidden. It had been selfish. Unforgivably adolescent. She was not the helpless victim of seduction. It didn't just *happen*. Pat chose it. She chose to escape from the horrible weight of her thoughts, from her fears, from her nightmares of a lifetime haunted by the ghosts of Destiny O'Connor, Shelby-Rose Dubois, and the countless victims of future cases unsolved. She had wanted time out and that's what Lauren had offered her.

Her eyes stung. It was time to do the right thing. But Lauren was in no mood for words, and what would Pat say anyway? The truth was sordid. She had used the younger woman, knowing how vulnerable she was.

It worked both ways, she rationalized. Lauren might think she was falling in love, but she was also escaping from reality. Once her attacker was caught, and she could return to her life feeling safe and confident, there would be no need for the happy illusion, and the feelings would pass. Lauren would not see it now, but one day she would understand that they'd both had their own private hells, and both needed the respite they'd found in one another.

Pat heard the villa door slam and gathered the rest of their belongings. She would fly into Raro with Annabel tomorrow and make the necessary travel arrangements. Then she would call Wendall Douglas and tell him she'd decided to return to the Bureau ahead of time because she'd had a break in an important case.

With any luck, they could be home within three days.

# Chapter
# Seventeen

"FORGET IT," LAUREN said. "I'm staying here."

"You know I can't leave you here alone." Pat sighed with frustration. "Annabel and I will be gone most of the afternoon. Get your stuff. You're coming."

Lauren remained on the sofa as if Pat hadn't spoken, shoulders rising and falling in the staccato rhythm of tightly coiled anger. White-knuckled, her hands gripped the paperback she was pretending to read.

Pat plucked the book away and tossed it across the room. "This is getting old," she said, injecting her voice with a calm she did not feel. "Your shitty temper is not going to get us out of here any faster."

Lauren's eyes gleamed bright and cold. "My temper is my own business, and you won't have to put up with it much longer." She slid her legs out from beneath her and stood. "I'm taking a swim."

Lauren was pushing her, Pat recognized, letting her know the time was fast approaching when they would have no more to do with one another, when Pat would no longer call the shots. In readiness for that happy day, she was making Pat irrelevant now.

If Pat chose, she could make this ugly. It was almost like Lauren was daring her to. Instead, she said placidly, "I'm not going to fight you. Let's agree on something."

Lauren anticipated her. "I won't say a word to Daddy." Facetiously, she added, "About *anything*."

Ignoring the jibe, Pat said, "I'll go to Raro without you, but I want you to spend the rest of the day up at Villa Luna."

For a moment it seemed Lauren would bicker over this, too, then she turned her attention from Pat to the paperback splayed open on the floor. "Whatever it takes. Give me five minutes." She swept by Pat with the air of a woman whose dignity was under siege, but who did not plan to yield an inch.

As soon as she'd left the room, Pat sank into an armchair and considered the wall. How had this happened? One day Lauren was in her arms, the next she was gazing at Pat as if betrayed. Pat wished she could undo what was done, yet the wish had a hollow insincerity to it. Would she really, if she could go back, exchange that kiss on the beach for the bland satisfaction of sticking to the rules? Would she elect to surrender the memory of Lauren's face, radiant in the throes of their passion?

Pat felt discomfited. She understood that the choices she'd made on this island had been fueled by a combination of lust and rebellion. Yet there was something else. For two days, since their quarrel on the beach, she'd put off traveling to Rarotonga because the thought of never seeing Lauren again made her stomach churn. Her heart knocked at her chest as Lauren returned.

She had changed and now wore a floral wrap-around mini-skirt over a black bathing suit that made her hair seem redder and her eyes almost tanzanite blue. They held traces of tears. "Ready when you are," she said with wan bravado.

For a few strained seconds they stared at one another, then Pat rose and walked to the door, aware that she was caught in one of those moments—a moment of possibility. She could tell Lauren had not quite closed the door on her. There was still a chance to do this differently. She did not have to deny herself, and Lauren, what was patently possible. All she had to do was reach for it. She sensed Lauren was waiting for her to speak, to seize the moment for both their sakes.

But knowing what she knew about herself, she couldn't do it. "I'll try and get us a flight for tomorrow," she said.

LAUREN TOOK BRIAR'S hand and wandered out onto the deep verandah that ran the length of Villa Luna. She felt numb, disbelieving. Even as Pat had walked off into the jungle, some part of Lauren had expected her to turn around. To come back. To insist they start again because there was something important between them.

But she hadn't.

"Pick me up," the little girl urged, and with some difficulty, Lauren lifted her onto the broad wooden railing.

"Better?" she asked, an arm wrapped around the child's middle.

Briar pushed her mop of black ringlets out of the way and lifted a small set of binoculars to her eyes. "Hine's there!" she said excitely. "She's my dolphin."

"Ahhh. I've met her. I thought she was a shark."

Briar lowered the binoculars and regarded Lauren solemnly. "Sharks don't smile."

Laughing, Lauren lifted the precocious child down and placed her on the wooden boards.

"I want to go see her," a small voice demanded.

"Not today, honey," Lauren said. "We have to stay here with Mrs. Marsters. I thought we could bake some cookies and –" She didn't get a chance to complete her sentence before the angelic face dissolved into tears.

Briar took a huge gulping breath and wailed, "No. I want to go. Now!"

"Hush. Shhhh." Lauren cast a look over her shoulder expecting to see the wide-hipped housekeeper emerge at any moment to investigate what torture the American visitor was inflicting on the apple of her eye.

As if Briar could read Lauren's mind, she redoubled her efforts, this time collapsing in a sobbing heap and pounding the boards with her feet. Mortified, Lauren tried to pick the child up, but Briar slithered from her grip and shimmied along the verandah, howling.

"Okay. All right." Lauren admitted defeat. "We'll go to the beach."

The sobs immediately evaporated into small, shuddering sniffs. Briar got to her feet and smoothed her sundress with her hands as if nothing had transpired. Suckered, Lauren thought. Were all small children this Machiavellian? No wonder they needed wranglers to work with them on set.

"This way. I'll show you." Briar sallied forth into the mango trees that screened the villa from the beach. After a few strides, she looked back over her tiny shoulder and inquired, "Have you got sun block?"

"Um, no."

The child paused, deliberating. "Okay. Don't forget next time."

"How old are you?" Lauren asked. Of the few small children she knew, none were as self-possessed as this little girl.

"Two and a half," Briar replied. "How old are you?"

"Twenty-eight."

Briar looked her up and down dubiously. "You can still be my friend."

CHRIS GAZED ONE more time around the clearing to which she and Penny had hiked, then began loading the remnants of their picnic into her backpack. "I guess we should be heading back to the Villa soon," she said. "I told Annabel we'd cook dinner."

Standing on a boulder, hands on her hips, Penny stared out at the view across the jungle to the Pacific Ocean. "I can't believe I'm going back to work tomorrow. It's been...perfect."

"Are you excited?"

Penny smiled in a way that made Chris feel weak. "I can't wait," she said, sliding down from her vantage point and helping Chris finish tidying up. "We're expecting to get divers into the hull this week. It's not the money that excites me, it's the artifacts, the stories they tell. It's as if, through the ages, someone reaches out and touches you. I know it sounds silly."

"No, it doesn't," Chris said, enchanted by Penny's candid wonder. Adulthood hadn't stolen that from her. Elaine had been the same, her outlook on the marvels around her unclouded by cynicism. "It's amazing to think of all that stuff sitting on the bottom of the ocean for hundreds of years," she added, embarrassed by her own prosaic perspective. "Will you find skeletons?"

Penny shook her head. "Bones dissolve in the sea after a few years. We find shoes instead. That's all that's left of human beings in most shipwrecks." Impulsively, she took Chris's hand. "You should come aboard one day and watch. I'll speak to Doug."

"I'd like that." Chris's hand was sweating all of a sudden.

She and Penny had spent most of the past five days together, and it had been a pleasure to get to know her. They hadn't moved beyond the boundaries of friendship in any way. After a few initial qualms, Chris had spoken frankly about Elaine, and it seemed they'd reached an unspoken agreement to take things very slowly.

She stared down at her pack, her hand still in Penny's. She wanted to say something, but she couldn't frame the words.

Penny filled the silence. "I had a nice time today."

"Me, too." Chris figured her face was probably brick red because Penny let go of the hand and swung her small daypack onto her shoulders, thoughtfully giving Chris time to pull herself together.

Something in her expression struck Chris. She knew that look. For years she had seen it in Elaine's averted gaze—disappointment laced with forlorn acceptance. Eventually it had given way to a compassionate tolerance that Chris, in her most honest moments, recognized as Elaine's way of excusing a failing in a loved one. Sensitive, romantic and idealistic, Elaine had found herself with a partner who avoided articulating her feelings and whose romantic vocabulary extended from A to B. After the accident that took Elaine's life, Chris had looked back on this aspect of their relationship and felt stricken that she'd failed to meet her partner halfway. Their compromise had been one-sided. Chris had almost never stepped outside her emotional comfort zone, and Elaine had almost never been able to occupy hers.

Now, here she was, starting off on exactly the same footing, making a woman she was interested in do the emotional legwork. Frustrated with herself, Chris dropped the pack she was hoisting to her shoulders and said, "Penny. Wait."

Her companion turned, those warm hazel eyes bright with hope. "Yes?"

Chris stumbled the few steps that brought them together. "I was trying to think how to say this, and instead I didn't say it at all. But I want to say it. I like you a lot. I think you're smart and wonderful and sexy, and I'm very drawn to you. I love being with you, and I hope I can see you again after—you know, once you're back at work. I mean, see you personally."  Chris fell silent, almost giddy with relief. Suave it was not, but a woman had to start somewhere.

She wanted to remember every detail of what happened then; the way Penny's happiness bubbled up and spilled over, the hands that slid into hers, the soft wind that lifted strands of honey-tipped hair to tickle Chris's cheek as Penny brushed a kiss there.

"I wanted you to care enough to ask," Penny said.

"I do." Chris kissed her in return, on the mouth.

It felt strange and sweet and right.

Against her lips, Penny murmured, "I'm so happy."

Chris framed her face with hands that shook slightly. "Me, too. I..." She struggled for the right words. "I didn't think I would get a second chance." The truth was, on some level, she didn't feel she deserved one.

Penny slid her arms around Chris and gathered her into a warm embrace. "I understand better than you think. One day we'll talk about this some more. There's plenty of time."

Chris dropped her arms to Penny's waist and allowed herself to be held. "I like the sound of that."

Penny drew back just enough to meet her eyes. "Promise me one thing."

"Okay." This sounded important. Chris willed herself not to look as apprehensive as she felt.

"Don't ever tell Doug you planted those coins."

Chris gasped. "How did you... How could you... Jesus!"

Penny's smile verged on the seraphic. "If you're very, very good, one day I might tell you. Meantime, it's our little secret. Deal?"

"Deal," Chris hastily agreed.

Penny hooked her arm into the backpack and helped lift it onto Chris's shoulders. "I guess this is nothing compared with hefting that gold bullion around," she remarked with wicked delight.

Chris groaned. "You have no idea."

AS THE DOLPHIN swam off, Lauren took Briar's hand and said, "Your Mommy Annabel will be home soon."

She felt a heavy sorrow. She and Pat would soon be leaving the island. They would return to their different worlds, proverbial ships that had passed in the night.

"Look!" Briar pointed at a distant speck on the vast Pacific sky. "There she is!"

Lauren squinted into the brilliant sun and had no idea if she were looking at a bird, a plane, or Superman. "We better hurry if we're going to make those cookies before she gets home."

Letting go of Lauren's hand, Briar scampered up the beach and onto the shell path that snaked through the trees. "Chockie chip. That's her favorite," she prattled happily. "Mommy Cody's favorite is Anzac biscuits." She skipped a few more paces up the path then turned to face Lauren, giggling. "Want to race? Visitors first."

With a big smile, Lauren made a show of running ahead. Briar was a real pleasure when she wasn't having a tantrum. And the little girl was strikingly beautiful with her rosy red cheeks, huge dark eyes and shock of black ringlets. For a brief moment, Lauren indulged herself in a fantasy of having a child. They would live upstate, she decided, conjuring a domestic idyll: herself looking on while her partner, who happened to bear a startling resemblance to Pat Roussel, pushed their daughter on a swing.

Lauren spun around at the sound of a sharp cry. Her heart jolted so violently, she could not draw breath.

He was there, and he had Briar in his arms. The impossible had happened. He had found her.

"I knew it was you right away," the lank-haired fan said. "They don't always have the best photos on Soapsite.com, and half the time it's not even the celebrity. But to someone who knows you like I do, I could tell right away the sighting was authentic." He tightened his grip on Briar. Indignantly, the little girl beat her fists on the arm around her middle.

"Please put her down," Lauren said as evenly as she could. "She has nothing to do with me." He wasn't holding a gun, she noted. It was probably concealed.

"I'll let her go when you do exactly what I tell you." Those watery blue eyes blinked double-time.

He was sweating profusely. Nerves, Lauren figured, trying desperately to stay calm herself. "What do you want?" she asked.

For some reason this prompted a harsh bark of laughter. Briar renewed her struggles, this time adding loud wails.

"Hush," Lauren tried to reason with her. "Just be very quiet, and he'll put you down soon, honey."

Above them an engine whined, and Annabel's B-17 made a low pass over the villa. Praying there was some way they'd know her assailant was on the island, Lauren tried to buy time.

Carefully, she said, "It upset me very much that a true fan like you would shoot me."

He flushed, adjusting his hold on Briar, who had fallen into the round-eyed silence of an animal sensing danger. "I felt real bad about those newspaper stories," he said. "After everything I did for you. I felt duped."

"You believed them?"

His blinks were punctuated with a tic. "What was I supposed to think? When it's in the newspaper, you think they wouldn't report it if it wasn't true. But then I saw that notice from the editor saying they made a mistake. I tried to find you to say I was sorry. It wasn't easy. The police are looking for me. I had to leave my job and move out of my apartment."

There was an accusatory ring to this statement, as if somehow it was Lauren's fault he was in trouble. She took in his appearance. Travel-soiled gray slacks hung from his frame like they were a couple of sizes too big, and his white short-sleeved shirt was limp with sweat. If he was concealing a gun, it had to be in his boot, she decided, spotting no telltale lumps anywhere else.

Forcing an understanding nod Lauren said softly, "I think you and I should talk. It's hard in front of a child. If you put her down and let her go home, we could spend some time together."

His eyes darted from Lauren to the surroundings. "Is that her house?"

"Yes. The people who own this island are her parents."

He vacillated for a moment, then set Briar down, urging in the high-pitched voice adopted by adults uncomfortable with children, "Go home and play with your toys now."

Briar stared at him, then at Lauren.

"I can't come right now," Lauren said. "I'm going to go for a walk with this man first. Tell Mommy we'll make the cookies when I get back. Okay?"

With another hard look at Lauren's number one fan, Briar ran off toward the house, leaving Lauren feeling like she was about to throw up. Sweat trickled down her spine. Forcing herself to breathe deeply, she tried to gather her wits. Within fifteen minutes of landing, Annabel and Pat would arrive at the villa and realize something was wrong. Mrs. Marsters knew Lauren and Briar had gone down to Passion Bay together. Hopefully, Briar would mention the man. If not, Pat would come looking anyway; and this would be the path she'd take. Somehow, Lauren had to keep this creep talking right here.

Calling on her acting talent, she said dulcetly, "Gosh, I don't even know your name."

"Hayden," he said, eyeing her cautiously. "Hayden Shaffer."

Lauren heard the B-17 coming in to land and lifted her hand to her face, flicking a wave of hair away. Covertly she peeped at the watch on her wrist and made mental calculations. She started improvising the script she needed to play out. *Scene One, take one: Lauren engages creepy Hayden in conversation to gain his confidence.*

"It gave me a terrible shock that day when you shot me," she said with a slight tremble in her voice. "I guess you didn't actually mean to hit me, maybe just to scare me."

Hayden licked his lips, evidently taken aback to be given the benefit of the doubt. "I was messed up," he said, cashing in on this stroke of luck. "I would never hurt you deliberately."

"Everyone makes mistakes. I know that you're a genuine person, Hayden. What you told me at that cocktail party at Mr. Garfield's house—you were right."

His pale eyes lit up immediately. "I noticed you were back to the old hair style in the last episode."

"And did you notice the line I improvised as a secret signal to you?"

The wet mouth dropped open. "A signal for me? You really did that?"

"Mm hmn. Just my way of saying thanks." Lauren sifted through memories of her script. She needn't have bothered. Her captive audience was engrossed in his own eager quest.

"Wait, don't tell me," he begged. "Was it when that fat lady with the dog said she had a Swiss army knife and you said—"

"—let's make that our little secret."

"Ha!" He drew himself up briefly, then lapsed into pained

self-criticism. "I had no idea. I should have known."

"I kind of expected a letter from you after that," Lauren said wistfully. "But nothing came."

"You must be very disappointed in me."

Detecting a hint of challenge in his stare, she said, on eggshells, "I'm never disappointed when a fan takes a genuine interest in my career. To be honest, I feel like I've let everyone down."

"No. You mustn't think that." He advanced a few paces to stand in her personal space. "We can solve this. I have some good news." He flipped his oily hair back for dramatic effect. "I taught him a lesson, and he won't be giving you any more trouble."

"Who?"

"That cretin who tried to blackmail you. That's the main reason I'm here. To let you know you can come back to the show now." Lauren must have looked as bewildered as she felt, because he slowed right down and, as if he were announcing a lottery win, declared, "After I found out the truth, I went after that coke-snorting slacker. I let him know it was his fault I lost control that day and shot you...by accident. Then I let him have it. Right here." He placed two fingers to his temple, his hand in a gun shape.

Stunned, Lauren said, "You shot him."

"He didn't deserve to live. When I get back, I'll take care of that bitch roommate of yours. The lawyer. I know where she lives."

"I don't know what to say." Lauren hid her shock behind an expression of awe. *Scene Two, take one: having obtained a confession of murder from a crazy man, Lauren must now keep him sweet and get the hell out of Dodge.*

"It was for both of us," Hayden said with heroic gravity. "You have a brilliant career ahead of you, and I'm going to be there to make sure no one will ever pull a stunt like this again. What I'm thinking is, I should become your manager. I know I'm not fully qualified yet, but I'm willing to finish college if I have to. I could do that part time."

He was on a roll, pouring out his fantasies of the future they would have together: the star and the man who knew her best. Lauren's flesh crawled. How many nights had this maniac lain alone in his apartment, gazing up at peeling walls, picturing the life he thought he could manufacture with or without her buy-in. And he had killed a man and almost killed her. That's how serious he was.

Lauren tried to look at her watch without being seen to do

so. Surely it had been ten minutes by now. Annabel and Pat would be nearing the villa. Pat would start looking the moment she saw Lauren wasn't there.

"So, the boat's waiting," her insane companion concluded. "All we need to do is pick up your stuff. I didn't have enough cash to buy an extra airfare for you but I figured you can change your ticket."

This was not the time to say *no*, Lauren decided. Weighing her words, she said, "I can see you've really thought this through, Hayden. I'll need a little time to make arrangements. Are you staying on Rarotonga?"

"I have a hotel package. There's two days left."

"Great. That's plenty of time." Trying to sound impressed, she said, "You know, I'm amazed you found this place. You're quite the detective."

"It was easy. I got most of the information off Soapsite, and when I landed in Rarotonga I told one of those charter boats I wanted to see where the shipwreck is at. We cruised around looking for the beach in the picture." From his pocket, he pulled a page obviously printed off a website and showed it to her.

Lauren recognized herself on the beach the day she and Pat quarreled, the day those guys in the speedboat came by looking for the *Aspiration*. They must have hawked their footage to the usual media, and someone had identified her. She was stunned. Her stalker must have bought his air ticket the moment he saw the picture. Wondering what to do next, she cast a nervy glance up at the villa.

Her brief inattention wasn't lost on him. "Who are you looking for?" he demanded, eyes narrow with suspicion.

Playing it cool, Lauren said, "The little girl. I wouldn't normally let her walk home alone."

His eyes darted left and right. "Where are the parents?"

"I'm not really sure," Lauren said vaguely. "This place takes a lot of work. I guess they could be anywhere."

"We better get moving," he said, as if they were in this together. "The boat's going to meet us in the next bay pretty soon."

Lauren hesitated. *Scene Three, take one: Lauren goes with the crazy man and waits for a chance to escape.* "I'll need to collect my things first, Hayden. I can't go anywhere without my passport."

"Okay. Where is it?" His tone became shrill.

Lauren pointed through the mango trees. "There's another villa over there. That's where I'm staying. It's not far."

He dragged a forearm across his face, then transferred the sweat to his pants. His tic was more pronounced. "I'll take care of that later. We gotta get going." The words spilled out in a breathless rush. Looking hunted, he grabbed Lauren's arm and hustled her down through the trees toward the beach.

Banking on the likelihood that by now Pat and Lauren must be close to the villa, Lauren broke free and bolted up the slope.

"Oh, no you don't!" He came after her, grabbing at her clothing and finally her hair. Wrenching her head back, he hissed in her ear, "I was hoping you would be reasonable after what you've put me through. But you don't care how I feel, do you?" He got her into a headlock and dragged her along with him, tightening his choking grip as she struggled. "Don't make me hurt you," he burbled and flashed something in front of her face with his free hand. A switchblade.

Lauren stopped fighting him and the arm loosened enough for her to pull a frantic breath.

"See," he said. "If you're good, I'll treat you like a princess."

# Chapter
# Eighteen


"WHERE'S LAUREN?" PAT asked Mrs. Marsters.

The housekeeper pointed toward Passion Bay. "They went to see the dolphin."

Flicking a glance at Annabel, who was busy unloading supplies onto the kitchen counter, Pat said, "I'll go get them."

She exited the living room and strolled across the verandah, squinting out to sea. She hadn't seen anyone down there when they flew over, but the trees obscured much of the beach from view. Pat hesitated. She had left both her guns on a closet shelf in Cody and Annabel's room when she went to Rarotonga. There was no reason to carry unless Lauren was with her; and doing so was illegal under the terms of her permit. Uneasy, she returned indoors. This was just another sleepy day on paradise, but she'd better be armed anyway.

Glock in hand, she descended the steps and was on the narrow shell beach path when an odd noise made her spin on her heels. A small whimper came from beneath the verandah steps. There, curled in a ball, her thumb in her mouth, was Annabel's daughter. Panic crushed the breath from Pat's lungs. Yelling, "Annabel!" she dropped to her hands and knees and slid an arm beneath the little girl, easing her from her hideaway just as Annabel's feet hit the bottom step.

"Oh, my God," Annabel gasped, arms extended. Immediately she bundled her child close. "Sweetheart, what were you doing under there?"

At that, Briar dissolved into tears and hiccupped. "I'm scared."

Pat's first impulse was to run frantically into the belt of trees and scream Lauren's name, but her training had brought with it the ability to close down emotion and focus on crucial detail. Until she knew why Briar was hiding, it was too soon to jump to conclusions. Over the mop of black ringlets, she met Annabel's startled amethyst eyes and mouthed in an undertone.

"Where's Lauren?"

Annabel carried Briar up the steps and sat on the cane chaise lounge at one end of the verandah, rocking her gently. "Sweetie, where's the lady who took you to see Hine? Where's Lauren?"

Briar pointed into the trees. "I want to make cookies," she stammered. "But the bad man hurt me."

Pat's gut constricted. Forcing herself to stay calm and listen, she sat on the edge of a chair and tried to convince herself Lauren wasn't dead.

"A man hurt you?" Annabel lost all her color. Hands shaking, she said, "Show Mommy where he hurt you."

Briar lifted her t-shirt. Across her midriff the skin was reddened.

Annabel's response was panicky. "Oh, my God. He must have punched her."

"I don't think so." Pat cut across her. To Briar, she said, "Honey, did the bad man pick you up and hold you real tight?"

Briar nodded. "It hurt."

"Where else did he hurt you?" Pat asked, keeping her tone as level as she could.

Briar pointed at her left wrist, which was mottled purple.

"He grabbed her hand, then lifted her and held her around the ribs facing away from him," Pat surmised out loud. "Was Lauren there?" she asked Briar.

Briar nodded, mouth trembling anew. "When she comes, we can make cookies."

Pat placed a hand on Annabel's shoulder. "I'm sorry," she said urgently. "I need to go. I think he has Lauren."

"Who is *he*?" Annabel rose, hugging Briar to her tightly. Pat could almost read the indictment in her expression. *What evil did you draw to my home?*

"Lauren was shot by a fan who was stalking her. I didn't think he'd ever find her out here, but—"

"Mrs. Marsters!" Annabel stuck her head in the door and the wide Rarotongan woman hurried across the living room. "Please radio the *Aspiration* and tell Cody she has to come home. Now! And take Briar." After passing the little girl over with promises of cookies very soon, she turned to Pat, and said unsteadily, "Let's go."

"No. Stay out of this, please," Pat urged. "Go inside and lock the doors. For your own safety."

Annabel looked like she was a millisecond away from punching Pat in the mouth. "Are you kidding? My child could have been killed by this asshole. Now where the fuck is that other gun of yours?"

"HE DRAGGED HER this way," Pat said, studying twin furrows left in the shell path.

Clearly Lauren had dug her feet in. The fact that she was alive suggested the lunatic fan had plans for her, otherwise they would have found a body already. The thought made Pat sick to her stomach. How could she have allowed this to happen?

"He's headed for Marama Bay," Annabel deduced and broke into a jog.

Following her closely, Pat swallowed the bile in her throat and willed her mind to clear. She needed to come up with a plan that would get Annabel out of harm's way. No way was she taking care of business with an irate mother tagging along looking for revenge.

Annabel slowed as they reached a dense stand of banana palms. In a low voice, she said, "The moorings are down there. Maybe he's got a boat waiting."

Hushing Annabel, Pat peered through the foliage. She spotted Lauren lying on a wooden platform, ankles tied, hands bound behind her. A few yards away a man was pacing back and forth, talking to himself. He brandished something in his right hand. Pat couldn't tell if it was a gun.

"Here's the plan." She handed the .38 to Annabel and kept the Glock for herself. "I want you to stay here and cover me."

Annabel looked uncertain. No doubt she was trying to remember what she had seen on TV cop shows.

"I'm going down," Pat continued as if these instructions were a clear as day. "And when I give this signal," she flapped her left hand over her head to illustrate, "fire a couple of shots in the air."

"Got it," Annabel said.

"Stay up here," Pat reiterated. She sliced some fleshy palm leaves into a pile and bundled it under one arm. "When the time's right, I want him to think he's surrounded."

"Okay. I can do this." Annabel straightened her shoulders. "Good luck."

"I'm so sorry this is happening," Pat murmured, and left Annabel in the safety of the jungle. She began a rapid, stealthy descent. As she drew within sight of the moorings, she slowed down and dropped the banana leaves on the ground one at a time to mask the sound of her feet crushing twigs. She was almost parallel to her target and could hear most of what he was saying.

Abruptly he stalked over to Lauren and yelled, "I risked everything for you, and you can't even remember where you put your passport! I thought you were better than that. I thought you were something special. But you're just like all the others. Stupid."

He was carrying a knife, not a gun, Pat noted with relief. It looked like a switchblade. He would have to get close, and even then he'd have to be very good to be any threat, given her training. She looked him up and down for any sign of a gun. If he had tried to bring one into this tiny island kingdom, it had probably been impounded. Pat had only got hers through thanks to a special permit.

It was time, she thought calmly. She stepped from the trees. He had his back to her, his gaze fixed on Lauren. Placing her feet with precision, Pat took several paces.

"It's in the blue bag inside the bedroom closet," Lauren said in a rasping voice.

"It better be!"

As he started to turn, Pat yelled. "FBI! Freeze! Drop your weapon."

His head jerked around, wishy-washy blue eyes wild. Releasing a noise oddly like a giggle, he took a small step toward her.

"Freeze! Or I'll blow your head off." Beyond him, Lauren's familiar form corkscrewed around. From the corner of her eye Pat could see her terrified face. She advanced a pace closer. He was actually contemplating running, she sensed with amazement. "Don't run," she warned with quiet authority. "If you run, I'll have to shoot you. Now drop the knife. Keep your hands where I can see them."

As she continued to speak, she moved steadily closer.

"Get back!" He choked on a sob.

"Hayden, please do what she says," Lauren pleaded with convincing concern.

"Shut up. This is all your fault." A long, wet sniff.

"You're surrounded." Pat adopted a more gentle tone. "It's over. Drop the knife."

His face twitched, then it was almost like a switch flipped inside, transforming the sobbing loser into something much more dangerous. In that split second, he made a desperate leaping dive for the wooden platform. Pat fired twice at lightning speed. He fell short of Lauren by inches. The knife dropped from his hand, and he looked back at Pat in shock. Hit in the shoulder and the leg, he squirmed in the sand, turning the white grains red.

Pat had longed to kill him. It could have passed for a clean shoot. But it would have been dishonorable. Containing her own shock and rage, she patted him down for any other weapons and bound his hands behind his back with one of the loose mooring ropes. She picked up the knife and quickly cut Lauren free.

"Forgive me," she said, taking Lauren into her arms and carrying her a safe distance away.

Lauren shook her head numbly. Leaning into Pat's chest, she wept with abandon. Pat felt numb. Her worst nightmare had happened. Lauren could have been killed and it would have been Pat's fault. She willed herself to focus on what needed to happen next, knowing that if she didn't, she would fall completely apart.

Annabel's chagrined voice broke in on her self-condemnation. "You didn't signal me." Crouching over the groaning man, she said, "Want me to finish him off?"

"He's not worth serving time for," Pat said, stroking Lauren's hair.

"I need a doctor," the victim moaned.

At the sound of an outboard, Lauren lifted her head from Pat's chest, and all three women watched as Cody raced across Marama Bay toward them. She cut the motor and neatly came about, tossing Annabel a rope. The two of them had obviously done this a thousand times, Pat thought, as Annabel looped the rope around a mooring and Cody climbed the steps onto the platform.

Hands on hips, the lithe Kiwi surveyed the scene with a long-suffering air. "Jeez, mate," she complained to Pat. "He's bleeding all over my beach."

# Chapter
# Nineteen

"I DON'T UNDERSTAND," Lauren stared at her father. "What do you mean, she's gone?"

Wendall Douglas held his cigar trimmer poised. "She's accompanying the prisoner back home. This is a matter for the authorities now, and obviously there'll be questions. So I released her from her contract." As an afterthought, he added, "Don't worry. She gets to keep her salary for the whole two months, plus I gave her a bonus."

That was it? Pat had pocketed the cash and left without so much as a goodbye? Did Lauren need it spelled out any more clearly that all she'd ever signified to the FBI Agent was a pay check and some sexual recreation?

"Yep. All's well that ends well." Her father lit up and puffed contentedly.

Lauren gazed around the hotel lobby, barely able to take in the blur of the past two days. After the shooting, Annabel and Pat had flown Hayden Shaffer to Rarotonga for hospital treatment. Pat had packed her stuff and told Lauren their flight home was booked in three days' time. They'd barely had five minutes to talk alone. She'd said she would have to stay in Rarotonga until then to help the police and get the ball rolling for extradition.

Two days later, Lauren had left Moon Island, expecting to find Pat waiting at the airport when she arrived. But instead, her father had sent a driver for her. Now here she was, sitting in a bar at the Rarotongan Resort hotel sipping a Mai Tai and listening to her father congratulate himself on hiring a bodyguard who had saved his babydoll's life.

"She told me to tell you goodbye," he said. "I think she was genuinely sorry not to get to say it in person."

"Lovely." With a jerky movement, Lauren deposited her Mai Tai on the nearest table. Deciding this was not the time for fru-fru cocktails, she waved for the waiter and requested a vodka.

As the chubby young man cleared the unwanted drink away, Lauren caught her father's eye and lifted her chin slightly.

"Everything okay, babydoll?" Wendall appeared slightly shocked by her abrupt transition to hard liquor.

"Everything's just peachy." She pictured Pat's face in front of her where she could slap it hard.

Unconvinced, her father cleared his throat and tried for diplomacy, never his strong suit. "You can't stay angry forever."

"About?"

"I know you didn't want to come here. Your mother wasn't crazy about it, either. She thought we should keep you home at St Michaels and use a couple of my security guys."

"I didn't know that." Lauren's curiosity was piqued. "What did she say?"

"That the whole idea sounded like trouble." He consulted his scotch dourly. "Turns out she was right."

In more ways than one, Lauren thought. "It was just plain bad luck that creep found out where I was," she said, not wanting her father to blame himself.

"And good luck I hired the right person to take care of that," he said.

Lauren could only nod. She wanted to throw her vodka across the room.

A FEW HOURS and several double shots later, she retreated to her room and lay on her bed staring up at the ceiling, a prisoner of blazing anger and pathetic yearning.

In her adult life, no one had ever made her feel as Pat did. Until Pat, Lauren felt as if she had existed in a mirage, accepting the shallow rites of sentiment and sex as standard currency in the land of veneer she occupied. There were times when she had wondered if this was really *It*, but she had dismissed her sense of emptiness as a character flaw. Other people were perfectly happy. Hers was an enviable lifestyle. What was the matter with her, feeling let down?

With Pat, she had stepped into a new reality. She barely recognized her own emotional landscape now. Everything had taken on a different hue. There were no familiar paths to traverse. Gone was the prospect of simple chocolate-box happiness served up by the convenient vending machines of dating and friendship. Pat had invited her into a foreign and wondrous interior and discarded her there. How would she ever find her way back to what she knew?

Lauren rolled onto her side and closed her eyes. She had lost the woman who had awakened her deeper self. Grief, humiliation and disbelief clawed at her. Tears poured down her face and soaked her pillow. More than anything, more than she could bear, she craved Pat. She craved the comfort of her presence, the bliss of being held by her, the intensity of their lovemaking. She craved the surrender and release that was Pat's gift to her, those moments of ripe, bursting happiness so pure they blinded her with joy.

How could she have found this only to lose it so quickly? Helpless fury overtook her, and she hated herself for whatever it was she had failed to be for Pat. There must have been something Pat needed that Lauren hadn't provided. If she only knew what that was. If only she could have their time again and be Pat's ideal mate. Lauren was overwhelmed with despair. She'd had that chance, and now it was gone. Pat was gone.

Lifting her hands to her chest, she wept anew. She could almost feel her heart breaking.

PAT STUDIED THE tattooed wrist handcuffed to hers. The name "Gillian" had been crossed out and replaced with "Lauren."

"Champagne? Juice? Water?" A flight attendant inquired, pretending not to notice Pat was attached to a groggy insect of man who had already thrown up once and occasionally lapsed into slurred ramblings about various television heroines, in particular Dana Scully.

The prisoner had been sedated for the trip, and they were sitting right at the back of business class where they wouldn't scare a coach cabin full of families homeward bound after their happy holidays. Thankfully he was asleep now. Hoping he would stay that way, Pat took a glass of water and requested a snack. She couldn't remember when she'd last eaten.

Rarotonga was four hours behind them. Pat could have waited another day or two to make the trip so that she and Lauren could have shared one of those awkward goodbyes. But what was the point? They had said all that needed to be said the day those photographers took the fateful pictures that drew Hayden Shaffer from his hiding place. Lauren had said then she never wanted to see Pat again and Pat had given her good reason. Subsequent events didn't change that.

Pat reviewed her conduct and felt disgusted with herself. Not only had she set her personal and professional ethics aside in getting involved with a client, she had made misjudgments that could have led to Lauren's death. It was only by sheer good luck that she and Annabel had arrived back on Moon Island in time for Pat to do her job. She had broken every rule in the book and walked away with a fat paycheck at the end of it all. Wendall Douglas had been so grateful, he had rounded her total up to 100K. Pat intended to return the payment as soon as she got home.

The flight attendant placed a club sandwich on Pat's tray table, and she consumed it, barely tasting the contents. She could not shake the sense that she had made a terrible mistake. Lauren was different from any other short fling she had ever had; in fact, to class her as a fling was a denial. Their connection was so much more than that.

Being with Lauren had invited Pat to dwell in the realm of possibility, to conceive of a life where her work came second. In a few short weeks, she had slid into a state of mind so foreign, it was scary. The truth was, the more time she spent with Lauren, the more emotionally naked she became, and Pat didn't like feeling vulnerable. It struck her that this was the real reason she had left, no matter how she might choose to rationalize it. She was falling in love with Lauren and had pushed her away; it was that simple. Years ago, she had made the choice to live without a mate and she had dressed it up as noble self-sacrifice. Lauren had challenged that. She had forced Pat to choose again, this time with very different stakes.

Pat stared down at her half-eaten sandwich and tried to fathom the choice she had made, the choice to deny her heart's desire. How had it come to this? When had she carved away the most tender part of herself and replaced it with armor? What exactly was she guarding against?

A boundless hunger bloomed within, displacing all in its path. It was as if a giant hand evicted the breath from her lungs and grasped her heart in a vice-like grip. Pat gazed sightlessly ahead. She recognized that leaving Lauren was more than a mistake. It was an act of self-punishment. She had dared to love someone, and the Pat Roussel she had become found that unacceptable.

# Chapter
# Twenty

ONE YEAR LATER

THROUGH A PALL of dust thrown up by the wheels of her Jeep, Lauren could make out two figures at the side of the road, a man and his daughter. Flies hovered around the girl in a swirling mass.

"*Tadias.*" Lauren greeted them in their language. "Mr. Debaba?"

The wiry man nodded and wiped his hand on his robe before shaking hers. His smile of relief was the one Lauren had grown accustomed to during her year in Ethiopia. Finally his daughter, Maiza, would be helped. Discarded by her husband, shunned by her village, deprived of her child, she was a pariah. She could not work, for no one wanted to work with her. If she tried to catch a bus, she was refused entry. She lived in a makeshift tent her father had rigged up outside the family dwelling.

Like most Ethiopian girls, she had been married off at fourteen to a man her parents chose and had fallen pregnant immediately. Birth control was not an option in her world. The few health agencies that had provided condoms and education had closed their doors after President Bush withdrew American financial support from the UN Population Fund and imposed the Global Gag Rule. These two measures had successfully ended family planning services in the poorest third world countries. As a consequence, the situation for the girls of Maiza's region was now worse than it had ever been.

Maiza's body was not ready for the ardors of childbirth, and after several days of labor without medical care, the damage had been extensive. Most girls in her situation simply died in squalor, a forgotten statistic, so easily preventable if anyone gave a damn. But Maiza had survived with holes in her bladder and bowel, leaking a steady discharge down her legs that dried on the one dress she owned, causing the stench that offended all those around her.

When Lauren had first arrived in Ethiopia, she could not come to terms with the plight of these girls and women. She was torn between disgust at their condition, outrage over their treatment, and impotent fury at the men they had married. She could not forgive the Ethiopian government that did so little to help them, or her own President for scoring moralistic points at the expense of the world's most vulnerable people.

Her reaction was perfectly normal, her mother had said. But they had work to do. The surgery performed at the Addis Ababa Fistula Hospital was life-changing. A woman who had been healed could return to her family and lead the best life possible for a woman denied the choices her sisters in the West took for granted.

Lauren opened the Jeep's door, and Maiza climbed in, her eyes downcast. Her father apologized to Lauren for his daughter and offered her a freshly baked *injera* and a piece of cloth with some coins wrapped in it. Because the operations were funded by overseas donations, Lauren wanted to turn down the hard-won money, but that would be an insult. Here at least was a father who cared enough for his daughter that he had probably sold some of the family's few possessions to make the trip. The precious sum symbolized dignity and a future for his child.

Lauren thanked him and placed the money in the pouch at her waist. "Twenty-one days from now," she said in Amharic, counting off fingers, "I'll bring her back to this place. Three weeks."

"Yes, Doctor Miss Lauren. I'll wait here." Again Mr. Debaba smiled. His eyes were tearful.

"Don't worry," Lauren said. "We'll take good care of her."

As she turned the Jeep and headed back along the road toward Bahr Dar, he walked after them, waving. His daughter waved back, her arm only falling when her father was finally out of sight. Then she sat hunched in the corner of her seat, her head bent in shame. This was another thing Lauren had grown accustomed to. The women who had Maiza's condition could not make eye contact. Their humiliation was too great. Lauren did not press her for conversation. That would come later, when she had clean garments and hope.

IN THE LATE evening, Lauren and her mother took tea beneath the awning in front of their tiny house on the shores of Lake Tana and watched the fishermen dragging their papyrus boats ashore. The temperature dropped sharply after the sun went down, and the cool was like a miracle. There was no air conditioning; in fact, there was no electricity. A kerosene lamp lit their cottage. It stood on a small table near them, radiating golden light. Beneath it, one of the trainee nurses sat with a textbook, making the most of this precious resource.

Sisay was Helen Douglas' protégée. Only seventeen years old, she had been discarded by her family, and there was no home for her to return to. Having taught the girl to read and write in her own language, Helen was now teaching her to speak English. She had high hopes for Sisay, who was brilliantly clever.

"Doctor Miss Lauren?" The girl handed Lauren her notebook and pencil. "Will you please check?"

Lauren had long ago given up trying to tell the women at the hospital and the people in the wider community that she was just plain "Lauren." It was apparently inconceivable to them that the daughter did not follow in her mother's footsteps. Doctor Mrs. Douglas was known to them from her previous visits. This time she'd brought her daughter to work with her. Enough said.

Lauren read Sisay's work. "This is very good. No mistakes."

A tiny smile tugged at the edges of Sisay's serious mouth. Lauren had never seen the girl laugh. Her baby had been stillborn, and her husband's family had thrown her out on the street to beg when they realized she could bear no more children. Helen and Lauren had found her several miles from the hospital. She had walked for three days to reach Bar Dahr and had asked to work in exchange for her operation.

Dr Hamlin, the founder of the Fistula Hospital, never turned a woman away. After a month of decent food and treatment, Sisay had her surgery. She had worked for several months, cleaning and doing laundry and had begged to remain. Now she was about to sit the exam for entry to nursing school with Helen sponsoring her place. It was a small triumph, but these made the daily tragedies bearable.

Lauren passed the notebook to her mother, who read it and told Sisay, "Your praise will make me vain."

Sisay's short essay about her reasons for wanting to be a nurse was poignant in its simplicity and compared her sponsor favorably with a legendary tribal queen and Mary, the Mother of God.

"Not feeling holy today?" Lauren murmured, lighting a new citronella coil to ward off the mosquitoes. Malaria was a problem in Bar Dahr.

"I shouldn't have lost my temper," her mother replied. That morning, she had sent a man running from the clinic after shouting at him over the state of his wife.

Sisay spoke up. "That man makes anger for me. I want to shoot him with many guns."

"He made me angry, too," Lauren said. "Ignorant, stupid man."

Helen said, "He doesn't know any better. At least he brought his wife to us."

"Seven months pregnant, and with a fistula condition already." Lauren could not contain her disgust. "What if she'd tried to give birth?"

"We can only be thankful she didn't. Now we can do a Caesarean, and eventually she'll have her surgery."

Lauren shook her head. "Some days I really don't know how you do it."

Her mother spent a moment in silent reflection. "It's going to be strange being home again."

"No kidding. Refrigeration. Hot showers. Salad."

"You could have gone back any time."

"I know."

At first, going home had been all Lauren could think about. But she'd promised her mother she would remain for a month, and besides, she'd had nothing to go home to. The network had killed off Dr. Kate, and the only offers Lauren was getting were for walk-on roles in B-grade mini-series. As the weeks passed in this far-off land, there was always another Maiza or Sisay she wanted to stay for and see recover. She and her mother had been assigned to the main hospital in Addis Ababa at first, then they'd moved to one of several newly built regional treatment centers, a small facility in the grounds of the Bar Dahr regional hospital in the northwest.

The area was beautiful, secluded in the purple and red highlands just a few miles from the Tiss-Issat Falls. Lauren loved its lushness and tranquility, the misty rainforests and curious monkeys, the shy but friendly Woyto people. This was the land where humankind originated, where the Queen of Sheba once ruled, a jewel of a place occupying Africa's highest plateau and surrounded by a hellish confederacy of neighbors including Somalia, Sudan, and Eritrea. History had left its imprint here in the hominid fossils of the Rift Valley, the tombs and fortresses of Axum, and in some of the oldest shrines in Christianity.

Lake Tana, the source of the Blue Nile, seemed a world apart, a giant inland sea dotted with islands. Lauren loved to stand on the shore at first light and watch the birds rise through the mist and hang as if inked against the pale morning sky. Out on the lake, medieval churches and monasteries still stood on many islands, somehow having weathered centuries of political turmoil. Occasionally, she and her mother took a woman who wanted to give thanks for her surgery to Ura Kidane Mihret, the only monastery open to both genders.

Lauren lived for the moment when these women emerged from the clinic wearing their brand new dresses — a gift from the hospital, huge smiles on their faces, their heads held high. She loved being able to look into their eyes for the first time and see what words could not express.

"I can see why you always stay over here longer, Mom," she remarked.

Helen Douglas gave a small, rueful smile. "I wish your father was so understanding."

When their six months had started looking more like a year, Wendall Douglas grudgingly flew out to visit them. It was the first time he'd ever seen the hospital, and he had been appalled. After writing a big check for the Jeep Lauren now drove and making a donation to the operating fund, he had gone back home promising he would speak out against the withdrawal of US family planning funds to third world initiatives.

His own race for the Republican nomination had grown ugly, he'd told them. His rival, a man to the right of Joe McCarthy, was running a smear campaign. A Rambo patriot who had taken a pass when it was his turn to die for his country, he had accused Wendall Douglas of deliberately stepping on a mine to get out of Vietnam, and described him as "a relic of yesterday's GOP."

Helen Douglas had suggested her husband take this as a compliment, but Lauren could see her father was shaken by the vicious attacks. He still clung to the belief that if people like him remained true to the original ideals of the GOP, they could turn back the tide of extremism that had swept their Party. Lauren thought he was kidding himself, but kept that opinion to herself.

"So, how do you feel?" Helen asked.

"About what?" Lauren guessed her mother had asked her something and she had not heard it first time 'round. "Sorry. I was miles away."

Helen smiled. "I was asking how you feel about going home — other than looking forward to ice in your drinks?"

"I feel different...in myself. I can't explain it. I feel older." Some things would never be the same, she thought. For a start, she would never take clean drinking water for granted. And flush toilets. Never again would she feel sorry for herself for more than a few seconds. Witnessing real misery and deprivation had put her own problems into perspective in a big hurry. Lauren grinned. "I'm not sure how I'll cope, listening to my friends bitching about bad hair days."

Her mother laughed. "Worried you might find it hard to sympathize?"

"Luckily, I can act," Lauren responded dryly. "I'm amazed at how little it takes for a person to be happy here. I mean, these people have *nothing*."

"Happiness is relative to expectation. In the world we know, people grow up feeling entitled to a great deal. Unless we have it all, we're not content."

"I get embarrassed every time I think about how spoiled I was. You told me this was going to be tough, but I had *no* idea."

"Are you sorry you came?"

"God, no. It's the first really good thing I've done in my life. I'm so glad I'm not Dr. Kate any more."

"It's funny you should say that," Helen mused. "I think you're more like Dr. Kate now than you ever were acting the role."

"Is that a compliment?"

"Yes, Doctor Miss Lauren, it is."

At that, Sisay lifted her head and laughed shyly, a hand across her mouth. "One day I am Nurse Miss Sisay."

"Yes," Helen replied softly. "And maybe one day, a long time from now, you will be Doctor Miss Sisay."

Lauren allowed her eyes to rest on the young woman. Her mother had said that if Sisay graduated nursing, she would pay for the girl to attend medical school at Addis Ababa University. The boldness of this dream struck Lauren forcibly. Here was a young woman who could not even read a year ago, and who had been brought up to feel worthless unless she married, had many children, and raised a few head of cattle. The women of her village spent half of every day carrying water and firewood so their families could survive. Yet here she was, against all the odds, aiming for the unimaginable—education and a profession.

"I was thinking," Lauren said, feeling oddly self-conscious. "When we get home, I'm going to apply for medical school."

Her mother raised her eyebrows. "Really?"

"Maybe I won't be good enough. I'm not as brainy as you." And I never had your noble instincts, she added mentally. "But I'm going to try."

"You have plenty of brains," Helen said indignantly. "You just hadn't decided how you were going to use them, that's all."

Lauren gazed out at the shimmering lake and sipped her tea in silence. Today her shoulder ached where the bullet had smashed flesh and bone. Although she no longer had panic attacks or nightmares, the pain reminded her that God had seen fit to spare her. She had been given a second chance, and she was not going to waste it.

One day, she would come back here as a doctor. Like her mother, she would make a difference in the world. Her life would have some meaning.

# Chapter
## Twenty-one

LIZZY DUBOIS KEPT a tidy home in the town of Hinten, West Virginia. The walls of her living room were freshly painted in a pale rose shade and boasted a collection of religious-themed art. She showed Pat to a plastic-covered sofa, also pale rose, and in her stiff-jawed Appalachian manner asked, "Can I fetch you'n something to drink, Agent Roussel? Sweet milk, pop, coffee?"

"I'm fine, thanks."

Lizzy took this for a yes. "I'll fix some coffee."

Pat fell into line. "Black for me, please." She unzipped her satchel and removed a tape recorder and notepad. Her pulse was racing. She had driven down from Philly at breakneck speed, making the seven-hour trip in less than six. That wasn't the only reason her nerves were jangling. On a gut instinct, she had phoned Lizzy a few months ago, deciding to press her one last time over Caleb Dubois' alibi for the day Shelby-Rose Dubois disappeared.

Lizzy had repeated the same story she'd told several years earlier, but this time there was a distinct lack of conviction in her tone. Wondering what had accounted for the change, Pat had called her periodically ever since, working on gaining her trust. On each occasion, usually over the sounds of screaming children, they'd talked about the case and the other victims. Yesterday, as if in passing, Pat had mentioned the lipstick missing from Shelby-Rose's backpack. Lizzy's reaction had been telling; she dropped the phone. When she started talking again, Pat had the distinct impression there was something she needed to get off her chest.

Lizzy handed her a mug of weak coffee and sat stiffly in an armchair. "It's rainin' like a big dog out there," she remarked, patting her rigid blonde waves.

Like any mountain-raised woman, she would have mixed feelings about discussing kin with an outsider—worse still, the FBI. Giving her some time, Pat said, "This room looks great."

A quick smile. "Oh, yeah. Last time you was here, it was that hideous yaller, weren't it?"

"Yes, ma'am."

"I always did like pink." Lizzy lapsed into thought, then set her coffee on the table with an air of determination. As if weighing her words, she said, "I sure appreciate you comin' all this way. Hope it don't turn out to be a waste."

"Anything you can tell me will help." Pat indicated the tape recorder. "Do you mind?"

Lizzy shrugged a thin shoulder. "It's okay."

"We've talked a few times about Duke, how he was with your husband that day. I was wondering if maybe you've remembered something else?"

"Well, it's proba'ly nothing. Folks would expect me to axe my husband afores I talk at the likes of you'n. But Jimmy don't have a lick of sense when it comes to that brother of his."

Pat sipped her coffee, allowing Lizzy to get to the point in her own way.

"I have this girlfriend, Dreema. She was my bridesmaid when I married Jimmy. Anyways, she's single, and time don't stand still, if'n you know what I mean."

Pat gave an empathetic nod.

"Well, she was seeing this guy, smelled like some'it the cat drug in, ig'nernt and liquored up day and night. So I gets to thinking, how's about I fix her up with Duke. You know, seeing as he's a wife short, and she could sure use a husband."

"You fixed your girlfriend up with Duke? This was recent?"

"Yuh-huh. They stepped out a few times." Lizzy studied her coffee for a moment. "It didn't go real well."

"In what way?"

"I don't rightly know what Duke was expecting. He's had some schooling, and he gets above his raisin'...if'n you know what I mean. Anyhows, Jimmy axes him what went wrong, and he says Dreema's plumb stupid. Well, that just chaps my ass. She's smart enough to have her own flower shop."

Pat deduced the obvious. "Sounds like your girlfriend dumped him, maybe."

"Yuh-huh." Lizzy lowered her voice a fraction. "Duke, he's got money, so he took her to fine restaurants an' all. Then he just drives her home. And Dreema's real fetchin'."

A wave of disappointment engulfed Pat. Had she just driven four hundred miles to hear that Caleb Dubois didn't kiss his date? "Dreema was surprised he didn't make a move on her?"

"At first she reckons he's being perlite. Next thing she's asking me if'n Duke is one of them...um..."

"Homosexuals?"

"Nuh-huh. When a man is lookin' to dress in women's clothing — what do they call that?"

"Transvestite? Men who cross-dress?"

Lizzy nodded, eyes darting anxiously to the picture above her fireplace. From what Pat could make out, it was someone's idea of God casting sinners into a fiery pit.

Pat asked, "Why would she think Duke is a cross-dresser?"

"Their last date, they goes back to his place for coffee. She figures he's got a mind for getting' to it, so she goes potty." She fell silent, then continued in a tone of bashful apology. "And while she's in there, she takes a gander in the medicine cabinet."

Pat's heart accelerated. She and Cicchetti had interviewed Duke several times, but they'd never gotten any further than his living room. When Cicchetti had asked to use the facilities, this had resulted in the cheerful suggestion that they all adjourn to the nearest burger restaurant in Duke's chain.

Lizzy lifted her eyes to Pat's face. "Now, sumpin' you should know is Jimmy and me, we use-ta visit with Duke ever' so often, and I swear, he ain't never had female company in that place."

"A real bachelor pad, huh?" Pat had formed a similar impression. Wade Dubois employed a cleaning woman to keep his place immaculate. The guy was a real neatnik, from what she had seen. And Lizzy was right; the house was devoid of female energy. Even Cicchetti had noticed.

"So it really throwed me when Dreema says she seed a lipstick in that cabinet. A real fancy looking 'un. Far'n."

Pat's breath caught in her throat. "How could she tell it was foreign?"

Lizzy gave her a quizzical look. "'Cause it said made in Paris. I know it sounds bad, her messing with his things, but she was curious."

Pat smiled. "I look in people's bathroom cabinets all the time."

"You'n the law."

"You know, just because Duke has a lipstick in his bathroom doesn't mean he's a cross-dresser," Pat said, digging a little more. "According to your husband, he has a lot of women friends. Maybe one of them left it there."

Lizzy shook her head, and her speech became more excited. "Thing is, it was wrapped up real purty in a big white ribbon. That got her thinkin'. What's a man doin' with lipstick and a bride ribbon? So when we was a-talkin' last night, I got chill-bumps after you said 'bout that lipstick missing."

"How big was the ribbon?" Pat wanted to run to her car, drive to Charleston and tear Caleb Dubois' place apart.

Lizzy demonstrated with her hands.

"I'd like to talk with Dreema."

Lizzy stood. "She's a ways from here. I'll fetch the address for her flower shop." Knotting her fingers, she blurted. "Duke don't have to know we've been talking, right?"

"This is just between you and me," Pat assured her. "You did the right thing in telling me."

A wistful expression softened Lizzy's bony features. "I loved that young'un. An' I don't owe Duke nothin'." The brown eyes narrowed. "Come to that, happen I know Jimmy's been coverin' up for him. That alibi. I reckon it's a lie."

# Chapter
# Twenty-two

PAT CLOSED HER front door for about the tenth time that evening and carried yet another small gift to her kitchen table. Caleb Dubois' arrest a week ago had brought with it a flood of attention from her neighbors and countless phone calls from smooth-talking agents who told her she stood to make millions. One had a book deal on the table. He'd even dreamed up a nauseating title: *Torn Petals*, billed as "the gut-wrenching story of the Kiddy Pageant Killer by the female FBI Agent who caught him."

Pat had said she would think about it. She and Cicchetti had already discussed doing something together, so he could earn enough money to buy a decent apartment. His divorce had left him broke and bitter, and now his ex was making it next to impossible for him to see his kids.

Pat wanted to think Cicchetti was probably to blame for his own misfortunes, and maybe he was. But her impression of Natalia Cicchetti was that the woman was a Class A bitch. She was already shacked up with another guy, and these days she had a Mexican housekeeper and a house with a pool. Not only had she traded up, she had moved to Miami, where her new man owned a chain of Italian restaurants.

If it was at all possible, her hair was even bigger, and her fake nails even faker when Pat saw her at the custody hearing a month ago. Pat was there to vouch for Cicchetti's credentials as a dad. A lot of good it did. Natalia had trotted out the whole Catholic-mother routine, painting her ex-husband as a callous detective too busy with the job and his buddies to remember his own son's birthday.

Pat shoved a couple of pepperoni Hot Pockets in the microwave and took a beer from the fridge. She opened the newspaper and found her face plastered alongside another salacious headline. The case was still big news, and she had even been interviewed for a *60 Minutes* segment that was airing tonight. She should feel more jubilant than she did. Her colleagues had been generous in their praise. Even the homophobic Dr. Stephanie Carmichael had actually managed to look Pat in the eye and congratulate her the last time they met.

But Pat felt drained. The banality of evil inevitably reduced her to helpless dismay. Maybe reading the newspapers was not such a good idea. The media and the public were obsessed with *why?* As if a rational explanation existed for the unspeakable, as if the formula that created a killer could be undone if it were understood.

People took comfort in the idea of a deranged individual driven by impulse, a misfit whose conduct was caused by some personal trauma. No one wanted to examine the awful probability that child murderers may be as much a product of their culture as corporate crooks like the *Enron* crowd. The ruthless pursuit of gratification was their stock in trade. They did what they did because they liked it. Pathological narcissists, they felt entitled.

Pat bit into her junk-food and listlessly turned on the television. One of the most dangerous of the breed was now locked up, but she could not solve the problem. The thought depressed her.

THE VAST KITCHEN in the St. Michael's home always made Lauren feel that her own apartment was the size of a closet. She'd been thinking of selling, but felt odd about it because it was her parents' graduation gift. All the same, since returning from Ethiopia, she'd had trouble settling there. It was like stepping back through time into the life she'd once led, only nothing seemed to fit any more.

She didn't like the décor. Every stick of furniture reminded her of Sara. Even her bed felt wrong. She'd grown so accustomed to a hard wooden base and a thin mattress that the enveloping softness of her bedding seemed smothering. Sometimes she abandoned it in the middle of the night, wrapped herself in a quilt, and slept on the floor.

It was not just the apartment. She had returned to New York City, but not to the world she had known. Her two closest friends from college had moved to the West Coast while she'd been away. Old Mrs. Rosen next door had died, and her apartment was now occupied by her son and his wife. They were doing noisy renovations and spent most nights yelling at each other, sometimes in the hallway right outside her door. The janitor had left his job, and the new guy smoked anywhere he liked in the building and wore a ball cap with embroidered ducks above a slogan that said "If it flies it dies." Lauren got the creeps thinking about him poking around in her apartment while she wasn't there.

It should have been comforting to return to the familiar, but she felt like a displaced person. She could hardly wait to get to St. Michael's on the weekends and always had to force herself to leave when the time was over. It had only been a month, she reasoned as she waited for the kettle to boil. Maybe it took more time to adjust. She had returned to civilization after twelve months of what most people would consider hell on earth. Was it any wonder she felt disoriented?

Maybe she should move home to St. Michaels for a while. There was nothing to stop her, she decided, as she spooned ground coffee beans into the espresso machine. She could just pack up when she got back to the city tomorrow, list the apartment with a realtor, and stay in the Chesapeake while she waited to get into a medical school. Her parents had met at Harvard, and they seemed to take for granted that she would be accepted at their alma mater. But Lauren was less confident. She would apply to several schools and see what happened.

Certain she could hear her mother's voice, she stuck her head out the door and called, "Is that you, Mom?"

"Quick. Come and see this," Helen Douglas responded from the TV room.

Halfway through pouring the coffee, Lauren hastened down the hallway. What wonder of the natural kingdom did her mother want to share now? Expecting *Gorillas In the Mist*, Lauren entered the room just as Pat Roussel's face filled the TV screen.

"Your bodyguard is on *60 Minutes*!" her mother announced, cranking up the volume. "It's all about that dreadful case of the child beauty queens. I had no idea she was the one who caught the killer." She picked up the remote again. "I'm going to record this for your father. He'll want to tell everyone he hired a famous FBI detective to look after you."

Lauren sat down because she felt like her legs wouldn't hold her. Blocking out her mother's chatter, she tried to focus on what Pat was actually saying. But she was strangely transfixed by the shape of her mouth moving, the structure of her jaw, the way her eyelids drooped slightly as she concentrated. For the interview, she was wearing a beige turtleneck tucked into black pants. She looked relaxed. Well rested. Incredibly, outrageously hot.

Lauren lowered her eyes, waiting for a commercial break before she dared confront the screen again. Her blood rioted through her body, making her head pound. She was aware that she was breathing in short sharp gasps, but could not slow the rhythm. "Amazing," she managed in a squeaky voice.

Her mother gave her an odd look. "Are you okay?"

Lauren tried to speak, but her attention was riveted once more to the screen. Pat was talking about the people she worked with, giving them most of the credit for the big arrest. Lauren followed her hand gestures with strange fascination, almost feeling her caress. A rush of longing consumed her.

Helen Douglas muted the sound as a cheesy Coca Cola ad played. Her eyes were glued to Lauren's face. They narrowed a little, and she asked point blank. "Are you in love with Pat Roussel?"

"No. Of course not." Lauren could hear the thin quality of her own voice. "Whatever would give you that idea? I hardly know her."

"Well, I don't recall ever seeing you have palpitations over Mike Wallace and since he's the only other person on the screen..."

Lauren forced herself to get a grip. Wetting her mouth, she said. "I just got a shock to see her. That's all. It kind of brought up — everything."

"Ah." Her mother looked skeptical. "Well, I'm sorry about that." She continued to stare at Lauren as if she could see right through her.

An uncomfortable silence ensued. "Okay," Lauren admitted finally. "We did have kind of a...thing." There was no point lying. Her mother had always been able to read her like a book. "But she — we decided it was the wrong time. You know. It wasn't appropriate." Trying to make her mouth quit trembling, she bit down on her bottom lip.

"And you thought you would forget her and move on?"

"I've tried to. It's strange. We only spent a few weeks together. Maybe it was the timing. I think my feelings were out of proportion because of the shooting. I formed a strong attachment to her very quickly."

"Ah." Helen mulled this over. "I liked her. I think she has integrity. And she saved your life. That certainly scores points with me."

"She is a good person," Lauren said stiffly. "I wish things had been different. But I guess it just wasn't meant to be."

"So, are you saying you wouldn't be attracted to her now? That it was just a fleeting thing?"

Lauren caught her breath. The very thought of Pat's touch, the feel of her body, evoked a sharp physical response. She blushed. "I'm not sure. I mean, yes. I think so."

Maybe it would be different now, she reflected. Maybe, if

she met Pat, she would not feel this ache any more. A year had gone by. Even if Pat had not changed at all, Lauren was a different person. She no longer had the panic attacks that had punctuated the months after her shooting. She felt confident, calm, and in control of her own destiny. How could she be so undone seeing Pat on TV? It made no sense.

"There's one way to find out," Helen said, ever the pragmatist. "Phone the woman and have a drink with her."

Lauren shook her head. "I don't want to see her again. That experience is behind me now. I've moved on." Even to her, the protestations sounded tinny. She cleared her throat. "What I'm trying to say is that I can't see the point. It never works to go back and try and pick up where you left off."

Her mother nodded sagely. "That was then, this is now. What's the harm in seeing her, just to say hello?"

Lauren knew the mature response would be a sanguine willingness to see Pat in a social setting. To have a civilized conversation and come to terms with what could never be. But she felt a mixture of dread and embarrassment at the thought. In hindsight, she could see she had thrown herself at Pat Roussel. She had placed an employee in an awkward position. Had Pat felt sexually harassed? Lauren didn't think so, but she wasn't sure if she could trust her own judgment on that count. All she knew was that Pat had backed off, and the moment the job was done, she had left without saying goodbye. Could she have made it any plainer that she didn't want Lauren in her life?

Lauren caught her mother's eye. "To be honest, I doubt she would want to see me. It's kind of awkward."

"Because you were intimate? Is that what you meant by having a *thing*?"

Lauren groaned. This was something she did not want to discuss in any detail with her mother. "We did sleep together, yes."

"Let's not share that with your father."

"Good idea." Helen had a brooding expression on her face, the one Lauren associated with plotting and scheming. "Just leave it. Okay?" she said.

"I'm not sure if your father ever told you this, but Pat returned the check for her salary."

Lauren tried not to react. Absorbing the information, she said, "I didn't know that."

"At the time, I didn't understand why she would do that," Helen said.

Lauren had trouble swallowing. "Don't read too much into it," she said feebly.

Helen gave a tiny shrug and picked up the remote. "All I want is for you to be happy, darling."

# Chapter
# Twenty-three

PAT SHOULD HAVE known she would never make it in time for the pre-dinner drinks. Her puddle-jumper had gotten into JFK an hour late, and the taxi-ride in rush hour traffic was one of the reasons she would never live in New York City. The speeches had already started when she reached the dinner reception, and she slid guiltily into a spare chair at the back of the room. She would have to wait for a break between speakers before finding her table.

Helen Douglas's invitation had come as a complete surprise, and she'd been of two minds over accepting right up until the plane boarded. By the time she'd finally decided to back out, it was too late. Her plane was taxiing away from the terminal, and the guy on the other side of the aisle reached out and shook her hand, saying, "I hope they fry that fucking scum," before announcing to the rest of the cabin, "Hey, right here's the lady who nailed the Kiddy Pageant Killer." Which made Pat very popular with the flight attendants, who had to keep the autograph-hunters in their seats during take-off.

Pat had still been signing her name on paper napkins at the baggage claim and thanking God that her fifteen minutes of fame would soon be over.

Scanning the reception room, she tried to catch sight of Helen. A staff member had told her she was seated at the main table, a large one close to the front. But the room was in darkness, with only the stage lit. A woman at the podium was talking about poverty in the third world and what the National Organization for Women had done about it recently. Waving an arm toward the curtains behind her, she said, "And on that note, it is my pleasure to introduce the daughter of the woman we're gathered here to honor. Please welcome Lauren Douglas!"

Startled, Pat got to her feet with the rest of the clapping audience and sidled around the room to get a better view of the stage. Locating an empty table to one side, she took a seat and stared at the young woman who strolled to the podium.

Lauren had changed. Pat noticed her hair first. The heavy, shoulder-length red tresses had gone, replaced by a short bob that made her neck seem painfully vulnerable. She was thinner. Much thinner. The cocktail dress she wore revealed a body that had lost its soft curves. Her heart-shaped face was more elfin, her cheekbones defined, her eyes shadowed as if she hadn't slept properly in months. Pat was shocked. What the hell had happened to her?

"When my mother and I went to Ethiopia a year ago, I was a child," Lauren said, adjusting the microphone slightly. "A spoiled child. One of the most fortunate ten percent of the world's girl children. My parents had not starved me, sold me into sexual slavery, or sent me out to work when I was five years old. I went to school. I played sports. I became an actress and earned more money each week than many of the world's women earn in their lives." She paused, scanning the room, but did not see Pat in her shadowed corner. "My skills included pretending to be a doctor on television, pretending to be a heterosexual in real life, and...buying shoes."

This scored a laugh, but not from Pat. Lauren had spent a year in Ethiopia. She was stunned. It certainly explained why Pat had never found her in any of the TV listings she checked intermittently. Lauren continued her speech, describing what it was like to work with her mother in a women's hospital in Addis Ababa. The place sounded horrendous. Pat tried to imagine how she had coped—the woman who had to have bottled Italian mineral water. Not only had she coped, she had stayed there for a year.

"What can I say about my mother that hasn't already been said much better by the people at the *National Geographic*?" Lauren said warmly. "She is my inspiration, and my best friend, a model of grace under pressure and a woman who makes a difference in the lives of others every single day. I am honored to introduce Dr. Helen Morrow Douglas."

Pat rose with everyone else, loudly applauding as Helen took the stage and hugged her daughter, at the same time acknowledging the audience with nods and smiles. During the applause, Pat hastened across to the large table in the center of the room and sat down at an empty place, just as everyone else took their chairs. She didn't know any of the other women at the table but surmised from their thinness and jewelry that they were probably important donors.

Helen started her presentation by screening a video she said Lauren had filmed. The film left Pat thunderstruck, and she wasn't the only one. By the end, every woman at her table was discreetly mopping tears. And that was even before Helen's speech. Her chair angled toward the stage, Pat barely noticed someone had occupied the empty place to the left of hers until a purse landed at her feet and a hand reached for it.

"Excuse me." Lauren Douglas brushed past Pat and returned the purse to her lap. Her polite smile froze in place. "Pat?"

The sound of her name on those lips delivered a shock of joy so irrational Pat blinked in surprise. Trying to sound at ease, she whispered, "Hello, Lauren. It's good to see you."

"What are you doing here?"

Catching a "shush" from a grandmotherly woman nearby, Pat leaned close to Lauren's ear and murmured, "Your mother invited me. I didn't realize you were going to be here."

Lauren's mute stare was eloquent in its displeasure. Whatever Helen Douglas had thought she was doing, it had backfired. "I see," she said without expression. Waiting for her mother to finish speaking, she sat rigidly in her chair, her hands clasped over her purse, her face set.

Pat wondered what she should do. She had no intention of staying if it meant Lauren's evening would be ruined. At Helen's suggestion, she had checked into the hotel for the night and arranged a late flight for the next day. That was easily fixed. As soon as she had exchanged pleasantries with Lauren's mother, she would excuse herself on the pretext of work, arrange a morning departure and get a good night's sleep in the room she had paid for. The last thing she wanted to do was make Lauren uncomfortable. Helen obviously had no idea what had transpired between them. Perhaps she had imagined Pat's presence would come as a happy surprise for her daughter.

Amidst rousing applause, Helen left the stage and navigated her way toward their table, shaking hands and exchanging greetings on the way. She knew how to work a room, Pat observed. No doubt, as a politician's wife, she'd had plenty of practice. Pat glanced sideways at Lauren and was relieved to see she had been pounced on by a couple of eager socialites wearing oversized pearls. This seemed like an opportune time to slip away. She could phone Helen tomorrow and apologize for not waiting to speak with her.

Just as she backed her chair out, a hand touched her arm and Helen exclaimed, "Pat! How wonderful to see you." To the women at the table, she announced, "Ladies. Please let me introduce Special Agent Pat Roussel of the FBI, who we recently saw on *60 Minutes* after she solved the child pageant killings case. I owe Pat a debt of my own as she was also responsible for apprehending the man who shot my daughter last year."

Pat immediately found herself the center of attention with women throwing questions at her and inviting her to come and address other events. Out of the corner of her eye, she could see Helen speaking with Lauren, who occasionally cast uncertain looks in Pat's direction.

A woman in costly jewelry pawed her arm, "Agent Roussel, we were wondering if you were inspired by Jodie Foster in *Silence of the Lambs?*"

"Er..." *Inspired*. Pat scavenged for something to say. She met Lauren's eyes and caught a flash of amusement.

"Actually, it's one of Pat's favorite films." Lauren came to her rescue.

The woman looked gratified. To the friend with her, she said, "Didn't I tell you women joined the FBI because of that movie?"

As the two socialites began a high-decibel discussion of actresses they had met at fundraisers, Pat told Lauren quietly, "I was about to leave."

"Please don't."

Pat fought off a reckless urge to take her into her arms then and there. She hesitated, choosing her words carefully. "Your film was wonderful. I'm so impressed."

"I hope they open their checkbooks." Lauren glanced covertly around. "Do you think anyone would notice if we vanished for a while?"

Pat's heart jerked into a gallop. "You mother seems to have it all under control."

Lauren slipped her arm into Pat's and they took the shortest route through the tables and around the wall to the exit.

Once outside the reception room, Lauren took a deep breath and said, "I'm sorry. I just had to get out of there."

Pat's spirits dampened immediately. It's not as if Lauren would want to slip away just to be in private with her. Unless it was to slap her face.

"I could use a stiff drink," Lauren said. "How about you?"

"Absolutely."

They took the elevator down to the small, quiet bar in the hotel lobby and ordered drinks, barely exchanging a word.

"I feel shell-shocked," Lauren finally said.

"It was pretty full on in there."

"Not about the fundraiser." She seemed to be measuring her words. "About everything. Why did you leave the way you did?"

Pat had rehearsed any number of answers to that question

over the past year. Her reply was not one of them. "Because I had fallen in love with you."

Lauren made a small sound, as if air had escaped her lips, leaving them parted in surprise. "I don't know what to say."

"I was an idiot."

"If you're suggesting *that's* what I should say, okay." Lauren's tone was playful. "You were an idiot."

For a moment Pat was taken aback, then she laughed. "I deserved that."

In that moment, she realized Lauren was letting her off the hook. A woman conscious of her own power could do that. The changes in Lauren were not just physical.

Their drinks arrived, and they tapped glasses without making a toast. Close up, Lauren seemed so fragile that Pat's protective instincts went into overdrive. Yet there was a strength in her face that had not been there before and a serenity that reminded Pat of Helen Douglas. Lauren might look like a gangly fourteen-year-old in adult's clothing, but her level gaze and self-assured demeanor told a different story.

"Congratulations on cracking the case. I know it must mean a lot to you."

"Thank you. It does." In truth, without it, Pat felt rudderless. She was tempted to say as much, but did not want to sound ambivalent about this win. A monster was behind bars. They had a confession. Pageant parents could get back to exploiting their daughters with peace of mind. For Pat, there would be new crimes to solve, new horrors to confront.

Lauren regarded her with serious eyes. "You seem different."

"So do you. God, you're thin."

Soft laughter. "Let's just say it's for good reason Addis Ababa is not listed by the gourmet travel guides."

"Why did you go?" Pat asked softly.

"Instead of staying home, crying in my soup because I'd been discarded by the woman I wanted?" Pat flinched at the bitterness in her tone. "I suppose I felt lost. It wasn't a noble decision at the time. I just couldn't think of anything to do with my life and my mother kind of railroaded me into it." Lauren sipped her vodka. "Later, everything changed. I wanted to feel...useful. To do something that would count. You must know what I mean."

"Yes. I think I do." Pat struggled to keep her expression composed in the face of a steady litany of harried thoughts. *What was I thinking, walking away from you? Do you have someone else? Would you consider moving to Philadelphia so we could date?*

Observing her companion lost in thought, Lauren swirled her ice for something to do. Covertly, she took in the muscularity of Pat's legs through the fabric of her pants, the tanned, squarish hand resting on one thigh, the leashed power in her every movement. Did Pat feel anything for her now? Lauren thought she had caught a brief burst of electricity between them when they had escaped the reception, but perhaps it was her imagination. It felt odd to be sitting here with her so formally. Their roles were different now, of course. It was almost as if they had just met, yet they knew so much more than they should about one another.

Taking a risk, Lauren said, "Back then, before you left, I was in love with you, too."

"I know." Those intense green eyes met hers squarely. "The timing was all wrong."

"I see that now." With mild self-mockery, Lauren added. "I hated you for not saying goodbye. I was horribly disillusioned."

"Goodbyes were never my strong suit. I can't stand to see a woman in tears. Myself especially."

Lauren smiled over that. The old Pat would never have been so candid. "Are you happy? I mean, Is your life going well?"

"I have no complaints." Pat set her drink down. Lauren could sense she was leaving a great deal unsaid. "I got a promotion. And a guy from the CIA called me up and asked me if I wanted to work in Iraq."

Lauren's heart stopped, then started again with a jolt. Feigning nonchalant interest, she asked, "Are you going to go?"

"I told him no. But I've been thinking about it." Pat seemed restless all of a sudden, crossing and uncrossing her legs as she spoke. "I'm not a coward. I would risk my life if I thought I was doing something important for our country. But Iraq was always about money, never about anything moral."

"You're already doing something important. Besides," Lauren took a deep breath, "how would we get to see one another if you're in Baghdad?"

Pat's eyes shot up. A faint dimple appeared in her right cheek. "Are you hitting on me?"

"Maybe."

Pat's eyes glittered with a potent mixture of desire and amusement. "Don't stop. I've missed it."

She hadn't seen this woman for a year, but Lauren wanted very badly to crawl into her lap and be held before making passionate love. It seemed crazy after everything that had happened, but all Lauren could think was that she and Pat had been given a second chance, and all they had to do was take it.

For her part, she planned to do just that.

In a small voice, she asked, "Are you staying in the hotel?"

"As luck would have it, yes."

"I have an idea." Her heartbeat drummed in her ears. "Let's go to your room so we can talk without that guy over there staring at us."

Pat cast a sideways look at a crew cut hunk in a charcoal suit and a shirt too tight at the neck. "Your father's?"

Lauren nodded. "Dad says he's just a driver. As if. He's out here because Mom wouldn't let him sit behind the stage during the dinner."

"I feel for him," Pat said. "In fact, I'm going to buy him a drink."

Ignoring Lauren's laughing protests, she went over to the security guy and spoke with him for a few seconds, then returned, saying, "Now, where were we?"

"What did you say to him?" Lauren demanded, picking up her purse and smoothing her dress over her hips.

"That you're all mine. Maybe not in those exact words." Pat placed a hand in the small of Lauren's back as they walked to the elevators.

The slight pressure was almost enough to make Lauren turn, inviting collision. She thought everyone in the elevator must see the pink tide rising from her cleavage to her throat. Mirrored in the stainless steel door, Lauren could tell she looked like the proverbial woman going forth in sin.

The doors swished closed behind them at Pat's floor and Lauren found herself tongue-tied, her poise nowhere to be found. As if guessing this, Pat took her hand and they walked briskly along the over-bright hotel corridor.

"IT'S NOT AS nice as the last place," Pat said, flicking light switches. Waving a hand, she said, "Make yourself at home."

Lauren sat on the edge of a fantastically uncomfortable sofa and watched Pat remove her jacket and unbutton her sleeves. She rolled these halfway up her forearms, and asked, "Pellegrino?" At Lauren's nod, she removed a green bottle from the bar fridge, broke ice into two glasses and poured. "You turned me onto this stuff," she remarked. "My buddies think I came back from my bodyguard stint with fancy ideas."

Lauren took several large gulps and touched her fingers to her forehead. The skin felt damp. Why was she so nervous? Pat was being perfectly charming. No one had said they were coming up here for any reason but to talk.

Pat sat down next to her and drank in silence, joining

Lauren in the pretence that they were not being awkward with one another all of a sudden. In a conversational tone, she asked, "So, what are your plans now?"

"I'm going to train as a doctor, provided I can find a med school that will take me."

Pat grinned. "That's great. Your mom must be thrilled."

"She's already planning the clinic we'll open one day." Lauren stretched her legs out in front of her and slipped her feet from her pumps, saying, "I've been in flat shoes for a year, so these are torture. Do you mind?"

"Be my guest."

She looked criminally at ease, Lauren thought. What was new? Nothing ever seemed to get under Pat Roussel's skin. By contrast, Lauren thought her own discomfort must be written all over her. "I didn't come up here to sleep with you," she blurted out.

This scored a reaction. Pat laughed.

"What's so funny?"

"Us," Pat said. "This deeply unromantic room. We haven't set eyes on one another for a year, and we can hardly look at each other now. But you still need to let me know we're not jumping into bed any time soon. Good plan. Just in case I had the wrong impression."

"I hate you," Lauren said throatily.

"Really?" Pat reached over, took her glass, and set it on the coffee table. "You *want* to hate me. Not the same thing." Raising a hand to Lauren's cheek, she brought her face to face. Softly, she said, "I'm so sorry I hurt you. There was no excuse. I wasn't being honest with you, or with myself."

Lauren's eyes stung. She wiped each of them against the backs of her hands. "I thought you didn't care. That I was just a job."

"I ran from you because you were so much more than that," Pat admitted bleakly. "Back then, I felt like my life was out of control. You were just one more thing I failed to handle properly, and it almost got you killed. I couldn't forgive myself for that."

"You know what I think?" Lauren took Pat's hand and drew it to the valley between her breasts. "I think we met at the wrong moment. I believe it was meant to happen, but the timing was out by, hmmn, a year."

"You're saying we got ahead of ourselves?"

"Maybe."

"It was worth it." Pat smiled a slow, hot smile. "Any chance we can pick up where we left off?"

Lauren could feel her body responding to Pat's before they made it into one another's arms. Pat's mouth fused them together. Her kiss was everything Lauren had yearned for, night after night in her lonely, dusty bedroom in Bar Dahr. Intense. Profound. Naked in its craving.

Lauren reveled in the salty taste of her mouth, the familiar feel of her. Sense memories dragged her from present to past and back again, dissolving time and distance and doubt.

They made it to their feet, the kiss unbroken. Lauren's dress was unzipped and fell away from her naked breasts. Impatiently, she pushed the garment down her body, collecting her panties on the way, and stepping out of both. Pat's hands slid past her sides, spreading possessively over her hips, drawing her closer. When her mouth finally left Lauren's, it moved from her jaw to the slender column of her throat, branding the delicate flesh with small hot kisses.

Trembling, Lauren tugged open the buttons on Pat's shirt and pulled it from her pants, then fumbled with the belt buckle and zipper.

"Slow down." Pat's voice drifted into her ear and she took over, shedding the flimsy barrier of her garments.

They moved to the bed, caressing, stroking, savoring. The contrast of cool, clean sheets and hot skin was more arousing than Lauren could bear. Urgently, she dug her fingers into Pat's back, drawing her down hard, loving the crush of their bodies, the merging of breath, the primal communion of heart, mind and body.

Pat drew back, her face unguarded, eyes clouded with desire. "God, I've missed you." Her thumb skimmed a nipple. "Just let me touch you for a while."

Compliant, Lauren melted back against the pillows as Pat explored her slowly and thoroughly, her hands lingering over breasts and belly, her mouth tracing its own path across quivering skin. In the haven of their shared passion, she allowed herself to watch as Pat made love to her, slowly, silkily intensifying her arousal. The sight of that dark head descending between her legs, the feel of a bracing hand in the hollow of her back, made Lauren whimper. A hand took one of hers. Their fingers knotted.

Lauren closed her eyes, lost in sensation. She felt a strange awe as her sex was enveloped. It was as if she'd had no other lover, never given herself this way. Surrendering to the insistent pressure of Pat's mouth, the hot teasing torture of tongue and lips, she lifted her hips in rhythm and released Pat's hand. She slid her fingers through the straight dark hair, urging her, needing a little more.

She knew she was making the soft moans she could hear, but was helpless to control her own responses. The pressure against her clit increased unbearably. When it was joined by the fullness she craved, Lauren's womb contracted. The tension in her body built. Cresting, bearing down, she uttered Pat's name over and over between small sobs of pleasure until she let go and floated. Limp and sated, she couldn't move, or think, or speak.

Eventually she became aware of Pat's weight shifting, of the bed rebounding slightly as she left it.

A moment later, she placed a bottle of chilled water in Lauren's hand. "Drink?"

Lauren dragged herself into sitting position and gulped down a few mouthfuls, conscious all the while of her companion's steady regard.   She returned the bottle and watched Pat drink, savoring the raw beauty of her, strong and perfect and just a touch away.

Pat set the water aside and turned her head, eyes smoky and assessing. Slowly, almost imperceptibly, she smiled. It was a smile Lauren had never seen before, palpably sexual, candid in its invitation. Extending a hand, she trailed her fingertips along Pat's thigh. The skin flinched slightly at her touch and she heard Pat's breathing change. Yearning to explore the body denied to her for so long, she moved closer and extended her caresses to Pat's belly, then her ribs, marveling at the unique geography of flesh and bone.

Beneath her hand, Pat's skin felt smooth and hot. Lauren encompassed a breast. A nipple nudged her palm as it ripened in arousal. Working it back and forth, she said, "More?" and released a small gasp of delight when Pat captured her hand and placed a sensual kiss in its palm.

"Tease," Pat whispered hoarsely. "I've never wanted a woman the way I want you."

Lauren slid her free hand between Pat's thighs and found her wet and swollen and completely unresisting. Groaning, Pat eased down the bed drawing Lauren with her. Wordlessly, they faced each other, Lauren resting in the circle of Pat's arms.

"I won't ever shut you out again," Pat whispered, her mouth brushing Lauren's.

Emotion and desire inseparable, Lauren kissed her deeply in return and once more sought that welling core. Guided by the movements of Pat's body, she slid her fingers slowly back and forth, increasing her pressure until Pat's breathing grew ragged and she rolled onto her back.

Moving with her, Lauren was consumed with heady wonder

at the body that was now hers to pleasure, at the way Pat lost herself in sensation yet remained fiercely present, constantly seeking Lauren with eyes and hands and mouth. As she sensed Pat's arousal starting to peak, Lauren held back slightly and, kneeling next to her prone lover, began a meandering exploration with tongue and teeth.

"Baby, you're making me crazy," Pat finally gasped out.

Lauren lifted her head. "Is that you, begging for it?"

Pat made a sound that was more of a groan than a laugh. "You're damn right it is." Seizing Lauren's shoulders, she pulled her roughly into a passionate embrace.

Slick with sweat and shivering against one another, they kissed with such intensity, Lauren felt profoundly shaken when they surfaced for air. Tears welling, she kissed her way down Pat's hot, damp skin and almost collapsed between her legs.

As she took Pat in her mouth, it was all she could do to be gentle. The taste and texture of her, the lift of her hips, the husky gasps, the fingers laced between hers, thrilled Lauren beyond any fantasy. At the point of release, Pat cried out in wild rapture. Then she reached for Lauren, gathering her close and quietly weeping against her. For a long while, they lay in a panting heap, their hearts pounding hard against one another.

"I should move," Lauren whispered. "Before I squash you."

Pat's arms tightened around her. "Don't. I like you on top. Sometimes."

Lauren pushed herself upright. Changing position to straddle Pat, she said, "I think I need more practice."

Pat's lake-green eyes flashed up at her. "I could help with that."

Lauren grinned, "I was kind of hoping you might."

LATER, CRADLED IN Pat's arms, sleep fast approaching, she said, "I love you. I never stopped loving you."

Pat kissed the top of her head. "I love you, too."

"What are we going to do?"

"Sleep sounds pretty good right now."

Lauren prodded Pat gently. "You know what I mean."

"Well, we could get married and live happily ever after."

Lauren propped herself on an elbow and looked down at Pat. "Do you mean that?"

Pat's eyes sparkled. "Put yourself in my shoes. Do you think I'm going to tell your father I just want you for sex?"

Lauren laughed. "Ask me properly," she demanded.

"I love you, Lauren Douglas. Will you marry me?"

Lauren brushed Pat's lips with her own. "Name the day."

# Epilogue

ANNABEL DUMPED THE mail on the kitchen counter and said, "We have a wedding invitation."

Cody groaned. "I still feel sick from those ribs at Whetu Parata's bash."

"This one's in Vermont. Pat Roussel and Lauren Douglas are tying the knot."

"You're kidding. I thought they were history."

Annabel unfolded a couple of pages torn from a magazine. "Check this out. Lauren and her mom are in the *National Geographic*. They've been doing medical aid work in Ethiopia."

Cody read the letter that came with the invitation, her disbelief palpable. "Pat says Lauren's starting med school soon." She read a little further. "And she's made a documentary about this hospital in Addis Ababa. She's won prizes at film festivals."

"I guess she's not a soap actress any more," Annabel said.

"I always thought she had more brains than that." Cody finished the letter and skimmed through the *National Geographic* article. "Let's send some money to this place."

"I already do. The Fistula Hospital is one of the charities we support."

Cody looked shame-faced. "I should take more of an interest in your trust."

"You run the island, sweetheart."

"I admire Lauren," Cody said pensively. "I never picked her for the type to do something like this."

"Well she won't be a celebrity any more. You don't get famous for helping people."

"Weird, isn't it, when people who *act* the parts of heroes in the movies are more famous than the people who really *are* heroes."

"Luckily for us all, the real ones don't do it for the glory."

"I was thinking." Cody folded the *National Geographic* pages, her face suddenly very serious. "Briar could use some company. You know, someone her own size. Maybe we could adopt one of those little girls nobody wants."

Annabel was speechless. Before Briar came into their lives, Cody hadn't wanted children at all. Now, she was suggesting they increase their family.

Apparently reading Annabel's silence as dismay, Cody said, "It's just an idea. I know you'll need time to think about it. But I think we're pretty good with babies. And I could build another room onto the house."

Laughing, Annabel took her partner's earnest face between her hands and kissed her tenderly. "I don't need time. I think it would be wonderful for Briar to have a sister."

Cody brightened immediately and kissed her back. "Hey. I know! We could call her Xena?"

"Wait a second. Am I hearing this? You want to name our next child after a TV hero?" Annabel gave her a sharp prod.

Cody caught her hand and pulled her into a clinch. "Xena's not just any hero."

"Uh huh." Annabel brushed her mouth across Cody's. "I'm thinking Amelia has a nice ring to it."

Cody unfastened Annabel's shirt buttons and steered her toward a sofa. "We're not naming our baby after someone whose plane went down in the Pacific."

"Spoilsport," Annabel murmured, as Cody kissed her throat.

They sank into the soft upholstery.

"What if Briar wakes up from her nap?" Cody paused between discarding garments.

"We'll just tell her we were getting ready to go swimming." They stared at one another. Briar was getting more curious by the day. "Rain check?" Annabel suggested, reaching for her shirt.

"Tonight," Cody said. "Our bed. Eight o'clock?"

They kissed, the long, slow kiss of lovers who have time to savor one another. Annabel smiled in contentment. After six years, Cody's touch still made her melt. "I love you. I love our family."

Cody nuzzled her. "Me, too." She helped do up Annabel's buttons. "Remember when you first told me you wanted a baby?"

"How could I forget?" The fight had been the worst they'd ever had.

"I was an idiot." Cody sighed. "Looking back, I think I really believed if you had one, you would love me less."

"The pumpkin pie theory of love—there's only so much to go 'round?"

"Something like that."

Annabel took Cody's hand. "It's the opposite. I love you more."

"I don't know why, but there's this part of me that gets afraid." Cody's voice was uneven. "I keep thinking I could lose you — and Briar — everything, just like that. That's another reason I didn't want a baby at first. If there's more to love, then there's more to lose."

Realizing her lover had finally dealt with some very old issues, Annabel asked, "How do you feel about that now?"

"Like a total jackass."

Annabel gathered her into a warm embrace. "I never thought I could love you more, but I do."

Solemnly Cody met her eyes. "Everything I know about love, I learned from you."

Their mouths fused, softly pledging what their hearts knew. That they belonged to one another. Now and always.

THE END

Also available from
Yellow Rose Books

# *Passion Bay*

*Book I in the Moon Island Series*

(2nd edition)

Two women from different ends of the earth meet in paradise. Mourning the death of her favorite Aunt, Annabel Worth is stunned to find she has inherited two things—an island in the South Pacific and a mystery that can only be solved by traveling there. Disillusioned with life as a securities trader in Boston, she rashly decides to exchange one world for another. New Zealander Cody Stanton has made the same choice. Dumped by her lover, laid off from her job, she rents a beach villa on remote Moon Island, expecting to take comfort in sea, solitude and simplicity. Then she meets Annabel.

Haunted by a secret that threatens to derail her relationship with her mother, Annabel resists their powerful attraction. Cody, too, is burdened with a secret that could destroy the passion growing between them. When Hurricane Mary strikes the island, each woman must make a choice that will change her life forever.

A runaway bestseller with seven reprints in its first edition, *Passion Bay* has been re-released in a second 'author's cut' edition, extensively revised, updated and expanded.

**Here's what the critics say:** "Send your customers looking for the perfect beach book to *Passion Bay*...this novel absolutely has it all." ~ Feminist Bookstore News

ISBN 1-932300-25-2

# Saving Grace

## Book II in the Moon Island Series
### (2nd edition)

Champion swimmer and Olympic hopeful, Dawn Beaumont has been injured in a car crash she caused. Haunted by guilt over the death of a passenger, her career in ruins, her body damaged and scarred, she flees to Moon Island. Scientist Grace Ramsay welcomes her cute new neighbor, imaging Dawn could be a pleasant diversion from her secret mission to evaluate Moon Island for corporate purchase by a chemicals giant looking for a waste dump far from civilization. But Dawn won't play ball, in fact she denies she is even a lesbian. Beset by troubling nightmares rooted in the past, and increasing ambivalence over her job, Grace sets out to prove otherwise. Meanwhile Annabel Worth, the owner of the island, is determined not to sell her home to a chemicals conglomerate. But then her plane goes down in the Pacific in suspicious circumstances.

**Here's what the critics say:** "*Saving Grace* has all the elements a reader looks for in a good novel: romance, adventure, danger and intrigue. Jennifer Fulton has taken these ingredients and created a novel the reader will have a hard time putting down." ~R. Lynne Watson, Mega-Scene

ISBN 1-932300-26-0

# The Sacred Shore

## Book III in the Moon Island Series

A page-turning journey packed with romance, adventure, humor, spirituality and steamy eroticism. Third in this unforgettable series, *The Sacred Shore* brings together a group of women at crossroads in their lives. Successful tech industry survivor, Merris Randall does not believe in love at first sight until she meets Olivia Pearce. But Olivia is deeply scarred from a damaging relationship, and has no plans to love again. Thrown together in a sensuous paradise thousands of miles from home, each comes face to face with her destiny. Anthropologist Dr. Glenn Howick is also on Moon Island, but romance is not on her agenda. Chasing the career-making discovery of a lifetime, Glenn must decide whether she can exploit the spirituality of another culture for her own ends. Another moral dilemma looms in the form of her research assistant Riley Mason, a post-grad student whose love for Glenn threatens both her reputation and her most secret self.

After five years of bliss, life seems complete for the island's owners, Cody and Annabel. At least Cody thinks so. But Annabel has recently woken up to the sound of her biological clock ticking. With preparations underway for the secret rituals local women perform to celebrate the goddess of the island, the topic is consigned to the back burner. Then Annabel's cousin Melanie shows up with a young baby and a desperate problem.

ISBN 1-932300-35-X

Other Jennifer Fulton books to look for in the
coming months from
Yellow Rose Books

# *Solace*

## *Book V in the Moon Island Series*

Rebel Monroe is a Californian yachtswoman sailing solo around the world. When her yacht - Solace - capsizes in a perfect storm near the Cook Islands group, she puts to sea in a lifeboat expecting she is not going to make it. Eventually she washes up half-dead on the shores of Moon Island, where she is found by ex-nun Althea Kennedy.

Althea, who entered a Poor Clare order at 20, has recently turned her back on religious life after a traumatic experience in Africa. Questioning both her faith and the church, she is on Moon Island recuperating from malaria and pondering her options.

Rebel, considered a hero by the island's owners, is invited to stay a while and she forms an unlikely friendship with Althea. When this blossoms into something more each woman must rethink her identity, her demons, and her life choices before she can find real happiness.

# *Dark Dreamer*

Rowe Devlin, author of best-selling horror novels, buys an old Victorian house in Maine expecting a tranquil writing environment and an enjoyable home renovation project. What she finds herself caught up in is a mystery more bizarre than anything she's ever written. Not only is Dark Harbor Cottage haunted, but her new neighbors are downright spooky. The Temple twins, Phoebe and Cara, are identical and seem to have something to hide. Phoebe, a forensic botanist with the FBI, knows remarkably little about plants. Her sister Cara is fiercely protective and seems to be frightened of something. The twins are profoundly alluring and Rowe is soon under their spell, unable to decide which one she is more in love with. Danger, intrigue, passion and suspense combine in this gripping romantic thriller.

Jennifer Fulton lives in the shadow of the Rocky Mountains with her partner and animal companions. Her vice of choice is writing, however she is also devoted to her wonderful daughter, and her hobbies—fly fishing, cinema, and fine cooking. Jennifer started writing stories almost as soon as she could read them, and never stopped. Under pen names Jennifer Fulton and Rose Beecham, she has published nine lesbian novels and a handful of short stories.

Printed in the United States
37968LVS00007B/1-51

9 781932 300376